Swiped

swiped

PAULA ROGERS

Choc Lit
A JOFFE BOOKS COMPANY

Choc Lit, London
A Joffe Books company
www.choc-lit.com

First published in Great Britain in 2025

© Paula Rogers

Cover art by Jarmila Takač

ISBN: 978-1781899120

To my loving family — Dad, Mom, Kent, Vanessa, & Elliot

CHAPTER 1

As the evening fog rolled over the city of San Francisco like a fuzzy cardigan, Natalie Lane had a choice to make.

"I'm telling you, Nat," said her roommate, Sara, through the bedroom door. "This party won't be weird!"

Nat instinctively shook her head. "So, you're saying that this time I *won't* get cornered by a tech bro telling me every possible detail about his creatine and microdosing regimen?"

"I had no control over that," said Sara. "It's like house spiders. You kinda have to assume there's gonna be one of those guys at every party, but hopefully they stay hidden in the shadows by the craft beer."

Nat let a smile warm her face as she watched the shadow of Sara's shifting feet by the bottom of the door. Making a link between creepy dudes and house spiders was exactly the kind of devastating but nonchalant insight that Sara was known to spout at any moment — just one of many reasons Nat loved her so dearly. If it had been from anyone else, the party invitation would have been an immediate no. Milling around a crowded house with a bunch of strangers, drinking cheap wine, and dodging hot takes was pretty much last on Nat's list of enjoyable ways to spend an evening — she preferred her cheap wine with pajamas and sci-fi TV shows. But Sara wasn't just a roommate; she was Nat's bestie

1

since college, and if anyone could screen through the multiple factors needed to make Nat even consider a social outing, it was Sara. She also knew exactly which buttons to push.

"Nat, do I need to remind you again of the reason for this little gathering?"

"No!" Nat dug around in her pillows for the oversized men's XXL T-shirt she wore every single night. The soft, cottony hug of her *Lord of the Rings* tee was a compelling argument for staying in. She could practically hear her body calling out for the sweet embrace of Aragorn's screen-printed face and her well-worn sweatpants.

"It's a dog's birthday party," Sara reported anyway. "A mini Schnauzer named Dino is turning three years old and, yes, he is a very small and fluffy boy, and yes, he will be wearing a tiny cowboy hat." She paused, readying her next weapon. "With sequins!"

Nat groaned and opened the door. Of course, Sara knew Nat's weakness for tiny dogs, and of course, she knew how it went double for dogs in just-as-tiny clothing.

Sara pushed in with a shimmery swish of her mermaid print dress and clomp of her combat boots. "Got ya!" she said, plopping down on Nat's bed. She tossed the cozy shirt aside, and Aragorn landed, handsome face down, on Nat's floor. "So? What are you gonna wear?"

Nat gestured to what was already on her body — her de facto work uniform of leggings and an oversized button-down. Her long hair was loose in her natural, if slightly frizzy, toffee-colored curls, and she may have put some mascara on that morning, but she couldn't remember. Being a coder, her job attire wasn't exactly formal, but how much effort was one expected to put in for a dog's birthday party, anyway?

"Nope," said Sara. "You haven't come out with me in *weeks*, so I think this calls for something a little more fun." She pulled a sour face. "Also, the start-up dudes are drawn to athleisure like flies."

"Fine, fine! But I haven't even decided if I'm going yet." Nat started to shuffle through her small closet. Half of the clothes inside were Sara's overflow of items that were way too busty and curvy for Nat's slim and straight build, but she didn't mind sharing the space. Her routine of waking up, commuting, coding, and coming back home didn't really give her much of a need for a dazzling array of outfits.

"Why not?" asked Sara. "Dude, I get the introvert thing, I really do, but sometimes you have to mix it up a little bit, right? Let the universe surprise you?"

"Most surprises are bad." Nat grimaced, once again repressing the memory of the time when the popular girls in third grade had "surprised" her with a square of chocolate cake they'd secretly covered in playground dirt. "Plus, these are *your* friends," she continued, willing her mind to stay in the present. "And you're bringing along a date, remember? So, I'll be the third wheel."

Sara shook her glossy blue-black curls. "Glad you mentioned it, lots of responses. One, this is my first time meeting this girl off the app, so it might go south before we even get off the train."

Nat flinched.

Sara gave a sheepish laugh. "Sorry, no offense!"

"What was your match score?"

"Sixty-one percent."

Nat nodded, satisfied. "OK, well, that's significantly higher than average, but nothing wild. I'd say she'll be around at least long enough to meet the birthday boy . . . *dog*."

Sara smiled, and her glittery eyeshadow sparkled. "Which brings me to my second point. You, as the creator of the dating app that introduced us, cannot possibly be considered a third wheel."

"Weird logic, but go on."

"Well, isn't this great data for you? Observing how one of your BeTwo matches goes IRL is kinda like working, right? And you love that!"

Nat's brain *did* tingle at the idea of data, even if the lab was going to be a party filled with people she barely knew. Sara really was a pro in the ongoing struggle to get her to be more social. In fact, Nat was pretty sure her mother was urging Sara on in the task, having walked in on them having a weirdly hushed conversation in Sara's room the last time she'd visited. They'd both gone silent and stared up at her with saucer eyes, as if she'd flipped over their rock. Nat had felt the need to announce, "I'm fine!" before adding, "Also dinner is ready!" and exiting the scene.

But the truth was that Nat was very used to her loved ones worrying about the amount of time she spent alone — it'd been happening since she was the little kid bringing home stacks of library books on a Friday night, who became the teenager running stats on how likely she was to have a good time at a given function based on past enjoyment at similar events (usually not great odds), who became the adult burying her nose and weekend hours in digital piles of e-books about sexy faeries.

After a mandatory school-wide personality and career aptitude test in high school, the counselor had characterized her as "an introvert's introvert," as he'd handed her a stack of STEM brochures.

"So, I'm weird because I don't like going to parties?" she'd asked, fully braced for a quick confirmation of what she'd been bullied into believing for her entire childhood.

"No, not at all," he had said, with a gentle smile. "Most people feel some level of ambivalence around social events. They want to go to the party and see friends, but some part of them wants to stay home, too. It's just a matter of which side wins on that particular day." Then he'd held up a laminated card with a black-and-white drawing on it. "What do you see here?"

"A duck," she'd said. "Does that mean I'm crazy? That I saw a duck?"

"Natalie, you're not crazy." He tapped the picture. "Yes, this is a duck and also, if you look at it a different way, it's a rabbit."

She'd squinted and sure enough, the beak became ears and the beady black eye flipped to peer over a small rodent nose. A rabbit head, as clear as day.

"See? It is two things at once," he'd said, slipping the picture back inside a well-worn file folder. "Everyone has both introvert and extrovert inside of them, at all times, and so do you." He'd rubbed his beard and smiled at her. "You very much prefer to be a duck, and that's OK. But don't forget that you also know how to be a lovely rabbit, too."

Now, over fifteen years later, she wondered if she'd shifted animal metaphors and fully formed as an indoor cat. As much as she admired Sara's endless flow of invitations to cool openings and events, she was genuinely happy staying in to work on her code, even if it would be nice to have a partner to share the time with. But although she'd had only a few "official" boyfriends in her life, each of those short relationships had died on the hill of how much of a struggle it was for Nat to venture outside of her own pursuits and plans and perfectly curated comfort zone. It was hard enough when there was a 600-page epic about smoking hot dragon riders that she wanted to finish. But her single-mindedness reached a new level when it was about staying in to finish some code for her very own app, and her dates fell behind. That was how Nat learned that the worst part about being an introvert was that no one expected you to feel sad when they left you.

"I'm not some kind of lonely freak, you know," Nat said, holding a long-forgotten black midi dress up to her body in the mirror. At five-foot-eight, Nat was tall enough to pull it off without heels, which was a data point firmly in the pro column.

"What are you talking about?" asked Sara, blinking her large brown eyes. "Did I say that?"

"It's not like I need saving, or something." Nat spoke from all the years of experience with the not-so-subtle hints and smiles of pity. Did other single people have to deal with the self-righteousness and semi-shaming about "putting yourself out there," or was it just the homebodies like her? She tossed the dress on the bed and went back to her closet for another outfit. A solid decision needed a viable second option for comparison. "It's why I created BeTwo's algorithm, remember? To meet someone in a way that was actually comfortable for people like me?"

"Dude, I know. I was there, remember?"

Nat could hear the genuine confusion in Sara's voice. She loved spending time with Sara . . . when they'd met in their college dorm as the undeclared student who couldn't "focus for shit" when she was alone in the room and the Comp Sci programmer who pretty much never left it, their friendship had seemed written in the stars. It still felt that way to Nat. So why didn't Sara understand that bringing a date would make Nat's own singledom more obvious to everyone? It was humiliating enough to constantly hear people crack well-meaning, if unoriginal, jokes about being the creator of a dating app who didn't have a boyfriend, but having a bestie who'd been single for maybe one week in her entire life didn't help Nat's ego.

Of course, this wasn't Sara's fault — she was gorgeous and witty and outgoing, and Nat thanked those lucky stars that her friend cared about her enough to try to be her personal ambassador to the world outside their apartment.

It was just that ever since she'd created BeTwo, social interactions tended to follow a very narrow route. After the questions about how to find the hottest people on the app, or the tipsy confessions from the non-singles about being "so curious", Nat would get peppered with questions about her own love life, and then, inevitably, her lack thereof.

"Of course, I believe in love," she would say, truthfully. "I started BeTwo to help people like me find a partner." Which, again, was also the truth. After all, for every one Nat's past relationships that died on the hill of her introversion, she sharpened her sword for the cause that there had to be other people like her out there — quietly alone and yearning for a way to be quiet and slightly less alone with someone else, but without having to subject themselves to clubs or bars or, God forbid, singles events. She did very much enjoy and very much miss sex, at the very least (hence the faerie books), and hookups were never really her style. But then Nat would smile wistfully and say the words that she'd workshopped with her Gen Z assistants. "But these days, my commitment to BeTwo is my most important relationship."

And this, despite being a carefully worded smokescreen to push more questions away, was truer than her interrogators ever knew.

Because the real reason there was never going to be an enticing enough dog birthday party, or cute enough outfit in her closet, was that Nat had her own favorite evening activity that was always ready at her fingertips, always asked only the right questions, and always made her feel in control of her romantic prospects.

Even if Sara had told her many times that she thought it was weird. "Except, it's not like you actually *go* on BeTwo dates, though, is it?" she asked.

Nat spun out of her closet. "Yes, I do!"

"Speed-dating your user base from the couch doesn't really count . . ." Sara hesitated. "Or seem all that healthy, to be honest?"

Nat winced. There it was — the pity and the advice. Anger flared in Nat's chest as she snatched the Aragorn shirt up off the floor. She wasn't going to the party. But she knew that, and had known that the whole time on some level. The show of an attempt was partly because Nat still liked being invited, but mostly because she didn't want to wound Sara's feelings. But somehow it ended up that Nat was the one feeling prickles of hurt in her chest. "But you going on, like, ten different dates a week is perfectly fine?" she snapped.

Now it was Sara who winced, and Nat instantly regretted her words. That was the trouble with old friends — they knew all too well how to hurt each other, even if they didn't really mean to. "I'm sorry—"

But Sara shook her head and held up a hand. "It's fine." She stood from Nat's bed and shrugged. "I tried. Have a good night."

"Wait!" Nat dug around in the makeup bag on her dresser. "Wear this one — it'll look amazing on you." She held out a plum-colored and expensive lipstick she'd bought for a work event — the best she could do for a peace offering at the moment.

Sara was gracious enough to accept it with a little twinkle in her dark eyes. "You know I love the goth shit." She slipped the lipstick into her pocket. "And good luck with your . . . *search* tonight."

* * *

Nat tugged her shirt over her hips and smoothed the wrinkles in Aragorn's smoldering, screen-printed face as she settled into the couch. She pulled her laptop close, took a fortifying sip of wine, and stretched her neck like an athlete getting ready for the big match. Then she refreshed the BeTwo user base data.

As the creator of the app, the codebase was her personal playground, and she could see behind the curtain any time she wanted. Yes, she did the routine maintenance like fixing bugs and monitoring how new features were being used — the kinds of heads-down coding work that people probably assumed was most of her job. But it was funny how it seemed like users forgot that apps were just things made by a person, not willed into existence by some kind of digital deity. So, every single part of an app was built by human design and therefore open to human scrutiny. For Nat, that meant the chance to vet her eligible male users for herself, all without having to create a profile or swipe or send messages.

Code sequences flashed on her screen for a few seconds and her data report blinked out its sum: twenty-seven. That was the day's number of new users who met her minimum pre-set compatibility factors: being straight, male, single, and active on the app for at least two months so she had some usage data to pull from. She also made sure to only include men with pictures in their profiles. She'd been running a dating app for a few years now, and still didn't understand why some people never bothered with pictures. Even the most basic assurances that someone was a real human tended to go a long way — and while she would begrudgingly admit that her AI-detecting code wasn't perfect yet by any means, she would also happily add that it was probably the best one in the dating app market at the moment. Nat tucked a wayward strand of curls behind her ear and started her dive into the twenty-seven prospects algorithmically lined up for the role of the love of her life.

Nat opened the first profile in her report, a thirty-three-year-old named Mike who pouted at the reflection of his tanned abs. Shirtless selfies *and* in a mirror? Those were two immediate no's, but she willed herself not to disqualify him right away. Then she caught a glimpse of an aggressive right-wing political meme that had somehow snuck past her filters and into his photo grid, and gasped out loud in the quiet of her living room. She knew for a fact that BeTwo had the highest standards for banned content of all the rival apps, because she took special pride in keeping her corner of the internet spic and span and sleaze-free, even if took constant vigilance. And yet here was Mike's meme disturbing her peace and parading around her app — these heinous things mutated faster than ooze-covered turtles. She chewed her lip in concentration as she zeroed in on the offending metadata and zipped up the BeTwo filters once again. Her racing heart slowed, and she toggled back to Mike's profile and his spray-tan torso. Now she felt vindicated that she wasn't being judgmental when instinct had told her to nix Mike as her prospective suitor just for his muscle-mirror selfie. She flagged the account and deleted the meme from her app forever; she was just seeing patterns in her data.

Next.

Nat genuinely liked the pics of the second guy — a thirty-six-year-old named Adam with curly hair and a studious expression and, promisingly, no exposed nipples. He was an Australian, in San Francisco for work as a pastry chef, which checked two of Nat's boxes: cool accent and cool, non-coding job. She knew from her nightly user searches that there was a myriad of interesting jobs among the field of eligible men, and so why not partner up with someone who could introduce her to the exciting world of forestry or neurology or lepidoptery — or pastry cheffing. Sure, Nat loved her work, but she probably didn't want to talk about it at the dinner table, right? Especially when said table could be filled with chocolatey, creamy cakes from a dessert professional. And as for the accent thing, well, sometimes things were added to the wish list just because they were sexy, and accents were sexy.

Nat read on about Adam, the sweets-master from Sydney. Under the question of what he values in a partner, he'd written, "I want someone who won't be afraid to absolutely roast me! Bonus points if it's in front of my mates or my mum." Nat frowned. She'd noticed that wanting to be roasted was suddenly everywhere in her users' profiles, and she had to say that she didn't get it. The desire to be made fun of in front of loved ones wasn't enough for her to nix Adam from the running, but it did give Nat pause.

So, she looked at his user metadata. No use learning how much he loved The 1975 and wood-fired pizza if he was the kind of creep who only messaged women under twenty-five or, God forbid, sent eggplant emojis to try and get around her finely-tuned anti-dick-pic filters.

She scanned his usage records and saw right away that Adam hadn't sent any messages in over six months. So why was he popping up as an active user? She scanned his swipe history. It was very active.

Now Nat was intrigued.

Like every dating app, BeTwo tracked which users got a lot of YES swipes and which ones got a lot of NO swipes. Unlike the other apps, however, Nat had opted not to use this information in her matching algorithm — she knew what it was like to be the nerdy, ostracized kid in school, and so put little stock in popularity to reflect anything about a person's actual value. What popularity did tell her, however, was how other people saw a user's value.

So, when Nat saw that Adam was only swiping YES on women who were ranked far above him, and only during work hours, it told her something very important. Coupled with the fact that he hadn't sent a message in several months, she could safely guess that Adam was actually in a relationship with — she checked the name of the last woman he'd messaged — Gina, and using the app to fantasize and fish for the kind of capital-H *Hot* women he knew he wouldn't actually have a chance with. Hence, the only swiping during work hours, when he wouldn't be seen by Gina.

Sure enough, Gina's profile had been deleted around the time when Adam had stopped sending messages on the app. Nat quickly opened the old message thread between Adam and Gina, whose data remained accessible even if her profile had been taken offline. Their last exchange had been to confirm the time and location of their date at a wine bar and included Gina sending Adam her number in case he was running late. Nat squinted into the glowing pixels on her screen. She could even see the time stamp of that last phone-number-containing message from Gina: 6:35 p.m. The time stamp of the last activity in the chat, however, was 9:57 p.m. when Adam had added a heart to Gina's digits message — a full three hours after her message was sent and, presumably, after their date. To Nat's eye, this was a clear indication that Adam had re-opened the chat to get Gina's number to text her that their date had gone well, and he was feeling so abuzz with the thrill of the good date and the wine they had almost certainly drank at The Beaut of the Vine that he had "heart-ed" the message.

Nat smirked at her screen. BeTwo, her app that launched a thousand 'ships . . . even if Adam was seemingly not a boyfriend for the ages.

Nat closed his profile with a satisfied sigh and drained her glass of pinot noir. She didn't need any more information on this particular mystery. The data could tell you so much and, unlike people, it never lied.

After refilling her wine and skimming a few more profiles, tossing out the immediate no's, and wielding her wish list like a weed wacker, Nat landed on her final prospect — a thirty-four-year-old man named Greg. He had sandy blond hair that swooped over his forehead in a sporty way, and wide-set blue eyes that shone with glee as he smiled over a meatball sub.

She skipped straight to his metadata.

Greg was a mid-active user, meaning he wasn't one of the ones who lurked on the app all day long, swiping through hundreds of profiles every hour. She could also see that his typical activity happened in respectably short twenty-minute chunks during the high-traffic times. For instance, his almost daily check-ins were during the pre-work hour in the morning, and Nat could reasonably surmise that they were done while Greg was running on a treadmill, given the repetitive motion without distance registered by his phone. So, Greg had an at least somewhat stable routine, and no red flags for desperation or emotional volatility behind his usage — like only logging in during the middle of the night, or swiping patterns that showed a huge difference in left and right-swipe ratios when done in the day (likely sober and discerning) versus at night (likely drunk and DTF).

Now Greg warranted cautious optimism, and an even closer look. Nat opened the reports containing his messages and scanned the last several weeks. Like most men, he sent out far more messages than he received, so that wasn't telling her anything. Nothing jumped out at her in terms of the number or frequency of his messages, and she could see that he hadn't been flagged by anyone for inappropriate comments. She ran a formula to search his messages for ten-digit strings of numbers, a clear indication that phone numbers had been exchanged and an IRL date was at least attempted. Greg had a phone numbers-to-messaged-users ratio of 1:5, which was way better than the average. Impressive. Now she knew that unless Greg's messages regularly contained random strings of numbers, a good number of women found him charming and desirable.

So, Nat began to read the messages.

The first time she'd shown Sara the amount of access she had into her users' every move within the app, her friend had physically recoiled.

"Yikes, you can see what I write to people?"

"Of course I can." Nat opened up a selection of Sara's messages to prove how simple it was. "Why does this surprise people? The architects see the pipes inside a house, right?"

Sara turned bright red and thrust her palm over Nat's computer screen. "There's nothing I'm ashamed of," she blurted. "But I just didn't think they'd be read by anyone else. Especially not someone I have to make eye contact with every morning . . ."

Greg, however, didn't have to worry about being embarrassed by his messages. True, he didn't seem too concerned with the difference between "your" and "you're," but his messages were polite and good-natured. She read through several of his opening lines, which seemed like a cut-and-paste template with a few personal details from the woman's profile inserted. *Hi, it's so cool that you like (hobby) and have visited (city)! What's your favorite (food) in the city?* But that was fine with Nat — a lot of people did it, and she honestly admired the balance of effort and efficiency.

Yet, as she read through dozens of threads where Greg asked only the safest of questions, like "Any plans this weekend?" and couched even the mildest of emotions with GIFs from *The Office*, polite and good-natured were still the only words she could grasp about Greg's personality, or lack thereof. She started to scan his conversations for any kind of strong opinion — and the cutesy ones about "(blank) is the best brunch food, fight me," did not count. She found nothing. And yet, here was Greg, milquetoast-ing his way to lots of IRL meetups, or at least agreements to meet up. Nat couldn't understand it. Inoffensive became offensive at some point, if you asked her. Plus, based on how quickly he was back on the app, lobbing more softballs at new matches after an exchange of numbers, Nat could surmise that his meetups lacked the spark of staying power.

She closed her laptop.

Because it was her code, she could spare herself that effort of picking a coffee shop, choosing an outfit, and making conversation with a relative stranger. Because it was her code, she could pass on Greg without ever being on his radar — no hurt feelings, no wasted time. Because it was her code, she could accomplish all this in her comfy clothes and sipping her favorite pinot.

She felt like a genius.

It didn't matter that this was how her search nights always went — she never found anyone whom she wanted to meet, or even anyone who motivated her to log in to her ancient beta-testing user profile (which was still blank) and send a message. The most she ever gained were new qualities to add to her mental wish list, and now she had "No excessive GIF use" courtesy of Greg, which was useful! Plus, there would almost certainly be a new crop of twenty to forty new prospects for her to look through the next night, and the night after that, and the night after that.

She rinsed her wine glass in the sink and shuffled into her bedroom in slippered feet. She pulled her hair back with a puffy headband, brushed and flossed, and slathered a thick, shiny layer of serum and moisturizer on her long, angular face. She slipped into bed, entered her bedtime in a sleep tracker app, and watched a little animated pillow tell her that she'd earned the Super Sleeper badge for fifty-plus days of going to bed at the same time every night. She turned off the lamp, arranged her six pillows around her body in a fort-like formation, covered her eyes with a towel, wedged a lumbar pillow between her knees, closed her eyes, and was asleep within a few minutes.

And so, if Nat had gone to the dog birthday party with Sara, where she would have had a bit too much wine to calm her nerves, and someone had asked Nat how she felt about the fact that she was the creator of one of the most popular dating apps on the market, and yet hadn't been on a date herself in almost two years, she would have answered honestly. She would have said she felt lucky because BeTwo made her feel completely in control of her love life, even if she didn't currently, technically have a love life outside of her app.

And that would have been very, very bad for the BeTwo brand.

CHAPTER 2

A few days later, Nat was bumping along in the backseat of a ride-share on her way to downtown San Francisco. Traffic was as thick as usual, and the car slowed to a crawl every few minutes, but Nat was secretly grateful for the delay. Normally, she'd be squished against the other commuters on the bus, but today, she was on her way to do some press for BeTwo and needed to arrive sweat-free and relatively at peace with humanity — two things that the San Francisco transit experience could never guarantee. Press was the part of her job that filled her with thick, existential dread. She hated being in the public eye. To cap that, no one ever asked her any decent questions about the app, and it wasn't always easy to hide her impatience, not when she really didn't want to be there at all.

But this time she wasn't heading to just any old interview or meet-and-greet.

Nat was speaking on the opening panel at the biggest tech conference in the country, Tech-Talk. She'd be sharing the stage with five other creators of the year's top apps, a fact that convinced her that maybe — just maybe — this event would actually be one where she could talk about her work rather than forced, blithe opinions on love and romance.

She decided to do a mindfulness exercise, while also hoping she would remember the steps correctly. Nat took a deep breath, mentally acknowledging the natural world, rather than the tight ache of nerves creeping into her stomach as they inched along in traffic. She focused on the morning sun sparkling on the skyscrapers. How it glared off the dozens of tech billboards with taglines that most people outside of the Bay Area would not recognize as coherent language. And there was the BeTwo billboard (comparatively normal tagline "The only modern way to date!"), shining in the navy, rose pink, and deep teal that had been workshopped ad nauseum by the board of investors that kept her app financially afloat. They were extremely hands-on with marketing, but hands-off with the code, and that suited Nat just fine. She had thought that adding a digital ticker of users to the BeTwo billboard was a little gimmicky, but seeing it in person, she had to admit it was pretty cool. As her ride-share pulled off the highway and into the dense grid of city streets, she watched the count go up a few numbers under its pink cursive header, *More users looking for love every second!* The figure was in the two-million range — a number she never thought she would hit in her wildest imagination.

For all her nights staying in to burn the midnight oil, BeTwo was a full-fledged business, albeit with a small but scrappy staff, and a small but scrappy office in a converted warehouse shared with a dozen other tech companies. Once she'd gotten approved for funding from the group of app investors looking to strike gold, she'd hired her two in-house employees full-time, outsourced some of the production tasks, and focused on perfecting her code and satisfying her board — the latest version of the San Francisco dream. But BeTwo was still an indie app, and the investors funneled in cash for the sole purpose of being bought or going public, and them making bank on their investment either way. Until that time, Nat had to spread their money as far as she could to grow her users, lure advertisers, and justify a subscription model with ever more enticing features. That meant BeTwo wasn't currently turning a profit, and if she couldn't meet the board's numbers, she could lose her funding at any moment. And, poof, no more BeTwo.

Her phone buzzed with an incoming text. It was Jo Kwon, one-half of her assistant duo.

Jo: *Boss, you good?*

It would have been sweet of Jo to check in before the big event, but since "sweet" wasn't actually a part of Jo's personality, it was probably her way of doing pre-emptive damage control. But to Nat, that was more valuable than any sugary words of affirmation. No one knew how much Nat hated doing press more than Jo. Once upon a time, she had begged Nat to do more — until she saw how truly awful Nat was at it. Then she promptly "pivoted" to a new media strategy without once asking Nat to "step outside her comfort zone", or imagine audiences in their underwear, or change anything about herself. For that, Nat was deeply grateful.

Nat sent back a thumbs-up emoji and took a deep breath.

Jo: *The most hostile emoji*

Why?

Words please

The other assistant, who was Jo's twin sibling, Justin, started typing in the thread. Jo managed publicity, and Justin took on UX/UI design — between them, all of Nat's blind spots were covered.

Justin: *What we mean is good luck! You're gonna crush it*

Justin: *Or kill it*

Justin: *Or some non-violent way to say
you're going to do great*

Nat: *I'm not nervous! I'm fine.*

Nat sent it before she could really think if it was true. The problem was that she tended to speak frankly when questioned by reporters. Concisely, factually. She was a coder, not a touchy-feely love guru after all. But her responses weren't always enough for everyone. In the rare times she had given an interview, Jo's feedback tended to include words like "hella blunt," sweating emojis, or simply "Mark Zuckerberg: human or robot?" memes. Then Justin would chime in with copy-pasted personality descriptions of Cancers (Nat's sun sign) and angry crab GIFs, until Jo would end the discussion with not-so-subtle asks if she could follow up with the reporter herself.

Jo: *Just stick to the talking points and it'll
be over before you know it*

Justin: 🦀 🦀 🦀

"Here we are. Moscone Center." The car pulled to a stop in front of the gleaming glass doors. A huge banner reading "Tech-Talk 2025" fluttered in the breeze. "Excited for the conference?" the driver asked.

Nat shook herself out of her reverie. "Kinda." She held up her badge, emblazoned with a yellow ribbon that read "SPEAKER."

"Oof, public speaking," said the driver, turning to face Nat rather than look through the rear-view. She was a petite Chicana woman with a shock of purple hair running through a shaggy wolf cut. "Not for me."

"Me neither, really." Nat eyed the crowd. The sidewalk was already filled with people lined up around the block to register.

"You're gonna be great," said the driver, winking. "Trust me, I can tell."

But before Nat could utter any thanks for this kindness, the backseat door yanked open.

"Yo, for Anthony?" said the voice attached to a muscled, Omega-watch-wearing arm that now motioned for Nat to get out.

She shot the driver a look meant to convey *Thank you, I'm sorry*, and *THIS GUY* all at once. Gathering her bag, she scooched by him as Anthony barked into his phone.

"So, I sent a DM like, 'Bro, you know I was the one who told you that STOICoin was going to blow up!' No cap! Yo, that's why I'm the CTO, dawg!"

My people, thought Nat as she grimaced and looked for the speakers' entrance. At thirty-five, she was old enough to remember the screech of the dial-up modem handshake, mix CDs, and making it a Blockbuster night. Majoring in Comp Sci had still been decidedly uncool for the Indiana University Class of 2012, and being a twenty-something woman with ideas for computer programs hadn't made people think she was gonna be the next big thing. It had made people think she was odd, especially in Indiana.

But she loved her work, and she loved the rush of coding — making a function run faster or squashing a persistent bug. It was like she was constantly building and solving and then remaking a puzzle just for her, a decade-long conversation with her own mind. She'd poured thousands of blissful (if also quite stressful) hours into her app. The BeTwo algorithm had actually started as a way to sort fishing flies, her mom's then-newest hobby and source of frustration. A professor had suggested she look into using it to sort personalities instead, as she showed Nat printed-out Yahoo! articles about the promise of a future where every lonely soul could find their match through the World Wide Web. Her overwhelmingly male classmates would never take on such a "touchy-feely" area as love, so Nat saw an opening and dove in.

Then, as breathless coverage of Elizabeth Holmes dominated magazine covers and every winking conversation with her parents' friends about why she was going to grad school in San Francisco instead of getting a job, Nat began to notice a shift. Suddenly, she was the one people were listening to, even if she was usually the only woman in the room. Her ideas were the ones being seriously considered, especially when she "pivoted into disrupting the dating space". Requisite tech bro jargon aside, it had seemed like there might actually be a seat at the table for her. She wanted to take it.

She paused outside a conference hall placard that read *Tech-Talk Opening Panel: Top Indie Apps of the Year*. A grid of app logos and names dotted the sign, including her own — *Natalie Lane, creator of* BeTwo. She counted half a dozen featured apps and felt her nerves relax a little. There'd be five other people on stage, plus the moderator. How much talking would she even have to do? This would be fine. She snapped a quick photo of the sign to text her mom and pushed through the doors.

* * *

On her way backstage, someone handed Nat a room-temperature bottle of water and a tote bag stuffed with stickers, pins, coasters, and flimsy sunglasses. In the green room, a dozen or so tech journalists hunched over laptops and smartphones, fingers furiously working their keyboards as their eyes scanned the room every few seconds. The biggest outlet and the event's biggest sponsor, the online juggernaut *BuzzFill*, had already commandeered an entire corner of the room — a teeming beehive of writers, interns, and audiovisual techs. Some of the panelists were already chatting up the reporters. Nat watched a twenty-something woman with wild pink curls gesture dramatically as she talked into a mic held by another twenty-something with asymmetrical hair and tattoos. She felt like she had only just landed where she wanted in her career, and yet she already felt the pressure of being replaced.

Nat was giving the journalists a wide berth when a hand suddenly grabbed her shoulder.

A petite producer with a *They/Them* shirt and a green pixie cut scream-spoke into a headset while holding up one finger to Nat's face. "I don't want excuses, Connor! I want any and all normies to be kept on the balcony!"

Before Nat could decide whether to defend herself against being a "normie" or jump at the chance to escape, they stopped yelling and smiled at her. "Speaker badge, yay! Panelists are over here."

"Hi, sorry," said Nat, as they scooted her toward a cluster of folding chairs and an oh-so-80s floral sofa that was probably a decade older than most people in the room. "I wasn't sure where to go."

"Just chill here," said the producer, whose name badge read V. "And help yourself to the spread." They gestured to a table piled with sweating cans and bottles and deli trays. "We've got sparkling water, all the flavors, though I wouldn't because the bubbles come back as burps onstage."

"Oh, that would be bad," Nat murmured as she took a seat against the screaming pattern of bright pink tiger lilies and palm leaves on the old sofa.

"Disaster. And we got a cheese sampler, but depending on how you do with dairy, that's basically gonna coat your throat in mucus. Saliva is already gnarly enough in a microphone, you know?"

"Totally . . ." Nat felt her chest tightening. "I probably won't eat the cheese then."

"Good call. Oh, and there's a keg of craft vodka tonics on tap." V took a breath and squinted into the distance. "Though, alcohol? Really? During a livestream?"

"Livestream?" Nat had a vague memory of Justin and Jo mentioning this, but it was actually too vague, almost as if they'd been trying to keep her from remembering it, which was why they were so good at their jobs.

V looked at Nat with a mix of bravado and pity. "The internet. You know how it is."

"Totally." Nat swallowed what she hoped was a normal amount of saliva and mucus. "Totally," she repeated.

"So, yeah, help yourself to the snacks. You're on in ten."

They stormed off, barking more orders into their headset, as Nat tried to take deep, calming breaths. Instead, she felt her body stiffen against the lumpy sofa cushions. Was she sweating already? She started to open the water bottle, then caught V giving her side-eye. OK, so it was a no to the water, and a yes to the sweating. She pulled out her phone to text the twins a question about maybe, just thinking out loud, maybe not doing the panel? — when someone plopped onto the sofa beside her.

"So, I guess I shouldn't have been downing all those gin-and-brie martinis, then?"

Nat laughed and turned to the voice. "I've never been so terrified of cheese in my life," she said. Beside her was a thirty-something man with deep olive skin and shiny black curls cropped above a boyish face. And he was smiling at her. Nat couldn't help but smile back.

He had thick eyebrows and dark eyes that sparkled as he gestured to the couch and said, "Here, let this weirdly tropical sofa soothe you into believing you are far, far away. Somewhere like . . ." His full lips turned up in a little smirk as he finished his thought. "Like at a Best Western in the year 1998."

Nat laughed again, and some more of the tension eased out of her chest. "'98?" she said. "I wish!" She turned toward him with an ominous creak in the couch, and scanned for his badge, but didn't see one. "Then I could just ride my bike to Blockbuster, and stay up all night eating Gushers and trying to find Carmen Sandiego."

Her companion smiled and shook his head. "I had a theory about that game and it wasn't popular around the school lunch table."

"Neither was I," said Nat. "So, let's hear it."

His brows knitted together, and Nat couldn't help but notice the way his boyishness sharpened into something more dashing when he was in thought. "Carmen Sandiego doesn't want to be found, right? And so, if we stop looking for her, she's free. We're both free." His dark eyes twinkled at Nat again. Mischief looked good on him. "So why catch the butterfly? Just observe its beauty."

Gorgeous eyes aside, Nat cringed. "Yikes! You said this out loud? In middle school?"

"I wasn't wrong!" he said as she laughed. "My point is, nothing you could say out there could possibly go over as poorly as my extended butterfly analogy to a group of seventh grade boys."

"I believe that," said Nat, as he paused, suddenly serious.

"Unless . . ."

"Unless?"

"Unless Brian K. is out there in the audience. Because in that case," he held his palm up to his face, "it doesn't matter that your hand is smaller than your head because you're about to get a bloody nose."

Nat laughed the last clench of nerves out of her stomach as she sank into the sofa. "Yeah, obviously." She smiled at him as the sudden desire to look super, super cute flooded her body. She remembered that a guy she dated in college had always liked it when she tossed her hair. "And thanks," she said, fluffing some of her honey brown curls across her shoulder and leaning toward him. "I've never done one of these before."

She watched his approval of her gesture flash across his face as he said, "It's nothing. You looked like you were about to pass out, which usually only draws more attention." He raised one eyebrow. His eyes flared with secret mischief again. "Counterproductive."

Nat felt his gaze with a flip in her stomach. *Speaking of butterflies . . . It's been a long time.* "Hi, I'm Nat." She held up her badge as if he needed proof, remembering how she behaved like an anxious nun when she was nervous.

"Well, that's shitty luck," he blurted. His face fell before he picked it back up into a forced smile. "I mean, hey there."

Nat mock-frowned. "I always kinda liked my name, but to each their own," she joked, still too charmed to fully register the sudden shift in tone. "And anyway, what's your name?"

He jittered his leg up and down as he looked at the ground. "I'm Rami." Then he turned his eyes — colder and far less sparkly — to her. "And you're Nat Lane, creator of BeTwo, the only modern way to date."

"Well, yeah!" This time, Nat felt a swell of pride instead of dread for being recognized, and having her app's tagline quoted back to her no less. Now she practically wanted to crawl up and kiss the BeTwo billboard . . . and maybe this cute guy with the soft-looking lips too, while she was at it. "Glad our ads are working." She offered her hand. "Nice to meet you, Rami."

Rami just nodded and gave her a quick handshake before fishing out his phone.

Nat frowned in earnest this time, and watched him tap away. Was he nervous to meet her? The twins had told her this would start to happen, even though she'd never believed it. Who got nervous around a coder? But they *did* have that billboard on the freeway. She *was* here to be the top speaker at this panel. Maybe this was her first star-struck fan? It was actually really flattering, and since it'd been almost two years since she'd flirted with anyone, she'd take any help she could get. She smiled and tossed her hair again. "So, you use BeTwo?"

Rami grunted a laugh. "Yes, I have." He grunted again, and his face lit up at some interior joke. "Though now I just go straight for a root canal when I feel like inflicting that much pain upon myself."

Nat blinked in shock. *Pain? Upon . . . ?* "Excuse me?" she said.

Rami sighed and ran a hand through his thick curls. "Look, you seem like a nice person, but your app is . . ." He hesitated.

"Brilliant?" suggested Nat.

Rami smiled. "Evil."

Nat's mouth literally dropped open, and she had a second to register that such a cartoonish thing actually did happen in a state of outraged disbelief. Then V's neon pixie cut flashed into view. Clapping loudly, they bellowed, "Panelists! You're up! Form a single-file line along the yellow tape, not the red tape!" They clapped a few times after each word as they added, "Not! The! Red!"

Nat stood and tried to fix Rami with her coolest stare. But the butterflies only fluttered harder in her stomach when she saw his full frame—strong thighs in dark denim and broad shoulders in a neat gray button-down. "Well, sorry to cut this short, but I've got to get in line."

But instead of withering into the sofa as she'd hoped, Rami stood also. Now his espresso eyes were above her line of sight just enough to force her to look up and lose the high ground. "Yeah, me too." He fished a SPEAKER badge from his pocket as he added in a singsong voice, "See you out there!"

V clapped again. "Now, panelists, listen. Do not just silence your cell phones. I need them off. O-F-F!" They herded the panelists into a line along the yellow tape. "If those phones buzz in your pocket onstage, trust me, it's gonna sound like you just ripped a huge toot up there."

Nat fumbled for her phone as she followed Rami toward the line. "Wait, you're on the panel?" she hissed.

"Yeah, I made App Number Six, Whither, Weather. And yes, I know that's the last place on the panel, OK?"

The mention of his app almost caused Nat's mouth to drop open again, but she was guarded against that now. Yet on the inside, her butterflies were now flying in loops and tossing glitter around. She swallowed back the excitement and sputtered, "What? I love that app!"

Rami shrugged, unmoved.

"How did you get it to be so accurate?" she whispered, aware that this situation had now gone so completely off the rails that *she* was the star-struck fan of an app, albeit one with what she could only describe as symphonically beautiful functionality.

"Hard science," said Rami, rolling his eyes. "And an algorithm that doesn't prey upon emotional vulnerability." He smiled, and Nat clocked an infuriating set of dimples. "You should try it."

"First of all," said Nat, no longer even trying to whisper. "Have you ever seen my code? Because it'd make your mother weep, it's so fucking spotless—"

"Yes, exactly!" Rami spun to face her and leaned closer. "Your code makes all kinds of people weep. What have your BeTwo dates been like? Because as far as I can tell, your app only opens up a portal to a personal circle of hell for anyone who uses it."

The flips in Nat's stomach now turned to fire. Now he was talking about her baby. She leaned closer, too. "It's OK, just admit you're jealous of my work!"

"Right." Rami laughed to himself, a soft, dark sound that rippled against Nat's skin. "How about you answer a question for me. You've used your own app, right? I assume that's why you're normally about as public as Emily Dickinson?"

Nat stammered. His combination of a novel way to insult her introversion, mixed with a jab at her whole lack-of-a-dating-life thing, was enough to cross the wires in her brain, even when she was fired up on righteous rage and a handsome target. Rami's eyes lit up, but she didn't like their sparkle this time. She didn't like it at all.

"Oh my God," he said. "You've never used your own app, have you?"

"I beta-tested it for years . . ."

Rami leaned in even closer toward her. He bit his plump bottom lip in thought, and his long lashes fluttered as he searched her face. "But you've never actually used it to date?" He watched her squirm as his face hardened into the full realization. "Classic," he declared.

"Nat Lane! BeTwo!" V bellowed from the front of the line. "You're our top app, so we need you up here!"

"One minute!" Nat called to them. She turned back to Rami. Her cheeks blazed with heat, and somewhere in her mind, she hoped that the flush was making her look pretty and not deranged. "So what if I haven't used BeTwo?"

"So, you have no idea the utter swamp of social depravity that you've created!"

Nat recoiled. "OK, so like, how many BBC period dramas do you watch on a daily basis to talk like that?" She watched him smirk and nod, clearly used to being called out on his word choices. Good. She was the creator of the top app at Tech-Talk! He should be asking her for advice, not judging her work. It wasn't something she usually did, but she needed to flex . . . just this once. "And as for the 'depraved swamp,'" she said, "my two million users and counting would say otherwise!"

"No, they wouldn't!" His hands were clenched, and now it was his voice that was getting louder. "Everyone hates online dating, but we all do it because it's all there is now that your garbage app has ruined everything!"

V stomped toward her, but Nat kept her eyes locked on Rami. She closed the gap between the two of them with a step toward his steely, crossed-armed stance. Every thrumming cell in her body was determined to play this out. Her *garbage* app?

"Oh, so, you want to wait around for a meet-cute?" she asked. She ran her eyes down him and noted his lean figure despite her boiling anger. "You want to have to walk up to people in bars? Lock eyes on the subway? Fall for the guy who hits you with his car?" She watched him scoff. She'd read the angry comments on Reddit in her dark moments. She'd seen the flare-ups in the discourse. "If only we could do it the old-fashioned way, right?" she said.

Rami nodded, his face as hard as stone. "Yes, exactly," he said. "By talking. To humans. Like humans."

"Inefficient," said Nat, crossing her arms as she made her ultimate argument. She stomped her foot, and her boot made a satisfying *clack*.

"The romance overwhelms me!" declared Rami, placing a hand on his heart in a mock swoon and tipping his head closer to hers.

They locked eyes. Rami's face was so close she caught his woodsy scent — a soft mix of sandalwood and juniper that hit her lizard brain like a shot of tequila. She clocked the shadow of stubble along his angular jaw. The way the swell of his lower lip jutted out just a little in righteous indignation. Nat felt a smile twist into the corners of her lips, even against the currents swirling inside her body. She remembered how people sometimes pointed out the prettiness of her stormy green eyes, and she felt her lashes flutter in response. Rami's gaze widened, and he bit his lip. He lifted his long fingers from his chest and inched closer.

"Seriously, folks," said V, an abrupt interruption as they snatched Nat by the arm. "We're running a dry finger along the razor's edge of disaster, here. Stand on your designated tape outline!"

"This conversation isn't over," Nat hissed as she forced her legs to follow V away from Rami.

"Good luck out there!" he called, waving from the back of the line with a gleaming, politician's smile. Still, his eyes followed her, even as they flicked down her long legs and back up to her loose curls. Nat never wanted to see his face again, and also, at the same time, she wanted everyone but him to vanish from the room.

V snapped their fingers in front of Nat's face. "Nat, you good? Deep breaths."

Nat nodded and fixed her eyes on the spotlit stage ahead of her. "Let's fucking go."

CHAPTER 3

The panel had mostly proceeded without any big surprises. Even Nat had to admit it hadn't been as terrifying as she'd thought to sit at a table with five other people and read off a prepared slide deck, as long as she'd kept her eyes on the moderator instead of the two hundred or so faces in the crowd and the whirring cameras fixed on her. It was also a nice distraction from the blow-up with Rami, which blared into her mind every time she let her thoughts wander. Everyone had made it through their portion of the presentation in much the same way — explaining the problem that had given them the idea for the app, the arduous development process, the sudden roadblock that had threatened it all, and then the equally as sudden breakthrough that saved the day and led to the app as it was known and loved today.

Being the creator of the top app, Nat had gone first, so it hadn't struck her as odd to hear the random bursts of applause and sitcom-style whoops as she described BeTwo. But then she noticed the audience was a lot quieter for the other apps, and she'd squirmed uncomfortably as Rami introduced his section for Whither, Weather by saying, "Now I realize predicting the weather may not seem as exciting as finding a date, but even BeTwo's best match can be thwarted by an unexpected rainstorm . . ." He'd gotten a few polite laughs out of the line. But mostly, Nat hoped that

31

he'd been too distracted by presenting to see how she'd craned her neck to catch every pixel of his slides, or to notice how fascinating she'd found the details of his process. He finished his section with the requisite shout-outs to team members and QR codes for socials as a production assistant snuck back on stage to give each of the panelists mics again.

"Thank you so much for that, Rami!" trilled the moderator, a Hollywood-ready BuzzFill star with real journalism cred named Tracy Goodwin-King. From her wavy black tresses to her flawless brown skin, she radiated the glow of destined success, even while wearing a branded T-shirt under her pink blazer. "Panelists, before we go to questions from the audience, I just want to give it up for you all one more time for these amazing insights!" Tracy paused, and from her perch a few feet away, Nat could see her eyes narrow and flash in her perfect makeup — a look Nat knew all too well from seeing it on the popular middle school girls right before they'd hit her with a devastating jab. Her stomach clenched.

"Special thanks to you, Christine," Tracy cooed into her mic, turning her now serene gaze to Panelist #4, a twenty-something with half-dyed hair and a manic, toothy smile whose app was a distraction blocker that rewarded productivity streaks with stickers of round, gleaming butt cheeks. "Who knew that a molting snake would make such a robust and detailed analogy? And *so many times?*"

As a few snickers rose from the audience, poor Christine flashed her grin and nodded along, unaware or unable to fight the joke at her expense. Sweat prickled on the back of Nat's neck. Tracy was a stunning, whip-smart alpha with a microphone and a captive audience. Nat hated to make any more animal metaphors, but there was definitely blood in the water.

"All right!" Tracy beamed into the crowd with a toss of her dark hair. "Who has a question for our panel?"

Hands shot up as production assistants scurried between the rows with mics. A young guy in a tech-logo T-shirt stood.

"Yeah, this question is for Nat," he said.

Feedback whined into the mic as Nat winced at the noise and the instant attention. "Hi," she said, her mouth suddenly dry. The stage lights flared in her eyes as the spotlights found her. She heard the question-asker clear his throat.

"So, Nat, can you get us some hotter girls on BeTwo?"

A roar of male laughter filled the room as the asker smirked at Nat. The producer frantically grasped for the questioner's mic just as he added, "I'll take my answer off the air." He raised his arms above his head in triumph and sat down to some scattered applause.

No thoughts came to Nat as she registered the producer mouthing her the words, *I'M SO SORRY!* She sputtered into her mic, only vaguely aware that she was making sounds at all. "Um . . . uh . . . I . . ."

"No way, nope!" Tracy boomed into Nat's silence. "Nat, do not even dignify that with a response." She winked at Nat before turning her full, gorgeous fury toward the audience member. "And you, never speak into a microphone again."

A few hoots and some more applause rose as Nat shrank in her seat. She shot a glance at her fellow panelists. Christine gave her a double thumbs-up and a grin. Rami was shaking his head, staring at the table, and drumming his pen against a notepad. Nat felt puddles forming in her armpits as she reached for her lukewarm BuzzFill-branded water bottle.

"OK, can we get another question?" asked Tracy. "A real one this time?"

From the back of the auditorium, a tiny figure with a chest full of lanyards and badges rose. "Yeah, this one is also for BeTwo," he said.

Paula Rogers

"Careful," Tracy warned.

"No, no, it's serious!" the asker insisted. "So, my question is, what's the data on how to get the most girls to respond? Like you must know the most successful opening lines, or the stuff that gets the most right swipes in profiles?"

Tracy turned her glittering eyes to Nat. It seemed like this question was going to be allowed. Nat swallowed and raised her mic. "Well, running correlations on our backend data wouldn't necessarily give us any insight into causation for something so personal," she said, feeling her words echo into silence. "So, I don't have a magic formula. But I like to think—"

"OK specific scenario!" the asker interrupted. Nat could see his small figure in the back row, waving his hands to cut her off as he continued his thought. "What's better: having a little kid in your pics or having an unusual animal, like a hedgehog or a pot-bellied pig? Because I have access to all of those options, but I just want to maximize my impression, you know?"

Nat felt Christine perk up as the question, impossibly, continued.

"And if I go hedgehog or pig," he said, "would girls just think I'm some weirdo whose apartment smells like wet Cheerios? Because it doesn't. Thanks."

He sat as Christine raised her mic. "Some women enjoy the smell of wood chips."

"Yes, well, this is actually an interesting question phrased in an unusual way," chirped Tracy, righting the ship once again. She flashed a dental brochure smile at Nat. "Nat, do you have data on what makes the most quote-unquote successful profile?"

Nat forced her eyes not to roll, and picked up her last thought, a line she'd actually rehearsed with the twins days before. "Well, I like to think that all a profile needs to be successful on our app is to exist." She paused for a warm reaction, but none came. In fact, she thought she heard a scoff from Rami's end of the stage. She sat up straighter and turned to meet his gaze. She couldn't ignore the amused glow dancing in his eyes or the heat it sparked in her chest. "The BeTwo algorithm is so unique because it takes into account more personality factors than any other dating app, meaning that the more information you provide, the more accurate your matches will be. We like to let the users set how much they share."

Rami shook his head and drummed his pen.

"Sure," said Tracy with her Queen Bee poise. "But back to my question about the data. Do you take any steps to ensure that your app doesn't just replicate toxic, patriarchal standards from IRL dating?"

This time, Nat felt her nerves ease up a bit. Now this was her wheelhouse — talking about data, *her* data, and all the times she had painstakingly combed through it to ensure that her code sorted it in a way that was organic and true to the user pool. Unlike a lot of app creators, she thought of the vast set of data in the user pool as a kind of personal challenge-slash-conversation between herself and every person on her app. She let users input as many disparate variables as they wanted, and it was her job, and her joy, to figure out how to stretch her algorithm to respond to each one of them. She smiled in Rami's direction as she said, "Actually, I — we have one of the most diverse user pools exactly because we let people set a huge number of details about themselves from scratch, from preferred pronouns to polyamory and even asexual search filters." She sat up straighter still, visually flashing back to the hundreds of hours she and the twins had spent making sure the app could handle so much variety. "So, the hope is that each BeTwo user can look for what aligns with them so specifically that the search reflects them as an individual more than any kind of social norm."

Tracy gave an approving "Hmm!" but it barely covered another scoff from Rami's direction. He was now frowning and glaring at Nat like she had personally kicked him in the shins. She narrowed her eyes at him.

"Wow," said Tracy. She pursed her glossy lips. "So it sounds like you're saying that BeTwo actually endeavors to break bad social cycles in the dating world?"

This time, the whole auditorium heard Rami's scoff. And what he said next.

"*Break* bad cycles?" he spat into the mic. "More like spawn them like locusts!"

Tracy grinned. There was blood in the water, all right. "One of our other panelists would like to weigh in?"

Rami looked a little startled at his own outburst as he ran a hand through his curls and nodded. "Yeah, yeah, I would." His brow furrowed in the way Nat had found so charming before they'd learned each other's names and personalities. "I mean, being ghosted used to just mean some glowing dude in a Civil War uniform was watching you sleep. And that's still preferable to what it means now, right?"

He got some laughs at this line, but Nat just shook her head. *Ghosting.* She couldn't believe that was his best shot. "Look," she replied, "we didn't invent ghosting or tell people to start doing it." Adrenaline swirled in her body. Maybe she could be a shark, too. "And if it keeps happening to you, well, maybe that's not about the app, you know?" She went for the kill with a little stage-y smile and shrug. The audience hooted as Rami fixed his stare on his hands.

"Sorry, just a joke," Nat continued, tossing her hair and gesturing for the crowd. She wasn't sorry. "But BeTwo is really only serving a very simple need. It's labeled as a dating app, which is true, but it's not a full-service love experience. We're not here to be relationship counselors — it's just about making introductions to get people on a date and letting them take it from there."

Nat smiled, proud of her answer as Tracy pressed a pink-manicured finger to her earpiece and frowned. "Let's move on," she said. "How about one more question, and please, not about BeTwo?"

Most of the hands went down as Tracy craned her neck to scan the audience. "I think I see someone over by the doors? Maybe?"

"Actually, I have a question," said Rami. *Of course he did.*

He leaned forward, poised with his arms folded on the table like he was chairman of the Model UN. *He probably even had a special gavel.* He looked into her eyes and grinned. A chill coursed through her spine.

"Just curious," he said. "Have you ever used your own app?"

A *whoosh* of panic roared into Nat's ears as all eyes fixed on her and his question hung in the air. The same question he had already forced her to answer backstage. Rami raised his thick eyebrows in a collegial way, eyes shining with a kind of sinister glee. She snapped, "As I've said in multiple interviews, I spent five years of my life beta-testing BeTwo every single day—"

"No, I mean, have you ever *really* used it to try and find someone to love?" He kept his eyes locked on hers with a wolfish smile. He gave little shrugs as if the words were just occurring to him, as if he were genuinely curious to find out her answer. "Thrown yourself into your pool of users? Put yourself at the mercy of a swipe?"

The rows and rows of people in seats swirled in her vision as Nat fumbled for something to say. She'd never talked this publicly about her dating life before — on purpose. "I want to find a partner someday, but for now I'm happy being single." The words felt small in the huge room as soon as she finished the sentence. The faces in the front rows stared blankly at her. "And when the time comes," she blurted, ad-libbing. "When the time comes, I'm sure I will create a profile, OK?"

Tracy seized the moment. "Now, that's interesting," she said, eyes narrowing. "Nat, you play Cupid for millions of strangers, yet you're happily unattached?"

Nat tried to smile. "Yes, but, I mean, it's just for now . . . While I focus on my business!"

Christine tapped her mic. "Girl, you could catch a man in a hot minute," she said, nodding sagely.

"Th . . . thanks," Nat stammered. "You too."

Christine cringed. "Gross, no thanks!"

Before Nat could say anything, Rami chimed in again. "So, since you've never actually engaged with your own app as a user, let me tell you what your data doesn't show."

Anger flared hot in Nat's stomach. *Keep my data out of your absurdly perfect mouth!* She forced out a more stage-friendly response. "I'm sure nothing will surprise me."

Rami gave her a sympathetic nod, almost apologetic. "Well, your app is single-handedly destroying the fabric of human decency. Did you know that?"

"That must have slipped my mind."

Nat gritted her teeth as Rami rose, seizing his moment like the smug debate star she'd always dreaded back in her Academic Decathlon days.

"I see. You talk about your nuanced algorithm, but the only thing your app creates are superficial snap judgments." He walked to the front of the stage, gesturing to the audience. "Swipe away anyone who doesn't fit your exact standards at that exact millisecond, because who cares? Have sex with someone and never call them again, because who cares? There's always a sea of new faces to fulfill all your custom desires." Nat watched in horror as several people nodded along in the crowd as he continued. "It's like buying a car. Leather seats, but not wood paneling. Blonde, fit, lucrative job, but not too short. Dear Lord, not too short!"

"You're describing the paradox of choice — the more options you have, the less satisfying your choice will be," Tracy chimed in, putting on a pair of black-rimmed glasses that she seemed to have materialized for exactly this serious turn. "That's a fair point. What do you say to that, Nat?"

Nat shook her head with a deep frown. "*No!* No, he's missing the point entirely."

"Really?" said Rami, striding over toward her. Nat stood and walked up to cut him off, meeting him halfway. They stood center stage and close enough to touch. "Or maybe I see the point better than you do because I've actually used your app?"

He fixed her with a look that she could imagine being very happy to see in different circumstances — wise eyes, soft smile, a shadow of stubble giving him a delicious edge. But then he had more to say.

"BeTwo isn't a dating app. It's a *shopping* app. And I think it's disgusting."

At that pithy indictment, the audience finally came back to life with a mix of applause, some cheers, and some booing. Nat felt her legs wobble. It was impossible for her to tell how many of the reactions were in her favor, but she knew she hadn't completely lost them . . . yet.

"Nat, any response to that?" asked Tracy.

"Over two million users would say he's wrong," Nat said, refocusing on Tracy's unflappable cool.

"Would they?" Rami interjected. She was determined not to look his way, but out of the corner of her eye, she could see him returning to his seat. "Or does this way of dating just seem normal because everyone is doing it? Except it doesn't even work! It's all hookups and dick pics and a thousand sad nights at a bar that might as well never have happened, except that each one crushes your soul just a little bit more."

"Wow, dramatic much?" Nat cracked over a few cheers for Rami's rant.

"Oh really?" Rami countered. "Who is finding a quality connection on BeTwo? Anyone?"

Nat laughed. "Tons of people! Every day!" Now it was her turn to work the audience. She gestured to them like a magnanimous queen. "Lots of you, right?"

Except she didn't get the rousing applause she'd expected — more like a few scattered, uncertain claps. She was losing them. She was losing this. And that couldn't happen.

Especially not with him.

"OK, fine!" she cried, collapsing back into her seat. "I'll make a profile and find a great guy to date on BeTwo. Done! It's not that hard!"

Rami flinched with shock as Tracy spoke up. "Now that is an interesting story. The guru tests her own medicine . . ."

"Or drinks her own Kool-Aid," he grumbled.

Ever the professional, Tracy turned to the audience. "What do you all think? Post on social with the hashtag 'BeTwoChallenge' and help me pitch this to my editor!"

The applause Nat had been looking for filled the auditorium, and she felt in her bones that something big had just happened. A surge of victory rushed through her as a few voices called out in the din.

"*Do it!*"

"This is getting off topic!"

"Snakes!"

She covered her mic and leaned back to call out to Rami. "Checkmate, asshole!"

He covered his mic and called right back, eyes gleaming as he smirked and hit her with his perfect dimples. "Rest in peace, BeTwo!"

"Well, the people have spoken," said Tracy with a dazzling smile for the cameras. "Keep an eye out for this BuzzFill exclusive series as we follow Nat Lane as she uses her own app to find love—"

"Wait!" cried Nat. "To be a true test, we need a complementary vector." She smiled at her rival as triumph pounded in her ears. "Isn't that right, Rami?"

"What? No!" His face fell as he bumped his lips on the mic. "I never said that."

Nat now rose and strode across the stage toward Rami. "It'll be a race." She stopped in front of him, close enough to smell his woodsy-sweet cologne and see the sweat rising on his smooth olive skin. "Can Rami, here, find a date before I do, but without using any apps?" She popped a hand on her hip and smiled at him like they were old friends. "You know, the old-fashioned way!"

"No way."

The audience booed as Nat laughed. "Aww, get back on the horse! When was your last date?"

Rami balked. "'Back on the horse?' Nice one, boomer. And it was only eleven months ago."

The audience laughed as Rami winced. Nat almost felt sorry for him as she watched him register that pretty much everyone else in the room actually did feel sorry for him.

"Those terms sound fair to me. Rami, what do you say?" asked Tracy. "Nat has to find a date online and you have to find a date IRL?"

Rami ran his hand through his curls and looked at Nat from under his thick lashes. She could practically see the resolve swelling up inside him, and it suited him. He stood and fixed her with a confident gaze. Nat's stomach flipped, despite the adrenaline surging around her body. "You know what? Yes." He smiled, and at the words, his chocolatey eyes softened, just like when they had been strangers joking on an ugly floral sofa. She couldn't believe that it had only been an hour ago. "Nat Lane and the only modern way to enter a depressive state," he quipped on her tagline as he held out his hand. "You're on."

The crowd roared their approval as she took his hand and gave it a firm squeeze. Through the noise, her mind pinged at how soft and strong his hands felt in hers, but she just tossed her hair and laughed. "Excellent."

CHAPTER 4

Technically, Rami beat Nat in getting off the stage first, but she made sure that she wasn't too far behind. She dodged the other panelists, the flocks of their people, and the congratulations of the producers as she tracked Rami backstage, closing in on his mop of dark curls and slightly sad posture.

"Listen, weatherman," she began as he whirled around. "Let's get one thing straight right now—"

"Please, can we not?" He waved his hands to his ears. "I'm pretty sure I just publicly humiliated myself on at least five different levels out there, and I just want to take a moment to really soak that in."

Nat scoffed. "Are you kidding? This was *your* idea!"

"I'm sorry, did you enter an alternate dimension and completely miss what you, yourself, said into a microphone in front of hundreds of people and the entire internet?"

"Did you miss the part where you told the entire internet that my app is garbage and that I'm garbage for not using it?"

He frowned. "Oh no, I stand by every word of that. Thinking of having T-shirts made, actually."

Nat felt her cheeks flare. "Good idea. You'll be needing a consolation prize for when I destroy you."

Rami barked a dry laugh. "Even if you didn't have a terrible personality, which to be clear, you absolutely do, Helen of Troy couldn't wrangle a commitment out of the cesspool of dating apps."

43

Nat laughed back at him, tossing her hair. "Well, the thing is, I've met you. So, I'm not too worried about you beating me to anything but the Reddit forums for 'sad bois.'"

They locked eyes for a silent moment before a wave of cherry perfume and the buzz of interns hit them. They blinked, and Tracy's arms were around them. Her skin was impossibly soft.

"Wow, you guys. That was brilliant!" she cooed as her minions took notes. "This is viral content gift-wrapped and delivered from the gods." She released her embrace and clapped her hands. "Can I get a producer over here? Have we gotten legal on the phone yet?"

V's green pixie raced forward. "Already have the contracts, standard terms and access, effective upon signing." They held out two packets of paper already on clipboards to Nat and Rami.

Nat grabbed hers right away. "Ready when you are."

Rami smirked. "Oh, I am extremely ready to crush you." He flipped through the papers. "And also, what are the terms, exactly?"

Tracy patted his hand for reassurance. "You both agree to meet up with me one month from now at the BuzzFill BuzzForce Expo, where we'll do an exclusive, live interview about the results of the race — did you get any dates, did you have fun, catch herpes, find your soulmate, blah, blah, blah."

Nat watched Rami's eyebrows creep up his forehead in fear as he listened to Tracy's explanation. "One month?" he repeated.

"Yes, and Nat only uses BeTwo," she continued. "Rami, I don't know, talks to strangers, I guess. Cool?"

Nat grinned. "Absolutely, and again, good luck with that."

Rami glared at her as V signaled to Tracy.

"Oh! One more rule!" said Tracy. "You absolutely cannot, under any circumstances, contact each other for the duration of the competition." She smiled and folded her arms, bracelets tinkling like bells. "So, are we good?"

"Perfect," said Nat.

"Perfection," said Rami.

V handed them each a pen. "Just sign on the line there. We'll email you copies ASAP. You have twenty-four hours to make any changes, but I wouldn't—" They stopped as both Nat and Rami immediately signed and handed their contracts back. "OK, then."

Nat took a deep breath. She didn't have to think about the unknown dates with unknown men lying ahead, the sudden shove into the public spotlight, or whatever the twins would have to say about this when she got back to the office. She just had to think about one thing — the look on Rami's face at that very moment. Sure, he'd puffed up his posture, and his pouty lips were twisted into a knowing smile. But his eyes? She held his gaze. There, in the warm cinnamon defiance, was a flicker. A quick glance away, and then a flash of fire when they met hers again. And that made Nat's stomach flip with excitement. "Game on," said Nat.

"More like game over," said Rami. His eyes darted again. "For you, I mean," he added.

* * *

The coworking space that housed BeTwo was sunny and calm as Nat pushed through the double glass doors. About half a dozen start-ups and ventures shared offices in the converted fruit-packing building close to the water. Slapped with a thick coat of white paint, and with the exposed concrete floors covered in gloss to make each pockmark seem intentional, the building had the blue-collar history that tech workers seemed to crave for their offices, as if in some subconscious apology for the more ephemeral nature of their fortunes made in code and ninety-nine-cent in-app purchases. Plus, the space was near the baseball stadium and at least three different indie microbreweries that were more than happy to take that tech money.

Nat had chosen it because they had given her a break on the rent — part of an initiative to get more female and minority-led businesses going in tech. When she'd moved in years ago with a fledgling BeTwo in barely workable beta, she was trying to make the most of her dwindling savings, and even a shabby spot in a tech office was good enough to give her credibility with investors. As months passed and she gained users and then seed money and her two employees, she'd stayed because the office turnover was high enough that by the time her office mates realized that they shared space with one of the top dating apps, their funding would either run out or come raining down, and they'd be packing up for a reset or a grander space before she had to field any pointed small talk around the ping-pong tables.

As such, the BeTwo office was nestled in a drafty back corner — really a cluster of two parallelogram-shaped rooms, one deeply overstressed kitchenette, a storage closet that mainly housed a giant, load-bearing beam, and two half-windows with partial views of the Bay Bridge and full views of the dumpsters of the organic grocery store next door, or as Justin called it, "San Francisco's hottest rat restaurant."

Nat could hear Justin squabbling with Jo before she even reached the doors. A glimmer of optimism shot through her that, hey, maybe they weren't freaking out about the stunt she had just pulled, but she knew better. She took a deep breath and walked in.

Justin and Jo were poised mid-argument, identical angry statues, as they clocked her entrance. Justin's long hair was pulled into its typical yoga-ready topknot, and his leather slides were scattered by the sofa, exposing his latest pedicure — gunmetal gray. "Hey there, boss," he greeted her in his soft patter. His voice always sounded both somber and sweet, like he was delivering world news to a kitten.

His sister, Jo, on the other hand, had a different manner. "We'd ask how it went, but, the internet," she said sharply, before raising her hands in a slow clap. On her frame, the topknot looked more spreadsheets than savasana, and her black patent loafers were very much still on her feet. In fact, Jo was almost always on her feet, which had their own pedicure that would never deviate from her standard rotation of cherry red, navy blue, and ballet pink.

"But, hey, you're a trending topic now," offered Justin, pushing Jo's hands down. "So, like, congrats! Although you're still pretty far below the Applesauce Bead Challenge."

Nat dumped her stuff and opened up her laptop in what she hoped was a no-nonsense and unbothered gesture. "You're up to speed," she said, frantically clicking her social feeds closed. "Good." As her email notifications reached stratospheric numbers, she closed her laptop altogether and started to pace in what she hoped was an authoritative and even more unbothered way. "So, obviously we need to start with my profile. Do y'all still have the data on what gets the most responses from our male users?" She tossed a casual glance at Justin, choosing to ignore the fact that she'd just used the word *y'all*, which she never used, which was definitely not the sign of an unbothered person.

He raised his eyebrows.

"We have it," said Jo. "But that was only for our investors, right? To get them to support our totally above-board and honest algorithm that we don't game in any way, remember?"

"What's your point?" asked Nat, smoothing out some wrinkles on her button-down.

Jo frowned. Nat knew how much she hated it when people weren't catching up with the obvious logic of a given situation, or pretending not to. It was one of the many things they had in common. "The most successful keywords for women in your age group were 'goat yoga,'" she said. "Do you even know what that is?"

Nat gave Justin a breezy smile and managed to quell her impulse to shoot him finger guns. "Yes, obviously."

Jo frowned deeper. "Oh, really?"

Nat crossed her arms. "It's an acronym."

Jo crossed her arms back. "Go on," she said.

Nat began to pace again. "Gluten-free," she began. "Obviously."

"The *O* is for *obviously*? Is that your final answer?"

"No! *O* is for . . . outdoor, obviously." She managed a laugh. "The *A* is . . . antibiotic . . ." She trailed off, pretending to watch something fascinating at the rat restaurant.

"And the *T*?" asked Jo.

Nat looked her in the eye. "Tanning," she said loudly, as the word echoed off the concrete floors and exposed beams.

"Wow," whispered Justin. "That was rough."

"Exactly," said Jo, flipping open her own laptop.

"Wait, is it just actual goats? Like from a farm?" asked Nat. A Google search would bring her dangerously close to checking her email and socials, and she couldn't risk that, no matter how much she wanted an answer.

"Just let her cheat," said Justin, eyeing Nat with clear pity.

"It's not cheating!" said Nat. "User data is just a tool in my toolkit. A toolkit that I built, by the way." She pulled a chair up next to Jo, who was already searching around BeTwo's backend reports. "So come on, hit me with the magic stats."

"It's much less shady when you say it like that," Jo muttered, typing as Justin hit the lights and cast her screen to the big monitor on the wall.

Nat grinned as reports and keywords filled the big screen. "Looks like the forecast calls for me to bring the thunder, weatherman." She ignored Justin and Jo giving each other one of their telepathic twin looks, aware that this signal was almost certainly about her. "Now let's build me the perfect profile."

CHAPTER 5

Justin stretched his arms tall above his head as Jo clicked rapid-fire around the BeTwo reporting interface. Nat pulled up a blank profile on her laptop and projected it to their other big monitor. *Just like any other user*, she told herself, before squinting into the analytics spinning on the adjacent screen.

"OK, so the data shows that mentioning international travel gets high engagement rates among straight male users," said Jo.

"Well, you kinda used to live in London, right?" offered Justin.

Nat flashed to the last time she'd been in that city — her undergrad study abroad program over ten years ago. Sara had stayed in Bloomington for a sports media work-study job, commentating for the women's soccer team — just one of the five majors she'd sampled in college. But Nat had made fast friends with a jock-ish guy named Jake, and fast enemies with her London roommate, a model-gorgeous mean girl on a dance scholarship named Katie. By the time London had influenced them enough that Katie was insisting on being called Kate, and Nat was downing several cups of PG Tips a day, their dynamics had been set. Nat was in love with Jake, who was in love with Katie, who was in love with Jake's attention.

The routine was that Nat and Jake would have hours-long chats in the pub, and swap homemade mix CDs before class, and marathon Monty Python DVDs together in her dorm, but Nat would all but vanish as soon as Katie swept into their tiny room.

Then Jake would jump up from where he almost always sat, on Nat's bed, and stutter and brush off his time with her like Cheetos dust from his fingers. Katie would inform Jake of what party they would be going to that night as she touched up her makeup, and Jake would turn back to Nat, suddenly sheepish when they'd been cracking each other up just moments before, and ask, "Uh, Nat, do you want to come with us?"

And Nat would reach for a book, pull on the drugstore reading glasses that she thought made her look sophisticated, and shake her head no. Katie would roll her eyes and scoff, and Jake would shuffle out behind her, floating away from Nat on a wave of Katie's fruity body spray and flat-ironed hair, while somewhere deep inside Nat's heart she believed that one night Jake would come back and choose to spend the evening with her, instead. Night after night, she clung to the hope that maybe a twenty-something guy on a semester abroad would see the romance of staying in and doing the crossword with her. After all, she thought it was pretty ideal.

He never did.

"We're not putting London in my profile," said Nat. She pulled her hair into a time-for-business ponytail and began typing.

MOST IMPORTANT THING ABOUT ME: I'm a total travel junkie, always down to visit a new continent. Wanderlust is my middle name!

Jo sighed loudly. "That keyword only works if you misspell it."

Nat blinked at her in confusion.

"W-o-n-d-e-r-lust . . ." Jo rolled her eyes.

Nat winced. She was trying to win this bet with Rami, yes, but she was also the same person who had won her elementary school spelling bee three years in a row, and asked for a trophy case for her birthday, and cried when she had gotten a bicycle instead. So, choosing between victory and accuracy was truly like choosing between her own babies, and yet, she knew her data wouldn't lead her astray. She changed the spelling.

"Wait, there's more!" Jo pulled up more analytics. "Men only respond to the international travel keyword if the travel is for pleasure, not work, and if the words 'itinerary' and 'spa' are not included."

> *I just go wherever the open road guides me . . . the only plans*
> *I make are for whatever seems F-U-N!*

"Too much?" asked Nat.

Justin frowned at Nat's projected profile-in-progress. "I mean, it doesn't exactly seem accurate," he said.

"How so? It aligns with the data Jo just presented."

"It doesn't seem accurate to *you*," he clarified.

Nat waved her hand as if shooing a fly. "But it's accurate to the *data*," she said, pointing to the screen. "That's how we'll win."

Justin leaned toward Nat with the delicate air of a besweatered guidance counselor. "But what would winning really mean in this situation, anyway?"

Jo shot her brother a loaded glance as she continued. "So, the word 'fitness' performs way above average, and you should use as many, like, sporty words as you can because each one of those is like a mating call for most guys, apparently."

"Easy," said Nat.

> *HOW I SPEND MY TIME: You can usually find me biking through the park or brushing up on my G.O.A.T. yoga. Fitness is super important to me! Almost as important as football, baseball, basketball, soccer, lacrosse, badminton, and bowling.*

"Nailed it," said Justin, nodding sagely.

"Again, 'goat' is not an acronym," said Jo, already exasperated. "It's literally yoga with goats. And I feel like you're just listing all the sports you've heard of."

Justin grunted and agreed with his sister. "Dude. And, actually, you do not want to date a badminton guy — they are such bad news. Trust me."

"What's just, like, one physical activity that you actually do?" asked Jo. "You live in California. There must be something."

The last time Nat had gone for a nature walk had been after Tech-Talk 2023, during her last romance, if you could call it that. She'd met him during one of the dozens of crowded happy hours where people wearing lanyards yelled over DJs and exchanged business cards, chintzy swag, and in the case of Owen, phone numbers because he was handsome, witty, and lucky enough to have met Nat before she'd started compiling her wish list.

So, they'd linked up for a stroll in Golden Gate Park, not exactly a hike but walking distance from her apartment in the Panhandle and definitely very beautiful. Their conversation had carried them past the entrance gate at the tail end of the Haight-Ashbury (neither of them were Grateful Dead listeners), past the Conservatory of Flowers (both of them had trouble keeping houseplants alive) and all the way to the California Academy of Sciences (Owen informed her that the penguins had a live stream. Nat informed him that the albino alligator was named Claude) before their chat had simply, inexplicably, dried up.

Nothing offensive had been said, nothing major had gone wrong, but Nat remembered looking around the objectively gorgeous park and the objectively gorgeous guy next to her and just feeling like suddenly all the air had gone out of the balloon. It was as if the switch had flipped to *OFF* between them, and she could see it all over Owen's face, too. Now his eyes darted around instead of winking at her. Now his stride was quicker, instead of leisurely, and matched to hers. Now he responded with one-word answers instead of volleying questions. There was no ignoring it — Owen radiated discomfort and, palpably, boredom.

And she felt the same way. It seemed like in the fated hourglass of their time together, they only had about twenty-five minutes' worth of sand. Which would have been less tragic had they not been in the middle of the park. So, they'd made strained chit-chat as they doubled back on the route that had unspooled around them so effortlessly before. Now every inch felt like an acre.

At some point, he'd asked for more detail on what her app did, and she'd revealed that she was working on a dating app called BeTwo, to which he blurted, "I haven't tried that one yet, but I will now!" She winced, and he managed an awkward laugh, but he didn't even try to cover the fact that he'd just told his current date that he was going to look for a new date. Some part of Nat had wanted to stick up for herself, say something to salvage the shreds of her dignity she felt slipping away like the wispy clouds in the sky above them, but she couldn't think of the right words.

The silence between them grew thicker after that.

Back at the gates, they managed a polite back-tapping hug before waving goodbye and, Nat assumed, thanking their respective gods it was over and vowing to never see each other again.

Her Golden Gate Park date experience had at least inspired her to make BeTwo sort users based on the most specific set of criteria out there, thus doing her part to spare anyone else the nightmare of a date running out of gas midair.

As it turned out, however, Owen also lived in Nat's neighborhood, so she'd started seeing him at her bus stop pretty regularly after that. They never spoke or even made eye contact. He radiated discomfort in a way that made it seem both compassionate to ignore him and impossible not to feel his presence like sticky syrup on her skin.

Then he started showing up with a girl who, Nat was not proud to admit, she immediately judged as beneath her. That was based solely on her haircut — flattering and fashionable and therefore, to Nat's wounded, bitter eyes, unoriginal. Then again, Nat was never very charitable before ten in the morning.

Still, basic haircut aside, for months and months, Nat had started every morning with the sight of her awkward date holding hands and sharing umbrellas and leaning on the shoulders of the woman he actually desired. And she had to admit it hurt.

It wasn't like she had wanted Owen, really. But she couldn't help the question that filled her mind as she forced her eyes toward a pigeon or an interesting cloud — why hadn't he wanted her?

Finally, the couple had stopped showing up, and Nat could only assume they had moved into a new place together. Mixed with the relief was the hope that one day it would be her turn.

Now she realized that it had all happened over two years ago.

Jo cleared her throat and tapped the screen with a square pink nail. "Is it really that hard for you to think of an actual sports-like activity?"

Nat blinked back into the present and looked at the list of certified sports words she had just entered into her new dating profile. She ignored the wet sting in her eyes and just replied, "This is fine. What else gets high message rates?"

Jo sighed. "OK, well this one is weird, but don't use any question marks."

"What? Why not?" asked Nat. The sensation of being surprised by her own data made her skin prickle with dread.

"Or semicolons," said Jo. "Colons are OK though."

"Semicolons I get." Justin scratched his chin and nodded. "Too symbolically loaded."

"A semicolon," Jo repeated, flatly. "Really?"

"Semi means half," Justin explained. "Body horror is not sexy." He smiled. "To most people."

"Gross." Jo buried her head back in the data.

The words on her profile stared at Nat like a puzzle, which happened to be one of her actual favorite activities. "What about exclamation points?"

"Strong positive performance," Jo reported.

MY PERSONAL MOTTO: Here's my philosophy: Let's have fun!!!!! Where we'll have it: Everywhere!!!!!!!!!!!!!

Jo scoffed. "Come on, no one is going to say anything about not letting women have their periods?"

Justin leaned in for a twin high five. "Nice one, sis!"

Jo let a smile creep onto her face. "I mean, the joke was right there."

Nat shot Jo an approving smirk. Jo had been her first hire, Justin had been a later decision, and although Nat had spent years designing BeTwo on her own, Jo felt as woven into it as the code itself. She was fastidious and focused. She was an overachiever who never stopped pushing for the best. She was, in Nat's mind, a younger and more socially savvy version of herself, and having someone who not only got her app but also got *her* as a person — it almost felt like family.

Nat clicked to the next part of the profile, where users answered a randomly generated personal question. She read the prompt aloud, "When's the last time I cried?" and choked on a dry laugh. "Yikes, did we really include that?"

"Oh yeah!" Justin piped up. "That's a good one. Our beta showed that asking the user at least one emotional question created a sense of buy-in, remember?"

Jo wagged her finger. "But then we also found that the responses generated way more matches for straight men, and way less for straight women, so we muted the answer on female profiles."

Nat breathed a sigh of relief, and not just because the honest answer had been earlier that week over an Instagram reel showing elderly dogs Photoshopped next to pictures of their puppy selves. "Cool, I'll just skip that one then."

Justin pumped his fist and sang out, "Time for the pics, boss!" He unfolded his gangly legs and sat up straight. As Nat's go-to for all things visual, from design to how they measured photo engagement, she trusted him completely. And yet, pictures?

Nat crumpled against her chair. It'd been mostly a full year of nights on her couch, overfilled glasses of wine, and takeout for dinner after working late, and she'd stopped even making excuses for why she wasn't going to the gym. So, she wasn't really feeling ready for pants with buttons, let alone a camera.

"User engagement shows that you need more than two full-body shots, outdoors, no babies, no group shots, no pets," said Justin.

"No pets?" asked Jo, offended. "Still?"

"Yeah, dude. Cats I get, but dogs?" Justin shook his head sadly. "Man, it's really tough out there."

Nat used their distraction to make a move, pulling her head-shot from the Tech-Talk conference panel website and making it her profile pic.

"A headshot?" Jo squinted into the monitors. "Do we even have data on that?"

"If we do, it's way down in the dregs," said Justin, searching the data.

"Great!" chirped Nat. "That means it's unique and will stand out."

"You know that's not how this works," said Jo, looking at Nat with a curious gaze. Nat had a sudden memory of a happy hour where she'd had one too many gin and tonics and told Jo about her nightly searches for her perfect date. Jo had looked at her then much as she was looking at her now, with a kind of ferocious pity.

"It's fine," Jo said, blinking her focus back to her screen. "I'll just crop some from your socials later when I do your posts for you."

"Have I told you today that you're the best?" Nat gave her a grateful smile and stood.

"Yeah, yeah." Jo shrugged in a satisfied little gesture and reapplied her lip gloss.

"Then I think that's it. We did it!" Nat gestured dramatically at her laptop as if coaxing out a spell from its LED glow. "And upload!"

But before she could hit the button, both twins cried out, "Wait!" Jo put her head in her hands as Justin cringed. They hated it when they accidentally spoke in unison.

"You need a headline, boss," Justin said, gently. "Remember? We added it last month to increase skim-ability?"

Nat froze in embarrassment. Of course, she remembered. The all-nighters to implement that functionality hadn't been that long ago. But why hadn't she remembered just now? "Totally, totally," she covered, hunching over to type.

NATALIE, F, 35 — Let me know if you want to meet up! Yay!

Now Nat clicked the button. "And upload!"

"Yay!" parroted Justin.

"Yay," echoed Jo, getting up to switch the lights back on.

Justin cracked open a sparkling water. "Did you guys ever read *Frankenstein?*" he asked. "I just started it again. That book is so cool."

Jo lit up, relieved at the new topic. "Um, yes, remember I was stage manager for our high school production of the play?"

"Wait, that's amazing!" cried Nat, also grateful for something new to think about. "Because I was stage manager for my high school production of *Young Frankenstein*."

"So that's like the prequel, right?" said Justin with true innocence.

And as both women turned to him, eager down to their very bones to explain the difference, they were all silenced by the telltale sound of a digital *ping!* from Nat's computer.

"Oh my God." A tingling wave of adrenaline ran through Nat's body. "My first message!"

Justin put his arm around Jo. "Our baby is all grown up."

Jo beamed, ever ready to see the fruits of her labor. "Well, come on. Read it!"

Nerves fluttered in Nat's chest as she clicked open the little bouncing envelope icon and started to read. "Hey gorgeous, any chance you're downtown for a happy hour?"

"That's his shot?" Justin rolled his eyes. "Snooze."

"Give the people what they are mathematically proven to want," said Jo, also rolling her eyes.

"Totally. Text me!" Nat said the words aloud as she typed them along with her phone number and hit send. She snapped her laptop shut. "Done and done."

Justin hesitated. "Uh, shouldn't we, like, look at this guy's profile first?"

Jo tapped away at her keyboard. "On it. Sixty-one percent match. He seems normal, no obvious signs of criminal intent or Jordan Peterson quotes."

Nat leaned against the window with a satisfied smile. "It's fine. It's just a date!" She watched some seagulls rip hunks off a sourdough loaf. "And I built this app, remember?"

CHAPTER 6

The hours since Rami left Tech-Talk had not been easy ones. After signing the contracts, he'd walked away from the meeting, down the cascading sets of stairs through the conference center, out of the heavy glass doors, past the throngs of attendees milling about in the nearby park, and then out into the gray grid of downtown San Francisco — and he'd basically not stopped walking since. He'd always heard that it was possible to traverse the entire seven-mile-by-seven-mile city on foot in a day. Maybe today he would test the theory. Because if he stopped moving, he would maybe have a panic attack.

How had this happened? Whither, Weather was pretty much a solo operation, plus the support of a few contractors scattered throughout the US and Europe. So, maintaining it took up a lot of his time, and it wasn't like the weather ever took a break. Being invited to the Tech-Talk panel had been huge for him, so huge, in fact, that he had put aside his many, many reservations and fears just to give his work the chance to be seen by the kinds of people who could make a difference in his career. Now, he would say that his worst fears had come true, but he hadn't been nearly creative enough to imagine the horrors that had emerged on that stage.

He squinted into the bright California sun and checked his app. Yep — it aligned with the current sunny and clear conditions in the form of an anthropomorphized cartoon sun who wore blue polarized shades and flexed gleaming yellow muscles. Rami had included this design element in his very first ideation of the app, the one drawn in colored pencil way back in a middle school science class when the idea of a pocket-sized weather computer had seemed outlandish. So, this dancing, showboating sun had been an inside joke to himself and the weird little comics he used to make before he spent all of his time on programming. It had nothing to do with the accuracy of his app. But then the internet had gotten wind of it, latched on to it with the force of a million memes, and made Fun Sun a viral hit. That, too, had nothing to do with the accuracy of his app, but it had made it shockingly popular. Still, something in him twinged a little bit when people praised his app for Fun Sun instead of its best-in-class prediction success rate.

But Nat had praised the accuracy.

Rami let out an audible groan. *Nat.* He turned down a side street that smelled rich and salty-sweet from a nearby dim sum spot. And there it was, back in his mind — his devil's bargain with not just one, but two of his personal *bête noires*, online dating and clickbait journalism. How had he let this happen? Because the first girl he'd actually enjoyed flirting with in months turned out to be the creator of an app that had brought him nothing but personal misery? Because he hated public speaking, which was part of why he had chosen to be a programmer in the first place, and since when did repping your personal brand have anything to do with your coding skills?

He was sweating now, even though it was a crisp 62 degrees Fahrenheit outside, and would definitely drop at least ten degrees once the fog started to roll in. His back hurt from lugging around his laptop for so long. His phone buzzed in his pants pocket, as it had been doing steadily since the panel. Rami kept walking. He didn't feel like talking to anyone about the mess he'd made for himself. At least not until his panic had given way to some sort of game plan for a solution. He groaned and heaved his backpack higher on his shoulders.

"Hey, take it easy there, cowboy." A man leaning against a liquor store eyed Rami with concern as he passed.

But the fact of the matter was that Rami's panic was partly, maybe entirely, because he already knew the game plan. There was really only one option. He had to start talking to women — asking them out, going on dates, *getting back on the horse*, as Nat had so infuriatingly put it on the livestream with that little impish smile of hers — the one that showed her pointed canines, one of his biggest turn-ons. But doing any of that was something that he'd been carefully avoiding for the past eleven months, as he had so humiliatingly confessed on the livestream.

Eleven months.

Had it really been that long? He heaved his pack again and rubbed his face. He felt clammy. His feet hurt. He stopped in front of a chalkboard sign on the sidewalk advertising artisanal espresso and looked in through the cafe's bay windows. A dozen or so people dotted the airy space, mostly solo, mostly women. He caught his reflection in the glass, not nearly as crazed looking as he felt, or at least nothing that couldn't be concealed by fixing his hair, having a coffee, and sitting down instead of pacing the streets. Yes, this coffee was probably going to cost him at least nine dollars. Yes, this cafe was infuriatingly named The Spaniel Project in an old-timey script font even though the sign also read, *Est. 2023.* But this was his fate. The one he had made for himself. It was time to face the music. It was time to cast himself at the feet of serendipity and pop culture references. It was time to talk to strangers.

* * *

Espresso in hand, Rami surveyed the spread of communal tables in front of him. Twenty- and thirty-somethings typed away on phones, tablets, and laptops, mostly insulated by Princess Leia-looking headphones. He grabbed an open seat between two pretty women who were not wearing engagement rings.

He turned to the woman on his right. She was wearing a fuzzy green cardigan and had long hair with heavy black bangs. She looked serious, like she read Russian literature and could tell him dry, existential jokes through rings of cigarette smoke, which was cool. Did cool people still smoke anymore? Why did he think he would know? He cleared his throat. "Excuse me, do you know the Wi-Fi password?" He smiled.

She took out one of her earbuds as he deflated inside. He hadn't seen those. "What?" she asked, blinking large blue eyes at him.

"Hi, how are you?" Rami said, smiling again. Or maybe just smiling broader. He wasn't sure if he had actually stopped smiling.

The blue eyes narrowed. "I'm fine?"

"How's your coffee?" asked Rami. In his mind, he leaned his chin on his hand in a charming, quizzical manner. In reality, he stayed perfectly frozen still.

"It's a chai tea," she replied.

Rami perked up. "Actually, 'chai' means tea," he said. "So, it's redundant to call it 'chai tea.'" He brought his hand to his chin, instead of the other way around, as he said, "Did you know that?"

His would-be literary lover rolled her eyes. "Wow great thanks," she grumbled.

"That doesn't matter. I don't know why I said that." Rami managed a little laugh. "Do you like the blend, though?"

Her eyes lit up, and she smiled back. Rami felt her prettiness clutch in his chest as she said, "Oh yeah. It's great!" She pushed her cup toward him. "But can I get it with a splash of oat milk this time? Thanks."

She popped her earbud back in.

"Oh, no, I don't—" he stammered. "I don't work here." She frowned at her screen and typed, oblivious to him. He looked around the table. Everyone was frowning at their screens and typing. He stood and went back to the counter.

One chai with a splash of oat milk later, Rami was back at the table. He set the drink down in front of the woman in the green sweater, who gave it, not him, a cursory nod as she talked to an invisible audience about the week's deliverables.

Rami pulled his phone out and opened up Whither, Weather after clearing a new crop of "WTF?!" notifications from his friends. He pretended to mull the display as he turned to the woman on his left, a petite blonde with a messy bun and an oversized men's flannel shirt. She looked sweet and fun, like she could introduce him to his new favorite band and make it so he actually didn't loathe the idea of going to a music festival. That could happen, maybe?

"Hmm, today's temperature is 5.3 degrees lower than the historic average," he said loudly. "How interesting!"

She, too, pulled out a concealed earbud.

"I'm sorry, did you say something?" she asked. She had fair skin and a round face with wide-set brown eyes rimmed in black eyeliner.

Rami gave his best casual shrug. "Oh, did I? I guess I just got absorbed in the successful app that I designed." He held out his phone. "Look, it's our newest animation."

Her face lit up and she actually clapped, *clapped*, as she watched Fun Sun bounce across the screen, blowing sunbeam kisses with his big, muscled arms.

"Whither, Weather! Cuuuuuuuute!" She fixed him with her wide brown eyes, which were now warm and glowing at him. "I love Fun Sun!"

"Great. Me too!" He started to feel an ember of something warm and glowing, himself. "I have some new outfits for him. Want a sneak preview?"

She pulled out her other earbud, set them both on the table, and scooched closer to him. She smelled like cinnamon gum and strawberries. She smiled at him, and he noticed that she had a little gap in her front teeth. And he was a goner, his mind already sporting flannels and listening to bands that played the banjo as he drove their #vanlife camper out into Yosemite.

"I'd love that," she said.

* * *

That evening, Nat stood in her room in front of a huge pile of clothes as Sara watched and sipped wine on the bed. Finding a potential date outfit for happy hour with Mr. Downtown, as they were calling him in a crooner's singsong, was proving to be a long and surprisingly sweaty task.

"How about this?"

Sara glanced up from the glow of Nat's laptop. "Maybe?" She squinted and frowned. "Not with that skirt, though."

Nat pulled off the shirt and fanned her armpits. "OK, but we can't alter too many variables at once." She tossed the shirt into the pile that was nearly to her knees. "It's inefficient."

"If you keep throwing clothes in that pile, it might gain sentience and murder us in our sleep," said Sara.

Nat dug through the heap. "I can't wear anything that I wore on a date before because that's just bad luck. And all of my new clothes have a vibe that's more . . ."

"'Fun' youth group counselor?" Sara offered.

"No," said Nat, tossing aside a chunky brown turtleneck.

"Time-traveling Puritan?"

"Stop."

"1950s accountant with a bad rash?"

"Nuanced!" Nat cried, pulling on an oversized Breton shirt with blessedly minimal wrinkles. "They're nuanced."

Sara handed her the wine. "Drink that." As Nat took a large swig, Sara turned the laptop around to face her. "And look! You've got a new match already."

"Oh, yes!" Nat took a second swig as she examined the man smiling out at her from the screen. "Oh no," she said.

Sara frowned. "Really? I thought he was cute!"

"No, I know him," said Nat. "Actually, I know his wife."

"Ouch." Sara refilled the wine.

"Should I say something to her?" asked Nat.

"Hell, no!" said Sara, taking back the computer. "You adopt that policy and you will be setting a truly exhausting precedent, trust me." She shook her halo of glossy curls in emphasis. "Anyway, you've got like ten other new messages."

Nat's eyes widened with a realization. "Wait, are lots of guys on here actually secretly married?"

Sara scoffed. "Ask Santa the next time you see him." She clicked around the messages as Nat stayed frozen in thought. "Um, hello, this guy's hot as fuck!" She leaned in closer to the screen as if inspecting an ancient scroll. "Why haven't I matched with him yet?"

Now, Nat shook her head for emphasis. "But if the user input data is inaccurate, then my algorithm can't—"

Sara turned the laptop and tapped her navy, coffin-shaped fingernail loudly on the man's picture on the screen. Long dark hair, hazel eyes with just the right amount of crinkle at the corners, a gleaming smile that was somehow both sweet and seductive, and a shadow of stubble across a chiseled jawline.

Nat melted inside while her body practically leapt to the computer. "Hello," she half-whispered. "Open his message."

Sara clicked.

Nat read it aloud. "'There she is.'" Nat smoothed her hair and felt a blush warm into her cheeks.

Sara gave a dry laugh. "Classic."

"Yeah," said Nat, swooning. "Classy."

"Um, that's not what I said."

"You know, I read somewhere that men really respond to a confident use of exclamation points," said Nat, suddenly sure of the Breton shirt.

"Why don't you open another message?" said Sara, nudging the computer.

"Yeah, you're right. I can't get attached to the first cutie I see."

"You sure can't."

Nat sidled up and clicked on the next message in her inbox. She read it aloud. "'There she is.'" She gasped. "Wait, what? Is this a joke?" She turned to Sara, stricken. "You open the next one."

Sara softened her face and lowered her voice like she was talking to a cornered raccoon. "Listen, you're gonna need a thick skin if you're gonna keep doing this—"

"Just open the message!" Nat hadn't meant to screech, but it definitely came out that way.

Sara sighed and opened a third message. "'There she is.'"

"What the shit is this?" Nat stood and grabbed the laptop. She clicked the next message. It just read, "hey." All lowercase but also punctuated? Was he trying to make her insane?

Sara refilled the wine. "So, a lot of guys online just take a shotgun approach," she said in the anxious possum voice. "It's a numbers game."

Nat whirled around. "A *numbers game*? Not my algorithm!" She kicked the clothes heap in frustration. "It's just a bad batch tonight." She ignored Sara's obvious frown of disagreement and closed the laptop. "And, anyway, this is what I'm wearing! Yay! Now I'm gonna go ice my eyes."

She tried to slow her breathing as she headed into the kitchen. It was fine. Just a bad batch. She dumped some ice cubes into a towel and pressed them to her eyelids. Her algorithm worked. *Obviously.* She heard the clomp of Sara's boots approaching.

"So, it's been a minute since you went on a date, right?"

Nat leaned against the cabinets and spoke through the cold darkness of the towel. "A year. And a half . . . maybe longer."

"Right, right." She heard Sara crunch on some chips.

"And before you say it," said Nat, "I'm totally ready to meet someone. I've just been too busy with the app."

"Totally, totally," said Sara. "Chip?"

Nat nodded and opened her mouth. "Wait, I think eating salty foods defeats the purpose of the de-puffing?"

"Maybe, but we finally got the honey mustard ones back in stock at the store."

Nat dumped the ice in the sink. "Oh, hell yes." Lately, Sara had been picking up shifts at a local co-op between her apprenticeship at a hair salon. She'd always rotated between various jobs, almost as a rule, but it was nice when the perks included snacks and haircuts. Nat grabbed a handful of chips and headed back to her room. "Are we sure about these shoes?"

Sara popped in holding up a pair of red ballet flats. "Maybe these?" She tossed them on the bed. "Anyway, I totally get the impulse to window shop like you do. No judgment."

Nat slipped on the shoes and held up her purse. "These are good. But with this bag, though?"

"Oh, try your one with the tassels."

Nat pointed at Sara like she was a star and dove back into her closet. "Brilliant!"

"But, I'm just glad you're getting out there," Sara continued. "Because, I have to say, it's also really hard to see you, like, kinda isolated so much, you know?"

"Well, I don't want to waste my time," said Nat, dumping out the contents of the tasseled bag onto the bed. "So, yeah. I'm fine with waiting until I find the perfect guy." She picked out the receipts, gum wrappers, and stray mints as Sara shifted uncomfortably.

"But perfect is, like, not a thing, right?" Sara asked gingerly. "For anyone?"

Nat looked up from prying melted gum off a quarter. "What do you mean?"

Sara stood. "Wait, no, hang on!" She dashed out and came back with a different pair of red flats. "I think the studded ones."

Nat crossed her hands over her heart. "Really? You love those!" She slipped on the shoes.

Sara sighed with satisfaction. "Oh my God, *yes*. I insist!" She watched Nat beam and pose in the mirror and took a seat on the bed again. "It's just that . . . no one person is ever going to be all the things for you, right?"

Nat stared at a few different colors of lipstick before dropping them all into her purse. "Well, you kind of are."

Sara winced and managed a dry laugh. "I'm not, actually. That's kind of my point." She shifted on the bed and fiddled with one of the piercings in her ear. "It's just really cool that you're branching out a little, is all."

Nat fixed her gaze on her mirror and applied another coat of mascara. "Don't worry, I won't replace you." She dropped the mascara into her purse, too.

Sara nodded. "Yeah, totally. But . . . you could if you wanted to."

Nat frowned and looked at her friend. Sara was squirming, but her face was firm. What was this about? "Well, no one is forcing you to be my friend," Nat said, instantly regretting how much meaner it sounded out loud than it had in her head. She was nervous. Her edges got sharper when she was nervous.

"You know I love you, and I love being your friend."

"But?"

Sara's face scrunched up in uncomfortable sadness. "Sometimes it's a lot of pressure for just one person, you know?"

Nat turned back to her mirror. She did know. It had always been her pattern to find one close friend and then consider herself done with the socializing stuff. The reasons why were numerous — it wasn't easy for her to make friends, and fewer friends meant lower odds that they'd turn into a mean girl (which technically hadn't happened since third grade, but still hurt). Plus, even Nat could recognize that she was a little on the unusual side as far as her female peers. It had all been covered by school counselors and concerned talks with her mother many times before.

In Nat's experience, people who actually liked her were rare, and the process of trial and error was agony. So, she liked to stick with success once she found it, or in the case of dating, try to set herself up for success as much as possible before taking a risk.

Nat sprayed a final coat of setting mist on her makeup. "I have other friends," she said. "You've met Jo."

Sara nodded with an approving grunt. "Jo is cool."

Nat forced a smile as she fanned her face dry. "Are you trying to freak me out before this date, or something? Did you place a huge bet on me losing this stupid competition?"

Sara's face lit with genuine warmth. "Just a cool milli, no big deal."

The two friends met each other's gaze in the mirror for a moment. Sara's round face and olive skin, with cat eye liner sharp around her brown eyes, button nose lit with highlighter, and pouty red lips that always seemed set to crack a joke. Then there was Nat's narrow face with her wide green eyes, long nose and thin lips permanently set in a wry twist. Sometimes, Nat wondered if she and Sara would be friends if they'd met now, in their thirties, instead of in college. But that line of thinking always led to her trying to imagine her life without Sara, and that was too lonely to consider, even for her. Nat stood and turned to her friend. "Well, sorry to make you lose your bet, because this is who I'm gonna be gazing at all night." She held out her phone with Mr. Downtown's profile pulled up. He wasn't quite "There She Is" Guy levels of white-hot gorgeousness, but he had a surfer boy cuteness, broad shoulders, and a confident smile.

"Oh, hey there, Eric," Sara cooed. "Six foot three, I don't hate that."

"That means he's taller than Rami," Nat blurted.

Sara's eyebrows shot up, and her eyes flared with amusement. "Interesting reaction."

"I just mean that he's hot! Eric, I mean." Nat shook her head. "I'm just nervous. Whatever." She looked at her finished look in the mirror and shook the random thought of Rami from her mind. She gestured to her finished look with a little twirl. "All good?"

Sara kissed her fingertips. "Beyond good. Gorgeous." Her eyes misted a little as Nat giggled. "So just . . . remember to sit with it a bit if it's uncomfortable, OK? Sometimes it takes a minute to feel a connection."

Nat shook her head and pulled on her coat. "Free drinks with a hot guy." She gave a loud mock sigh. "I'll try to enjoy it." Then she held out her arms for a hug, squeezed Sara's familiar softness with a burst of powdery, fresh makeup scent, and slipped out the door.

Sara sighed and refilled her wine.

CHAPTER 7

Rami paced the narrow lane between the bookshelves, record shelves, spiral-legged wooden coffee table, and overstuffed leather sofa in his living room. This is what happened when you let your trust-funder roommate bring in all their parents' old ("old," as in, perfectly good) furniture. He paused occasionally to sip the IPA sweating in his hand.

"I'm supposed to meet her in thirty-five minutes, and I don't even know her last name. I can't google her. I can't Facebook her. I'll actually have to ask her questions about herself. And I won't have to pretend like I don't already know all the answers!" Rami looked at said roommate, Ian, reclining on the sofa with a baroque bong and a lead crystal glass of rare Scotch. "The freedom I feel right now . . ." he said, extending his beer in a toast. "It's beautiful."

Ian sipped his Scotch and pondered, which it seemed to Rami he would be doing whether or not he'd just said anything. Ian's long face was somehow both much smoother than you'd expect a fifty-something's to be and just as weathered as you'd expect a lifelong surfer's to be, with a ruddy tan that almost matched his permanently windblown sandy blond hair. As such, he was ageless, a trait he used to great advantage on top of his already birth-bestowed advantage. His bemused expression deepened into a frown and he stretched his long ropey arms and adjusted his hemp hoodie with a satisfied sigh. "You know, man, I think it's amazing the amount of blind, almost foolish, trust that you're showing. It really makes me want to get back out there, start Ubering again, you know?"

Rami set down the beer. "What do you mean, 'trust?'"

Ian's face crinkled with a smile. "To dive so deeply into your shadow self."

"OK, you keep talking about that and I still don't know what it is, and how am I doing . . . shadow whatever?"

"Your shadow is the collection of all your weaknesses and traumas. Essentially the inverse of everything that's good about you." Ian blinked his large, watery blue eyes. "Like how you're really good with numbers, but very not-good with people."

Rami scoffed. "I'm good with people. I'm a people person!"

Ian shook his head with another sip of Scotch. "I don't think even the DoorDash guy would agree with that." He squinted up at Rami. "Shit, man, I thought you knew this?"

Rami picked up the beer again. "Oh, really? You thought that I walked around totally content in the knowledge that my friends and colleagues think I'm some horrible asshole from the shadow realm?"

Ian huffed a small laugh. "Shadow realm. Metal." Then he knitted his furry brows. "I mean, you do argue with people a lot." Ian pulled a piece of hard candy from his cargo shorts pocket. "Like, I stopped watching *Law & Order* after I moved in with you." He popped the candy in his mouth. "I felt like that itch was scratched, you know?"

"Perfect," said Rami. He downed the rest of the beer and set it down pointedly in front of Ian — he couldn't bring himself not to set it on a coaster, but still. A hostile gesture. His point was made! Even if he would definitely throw it out as soon as he walked back in the door, because Ian certainly wouldn't. "Thanks for the pep talk."

Rami pulled on his jacket and opened the door to the building hallway, with its blast of damp city-street air. He whirled around to Ian. "And so, you know, it takes two people to argue."

Ian nodded philosophically. "I suppose."

"Yes, because it's physically impossible for me to sustain an argument on my own, so to assume that correlation somehow means causation is a classic logical fallacy."

A soft, knowing smile spread on Ian's face as he closed his eyes and said, "Godspeed, conquistador."

Rami turned to leave again. "OK, see you later." He sighed. "Also, I brought you some leftover cheese from the event today. A brie. It's pretty amazing."

Ian stood up on his gangly, hairy legs and grinned. "My man!"

Rami waved and hurried out the door to his date.

* * *

The chilly fog poked needles along Nat's neckline as she clutched her scarf tighter and hurried out of the BART train station. The sidewalk sparkled between rolling tumbleweeds of trash and dark piles that shouldn't be looked at too long. She gingerly navigated through the mess in Sara's beautiful red shoes, checking her phone to make sure she was heading toward the right wine bar to meet Eric, aka Mr. Downtown. She was. The confirmation was neither a relief nor did it fill her with dread. It simply was.

She was simply walking to a wine bar to meet a man. She liked wine. She liked men. This was fine.

And yet.

Despite how blasé she'd been in agreeing to this date earlier, she had, in fact, looked at Eric's profile more closely once she was somewhere she knew she would be alone, namely a stall in the women's restroom at the office. His pictures were definitely cute, if worryingly outdoorsy and all taken on mountaintops and in parks and before sparkling lakes, but Jo was right — no obvious red flags in any of his answers. He liked to travel. He liked spicy food. He liked concerts. He wanted to have fun. Nat had read his responses over and over like she was scrying for long-lost secrets, but Eric was, by all three-hundred-character-limited indications, a regular guy. A sixty-one percent match was, statistically, pretty high. And he was tall. Six foot three! So, he had at least one of the qualities on her checklist, and even if she would've culled him from her nightly reviews for his repeated use of the word "hella," he was, objectively, good-looking. Besides, he didn't have to be her match, he just had to be her date to the gala and help her beat Rami. So, she should just enjoy the simple pleasure of a handsome man, right? She'd closed the profile and gone back to work, and then home to get ready, and now here she was, walking to meet him.

Yet why were her palms sweating like she was about to give a school science fair presentation?

She'd always planned to go on real dates again at some point — that was the whole purpose of her personal BeTwo searches. Still, saying out loud to Sara that it had been almost two years since the Golden Gate Park disaster hadn't felt good. Was she being too picky? She'd been scouring her user database for so long, and that user base had grown so much during all those months, that she must have looked at thousands of profiles. Nat did some quick math in her head, almost reflexively, and arrived at a figure — she could reasonably estimate that she had reviewed over five thousand single men. Her heart fluttered in panic, and she ran the numbers again to be sure. That estimate actually seemed conservative, but to her credit, the number was probably less than ten thousand.

Still, that seemed like an impossibly high number of men for her to have churned through. And it wasn't as if they were all awful! It was just that she was waiting for a spark, a flip in her stomach, and for someone to check at least eighty percent of the boxes on her wish list.

She felt the familiar burn of righteous anger bubble up in her chest. She'd only started the wish list because of how many great things she saw in all those profiles, anyway. It wasn't desperation. It was inspiration and determination. In every other aspect of her life, her rigorous research was praised, so why should she suddenly loosen up when it came to matters of the heart — her heart? No one likes to waste their time. No one likes to be rejected. She was doing herself and the thousands of men a service by doing everything she could to spare them all pain.

She listened to the clicks of Sara's gorgeous shoes on the sidewalk with satisfaction. Besides, she was on her way to meet a real-life man at that very moment. She was taking a chance. So clearly, she could relax her possibly strict standards a bit, and the fizzy feeling in her stomach aside, it had been fun to dress up and have an actual outing to look forward to. Maybe she could even make a habit of it.

Her phone buzzed in her coat pocket. She had arrived, and from his text message, so had Eric. She looked up at huge golden doors, seemingly made for a race of wine-loving giants. She suddenly felt both impossibly small and lit by a spotlight. Were people looking at her? It was probably so obvious that she was going on a date. Her face flushed with embarrassment. Why did she have to wear the fancier shoes? A dead giveaway. She gripped a door handle and pulled. It didn't budge, and she stumbled backward a little. People definitely saw that. That wasn't great. She dug in her heels, apologizing to Sara for any damage, and threw her body weight into her tug on the door. It flew open with a blast of warm air, and she stumbled backward even more this time. Amazing. Awesome. She made eye contact with an elegant gray-haired lady watching her coolly from inside the bar. Perfect. Nat straightened her coat and stepped inside.

* * *

The wine bar was lit with warm amber sconces dotting dark walls lined with books. A low tin ceiling reflected the glow like they were all being held inside a soft, gauzy candle flame. Unfortunately, the tin ceiling was not as good for the acoustics as it was for the ambiance, and the place was a roiling ocean of noise. Pods of well-dressed people clutched highballs and wine glasses and yelled at each other over the din.

But it still wasn't enough to drown out the sound of Nat's heart thumping in her ears.

She approached the bar and looked around, trying to breathe through the panicked questions whizzing around her brain. How would she find him? Even a six-foot-something blond guy would be hard to spot in this crowd. What was she thinking? It was weird to be standing here alone. Was everyone looking at her? Should she just leave? She closed her eyes and tried to, as Justin would say, find her center. She was here because of her app. Literally, because that's how she'd found Eric. But also she was here to defend her app, her work, *her baby*, against attack. Specifically, the attacks that had come from Rami. Rami and his smug smile. She opened her eyes. On this particular night, it turned out that her center was a white-hot ball of competitive fire, and that definitely did the trick. She took a deep breath, just as she felt a tap on her shoulder.

"There she is."

Nat froze. The man standing in front of her seemed only vaguely familiar, but she had a sinking feeling that she should know him. He beamed at her with small brown eyes almost level with hers. He had a sparse beard, really more of a chin beard. Did she know anyone with a patchy chin beard?

"Nat, right?" said the man, still grinning. He pointed at himself. "Eric!" Nat's brain registered it only as nonsense as he leaned in for a hug.

She felt his definitely not six-foot frame smoosh against hers in a wan embrace. She patted his back, a move that instantly reminded her of awkward uncles at holiday parties. But was she the uncle in this scenario, or was he? She gave him another look. "Eric?" She repeated his name as if to force it to make sense with the person who stood eye-level in front of her.

"Guilty as charged." Eric nodded and slid onto a nearby bar stool. He pulled out a stool for her and patted the seat.

In a daze, she pulled herself onto the stool beside him. She squinted again at the man smiling at her, mentally pulling up his profile pics in her head like assembling a criminal investigation board. Egregious height discrepancy aside, there was a resemblance — or at least there had been several years ago. This current version of Eric had the patchy chin beard and also a pasty sheen to his skin that it seemed like Profile Eric would've left behind on all those mountaintop treks. What had looked like rakishly windswept hair in the outdoor pics now looked like a frizzy tangle in need of a haircut and styling cream. He was wearing a boxy khaki suit and, uncannily, a silver tie covered in tiny embroidered cubes like a graphic for a computer store in a 90s mall. Her mind reeled, at a loss for how to proceed with this very unexpected IRL version of Eric. Should she say something? But what could she say?

Then her social conditioning kicked in. Some long-buried zombie lich of her Sunday school teacher, her grandmother, the poor boy who farted in front of the whole class in the seventh grade and then cried about it, and her beloved childhood dog rose in her mind and she was wracked with a powerful combination of pity and duty. She didn't want to make him feel bad. She didn't want to be rude.

Eric tapped the bar top. "Care for a social lubricant?" he asked.

"Hey, there!" she said, finally. "Yes!" On cue, a twenty-something bartender with long, shining copper hair and a thick beard slid over two menus, and she made a point to look him in the eye with a loud thank you, because she was a normal person in a normal situation who definitely did not feel like she was in some kind of surreal play or maybe a waking dream? The bartender went back to his station.

Eric whipped open the leather-backed menu with a loud "Hmm." Nat tried to parse the gilded letterpress script font listing the long names and even longer list of ingredients of all the drinks, but the words slipped through her brain like water.

"So, Natalie," said Eric, his voice suddenly booming above the noise. "Tell me about you. Let's do this. First date rundown!" He slapped a hand on the bar. The woman next to him visibly jumped. "What do you do?"

Nat watched the woman scooch closer to her much quieter date. "I'm a coder . . ."

Eric scoffed. "Ya think?" A knowing frown twisted his face. "I mean, we're in San Fran, right? Everyone's a coder." He pointed out the window to a woman in tattered clothes huddled on the sidewalk. "I bet she's a coder!"

Nat cringed and stopped herself from pushing his hand down. "I don't think so . . ." she managed to say.

"It's a joke, relax!" Eric held up his empty hands in a shrug. "I work for a housing non-profit. No one's losing their leftie points here, OK?" He sighed and signaled the bartender.

Nat took another stab at reading the menu. One of the drinks had gin in it. That seemed good.

The bartender returned. "What'll it be for you two?"

Eric leaned in as if to share a secret, but without lowering his voice. "Hey, man, I'm not sure the John Lee Hooker cocktail here should have this kind of whiskey, right?"

The bartender blinked. "I can make you something that's not on the menu."

Eric shook his head. "It's just that, and I'm sure you know this, but a bourbon would be more authentic in the mix than a rye. Don't you agree?"

The bartender blinked. "Is that what you'd like? I can make it with bourbon."

Eric took a moment to ponder this. "Well, what do you think it should be made with, man?"

"I can make it with bourbon. It's basically just an old-fashioned."

Nat felt sweat prickling into her hairline as Eric snapped the menu closed and handed it back to the still-expressionless bartender.

"Why don't you make me whatever you want? Some crazy idea for a drink that you've been wanting to try."

The bartender took the menu. "How about an old-fashioned?"

Eric grinned. "Yeah! But totally different. Just surprise me!"

The bartender turned to Nat, who found it much harder to make eye contact this time. "And for you?" he asked.

She pointed at the menu. "An Edith Piaf, please."

The bartender nodded and slipped away, leaving Nat feeling like she was watching the last lifeboat sail away from the deck of a sinking ship.

Eric rolled his eyes, and turned toward her. "I wasn't asking for anything difficult, right?" He ran a hand through his wild hair and squinted. "Are you French? You look like you could be French."

"I'm from Indiana," she said. "But thanks?"

"I'm from all over." Eric drummed his fingers on the bar top. "I mean, my ex was *ob-fucking-sessed* with San Fran, but it's not the alpha and omega to anyone who's actually traveled, right?"

Nat smiled like she knew the answer to the teacher's question. "I love to travel!"

Eric peered at her with narrowed eyes. "So, first date," he said again. "Big!"

Nat gave an awkward laugh and tried to open up the conversation. This was for her app. "Actually, it's my first BeTwo date."

Eric scoffed. "Oh, come on. I've heard that before." He switched to a squeaky, high-pitched voice. "It's my first time, too!"

Nat shook her head, genuinely confused. "No, really. It is!"

Eric rolled his eyes then took on a tone like he was humoring her. "Uh huh. Well, if this is really your first time in the BeTwo swamp, let me give you some advice. One, buckle up. Lotta crazies out there. Two, lower your standards now. Save you a lot of time. No one's getting any younger, right?" He picked up the food menu that had been lying inert between them. "You hungry? I saw they have truffle fries and you like those, right?" He gave her another glance. "You look well-fed, and that's a compliment, by the way."

Nat flinched as the words landed, scattering all of the evening's previous insults from her mind. Before she could say anything, the bartender returned. He set a flute of sparkling wine and gin in front of Nat with a quick nod. For Eric, he produced an oversized hurricane glass filled with a bright pink boozy concoction and loaded with an orchid, a pineapple, what looked like at least three different stir sticks skewered with cherries and palm fronds, and rimmed with pink sugar. It was as big as a human head. The bartender quickly scurried away.

Eric grinned and clapped. "That's what I'm talking about!" he shouted. "Gender norms, my ass! I'm a real man now." He grasped the colossal candy-colored drink with both hands and lifted it in the way he might otherwise hoist a bowling ball. "Cheers!"

Nat tried to ignore all the people turning their heads her way as she gingerly tapped his glass with her flute. "Cheers . . ." she managed, as she took a deep breath and a long drink.

CHAPTER 8

Rami watched Lynn, his date from the coffee shop, study the Skee-Ball machine in front of her. They'd agreed to meet at a bar-arcade, and after he'd gotten them a couple of beers, Lynn had led them right to the machine as if pulled by magnets. She was definitely just as cute as he remembered — bubbly and warm with a cherubic, sweet-looking face and those big brown eyes. But he had to admit that it was hard, actually nearly impossible, to have much of a conversation between the jangling noise of the various machines. Even if it was an impractical choice, it was still a relief to have something to do besides stare at each other and exchange life details over pricey cocktails. The creeping melt of first dates into quasi-job interviews had been part of the reason for Rami's eleven-month retreat from the romantic arena. Other reasons included every conversation that suddenly went cold, every promising date that ended up ghosting, and every crushingly awkward IRL meetup that was one more brick in the wall of his growing belief that he was, probably maybe, terminally undateable.

The Skee-Ball machine rang out with a shrill siren and flashed its lights while a stream of tickets flowed out of the slot. Rami clapped as Lynn gave him a curtsy and collected her winnings.

"Damn! Baller!" he said, giving her a high five. "Like, literally. You are a skilled thrower of balls." He paused. "That sounded dirty, but that wasn't what I meant—"

Lynn handed him the tangle of tickets. "Dude, relax." She took a swig of her beer and surmised the rest of the machines like she was crafting battle plans. "I could do this in my sleep. My husband and I used to live right by this place."

Rami gave a polite laugh. "You said 'husband.'"

Lynn smiled at him and batted her wide, chocolatey eyes in the neon glow. "Did I?"

"You meant ex-husband," he offered.

"Um . . ." Lynn glanced at her beer. "No, I didn't." She took a cautious sip and watched for his reaction.

Rami blinked in shock. He felt the prickle of his conscience in the pit of his stomach as his mind raced for how he could possibly respond. Why was the first thing on his lips an apology?

"Look, I'm poly," she blurted. "It's an open marriage, so he's totally cool with this." She gestured into the space between her and Rami. "And so is my boyfriend."

"H . . . husband *and* b . . . boyfriend?" Rami stammered. His stomach fully lurched now, and his mind went blank, the instinctive apology now abandoned out of total confusion.

Lynn set down the Skee-Ball she was holding and faced Rami with a kind of defiant kindness — arms crossed, jaw set, eyes sparkling. "Serious boyfriend, actually. And then there's a guy I see whenever he's in town."

As it always did in times of great stress, Rami's brain turned to logistics for comfort. "Wow, that's a lot of people."

Lynn smiled, shrugged, and took his hand. She traced a finger along the inside of his palm and gave him a warm glance through her dark lashes. "I like to think of it as a lot of experiences," she cooed.

Rami frowned. "Wait, do all these guys also have other girlfriends?"

Lynn dropped his hand and nodded with a weary air. "Yeah, they do."

"So exactly how many people are in this relationship hydra?" Rami wiggled his fingers in the air as if to materialize a pen and paper. "Have you ever diagrammed it out?"

"We have a Miro board."

Rami grunted with a knowing frown. "Well, you'd have to." He drummed the stands of tickets against his chin as his mind raced ahead. "I mean, the scheduling alone produces a lot of data streams, not to mention controlling for the potentially calamitous overlap between social circles, and tracking sexual encounters for health records . . ." He trailed off, lost in the numbers already whizzing around his head.

Lynn tossed her long blonde hair and hooked her hand on the curve of her hip. "We think of it like swimming into deep waters — you don't know how far it goes, or how many people it's touched, only that it's nourishing you right now."

Rami absently twisted one of his curls. "Sure, it's water, but maybe put a few drops into a Petri dish and take a look every so often, right?"

Lynn's face drooped with a sad smile. "I take it this isn't your thing?"

"I'm sorry," he said, dropping his hands and facing her. "It's really, really not."

Lynn winced and covered her eyes. "Shit. Now you hate me."

"No, no!" Rami resisted the impulse to hug her as she shifted her weight in the classic pose of wishing to vanish into thin air. It was a pose he knew well. "But maybe you could have told me this before our date?"

A blush crept into her pale cheeks. "Yeah, I know. It's in my BeTwo profile, all spelled out." She shrugged at him, eyes full of regret. "It just felt way more awkward to say it in person."

Rami sighed. "Right. It's all online." His stomach sank with a different feeling now as he remembered Nat, her damned app, and their wager. Which he was now, it seemed, officially losing.

They both went quiet and watched the couples around them, all jamming arcade buttons, jumping for excitement in the whirring machine lights, and sneaking kisses between waterfalls of tickets.

Lynn pulled her purse in front of her body. "So, do you want me to pay you back for the beer?"

Rami shook his head. "No way, forget it." He ripped off a few of the tickets. "But I'm gonna take some of these because there's some pretty good candy over in the prize booth." He handed her the rest of the bundle with a quick nod. "Nice to meet you, Lynn."

She took the tickets and bit her lip. "Hug before I lose you forever?"

Rami whirled around. "Really?"

"Are you serious?" She winked at him. "You're a total babe."

The unfamiliar words hit him with a wash of confusion. And suddenly her arms were around him and her soft body was pressed against him and she planted a tender kiss on his cheek. His stomach flipped again for another entirely new reason. He froze, watching as she slid away with a flirty wave and wandered into the people milling about the arcade.

He was a babe. It had never occurred to him. He shook the stars from his mind and made his way to the prize booth to try and find some sour gummies.

Like a babe.

* * *

Nat drained her second drink as Eric hunched over the plate of truffle fries. He was stuffing them three at a time into his mouth and speaking between bites.

"Anyway, it turns out so much of my relationship shit is because of my trauma, and unlocking that was huge for me." He ate some fries. "Huge."

84

Nat nodded. She couldn't remember the last time she'd uttered a word. But she didn't know what she'd say even if Eric gave her an opening. It was painfully clear that they had nothing in common, and that even if they did, Nat would happily pretend that they didn't.

"I mean, I've been shopping for therapists for ten years and finally had a life-changing session yesterday." He grabbed some more fries. "Like, I haven't checked my ex's Insta at all today. Not once!"

It seemed like he wanted a reaction, and instinct kicked in as Nat said, "Oh, that's great!"

He nodded, taking the cue to continue. "Yeah, and she's swimming with pigs in the Bahamas right now."

Nat squinted. "Like, pig-pigs? Curly tails, oink?"

Eric peered sadly into the pink dregs of his drink. "Little floating porkers, yeah."

"Wow! Sounds . . . fun?" Nat considered the image. "I've always been a little scared of the ocean, but what shark would eat a human when there's fresh bacon nearby?"

Eric shrugged, as if discussing the weather. "It's an influencer retreat," he said. "They have all kinds of crazy shit at those things."

And with that, his monologue seemed to run out of steam. He pulled the last cherry off a skewer with a heavy sigh. Nat felt the silence grow thick between them. She knew Eric would not be her heart's match, or even a way to win the competition with Rami without driving herself insane. But she was here, she was slightly buzzed, and she was not one to ever let a research opportunity go unused.

"Cool." She leaned in and tossed her hair. "So, what made you message me?"

Eric blinked at her with confusion. "Come again?"

"What about my profile piqued your interest?"

Eric's eyes took on a faraway sheen. "I don't know, it's all the same girl out there. Just a blur of yoga poses and sunsets and," he held up his fingers in air quotes, "'casual' bikini pics of these straight-hair hot chicks who will probably be voting Republican in two years. And then you." He shot her a glance with an edge. "I mean, the fact that you used the word 'philosophy' and knew how to spell it? It was like fucking water in the desert."

Nat scoffed. The cocktails and her actual personality reared up through the objective of her date. "Well, thanks for noticing that I graduated high school."

Eric nodded, genuine and still morose toward his empty cocktail. "You're welcome."

Nat frowned. She wasn't sure yet if she would die on this hill, but she'd certainly endure a few hits. "I mean, it's a pretty normal word, right?" She watched as he seemed to remember her existence and looked at her. "It's not like most women aren't smart, right?"

"They're not." Eric sat up straighter, suddenly energized. "It's a bell curve. That's why I list myself as a sapiosexual." He stroked his patchy chin beard and squinted at her. "You know what that is?"

Anger flashed heat into the back of her neck. Somewhere in her mind, neurons were already sharpening their knives. But before she could respond, Nat heard her phone chiming in her purse — long and steady for an actual phone call.

"Hang on," she said to Eric, digging in her purse.

It was Jo, and either she was in trouble or, more likely, she knew Nat might need a rescue call.

Relief and gratitude hit her chest in a warm, sparkly wave. This wasn't the job of a publicist, but rather the move of a friend. "Oh, I have to take this," she said with a stage wince.

Eric rolled his eyes. "Classic. The rescue call." He glared at her. "I knew this wasn't your first rodeo."

She hopped off the stool. "No, it's not like that." She grabbed her purse, wondering if Justin was with his sister. "It's my — it's a work thing!"

Eric gave her an exaggerated wink. "Sure. Smart thinking."

"Sorry!" Nat cried as she picked up the call and rushed into the lobby. She plugged her free ear as she dodged people on their way in. "Jo? Hello?" But it was too loud. She could hear her voice, but not what she was saying. "Hang on!" She squeezed past a trio of laughing women in cocktail dresses. "Everything's OK, right?"

"I know, I just feel kind of trapped, you know?" Jo's voice was tinny and small.

"I can't hear you!" Nat shouted as she ducked into the empty corner behind a large plant. "Are you doing a rescue call? Because I swear to God you are psychic and I love you so much right now—" She froze at the sound of Jo's cackling laugh.

"Oh, she is for sure gonna get eaten alive on these dates! Listen, Nat is amazing and I love her, but she's a lot. Total genius, but sometimes people are their own worst enemies and they can't even see it."

Nat sank against the wall. A pocket dial. She knew she should hang up, but she couldn't. She heard Jo take a drag of a cigarette, and she knew she had more to say.

Jo's voice came back. "But it's good for me to see, like, the kind of person I don't want to become, you know?"

Nat ended the call so fast she almost dropped the phone. Her heartbeat throbbed in her ears, and her hands shook. She stepped out from behind the plant.

From the lobby, she had a full view of the bar and the empty stool waiting for her return, and Eric, who was leaning over, waving a fully extended arm to signal the bartender. Tears pricked in her eyes, and her mouth drooped. A sob swelled into her throat as she ran for the ladies' room.

Inside the well-lit glare of the bathroom, Nat leaned against the sink and let the tears come. Gray, mascara-tinged drops hit the white marble. Her heart ached in her chest like it was a vacuum trying to suck her whole body into its dark void. She told herself she was overreacting because Jo was her assistant, and their relationship was professional. She scolded herself for being so needy. In theory, it should be fine that Jo didn't like her, and as the overheard words pinged around her mind like deranged moths in a lamp, it was painfully clear that Jo didn't like her.

Still, Nat's mind flashed back to the hundreds of laughs she'd shared with Jo over their meme-and-emoji shorthand, and the hundreds of times the intimate details of her life had spilled out in their conversations on the way to lunch or while they tried on online shopping purchases for each other over a coffee break — really, the ways in which she'd let her guard down around Jo were countless. Because she'd thought that she could. She'd thought Jo enjoyed her company, not just her *actual company*, but of course that was impossibly naive. Nat was Jo's boss, not her friend — even if Nat had believed otherwise.

She pulled a paper towel from the dispenser and dabbed at her red eyes. There was a kind of comedic cruelty to this all happening when she was in the middle of an absolute nightmare of a date. More tears ran onto the paper towel. *Eric.* The rude, self-absorbed conversation, the bait-and-switch of his height (like she wouldn't notice him being almost a full six inches shorter than he'd said?), not to mention the painfully obvious fact that she had willingly chosen to go on a date with this guy, supposedly an above-average match. It was humiliating to her person and her algorithm.

She looked at herself in the mirror. The paper towel was rough and stabbed into her puffy skin, only making it angrier. Her eye makeup was melted into black creases and smears. Her cheeks were blotchy, and her nose was red. At this moment, she could see why Jo didn't want to be anything like her. Who would?

Maybe she had been looking at her dating search all wrong. Maybe the hard part wasn't finding someone *she* could like. Maybe the real feat would be trusting that anyone could ever like *her*?

A stall opened behind her, and the elegant, gray-haired woman who had been watching her struggle with the front door emerged. "Oh no!" she cried, taking in Nat's appearance. "Are you OK?"

"Yeah, sorry," Nat said. "It's stupid." She managed a companionable smile. "Just trying not to look like a raccoon right now."

The woman drew close to her. "Let me show you a trick, sweetie," she said and pulled a tampon out of a glass jar on the counter.

Nat balked. "Oh! No, I'm not—"

But the woman held up an index finger to cut her off as she popped the tampon out of the applicator and gestured for Nat to take the soft white cylinder. "It soaks up the tears and it won't scratch your face."

Nat dabbed the tampon to her face and watched the mess melt into the cotton. It was soft as she wiped it under her eyes. "Oh God, thank you," she said. "I'm not usually like this."

The woman washed her hands with a casual shrug. "Don't worry. We've all been there." She smoothed her sleek bob and righted a twisted necklace. Her blue eyes met Nat's in the mirror. "You sure you're OK to go back out there?"

Nat crumpled her tear-soaked towels, tossing them in the trash, and nodded as they headed to the door.

The woman opened it for Nat and turned to face her as she walked out. "And trust me?" she said. "He's not worth it."

Nat sighed and headed back to her seat at the bar. Eric's stool was empty, and she was relieved to have another moment to herself before he came back. Now all she had to do was end this date as painlessly as possible. Even though she knew that the rest of the night would probably be spent crying into her wine glass with Sara and her cat, it was still better than being here.

The bartender approached with a tray, and Nat cringed, wondering if Eric had ordered another round while she was away. But he handed over a leather-bound book with an envelope sticking out. "He paid his half, so here's your tab," he said.

Nat blinked in shock. "He left?" she said.

The bartender nodded.

Nat opened the envelope. Inside was a bill from the restaurant splitting everything fifty-fifty, including Eric's massive drinks and fries. Eric had also left her a note scrawled on a napkin.

Hope you enjoy your "phone call" and <u>DYING ALONE.</u>

Stunned, she looked up and searched the bartender's impassive, bearded face as if he could somehow right this deeply wayward ship. "Ready to close out?" he asked.

CHAPTER 9

Rami watched the city lights go by through the dirty bus window. He'd gotten on close enough to the start of the route to grab a seat, but now every spot was taken and the aisle was jammed with standing riders who clung to the metal poles for dear life. His mouth was sticky with candy already, but he shoved another lollipop into his mouth. Even in the dark reflection, he could see the blue stains on his lips, but it wasn't like it mattered. The high of being called "a babe" had worn off by the time he'd walked a half-block from the bar. It'd been another wasted evening, and had gotten him one more person to dread running into at the grocery store or, the more likely scenario, he realized with some mild panic, to have to acknowledge on public transit. He looked around suspiciously for anyone who might recognize him, but it was too crowded for anyone to see much farther than the person's armpit in front of them.

Still, this was quickly becoming his sense of San Francisco — not so much his small but tight group of friends or even the familiar faces in his neighborhood, but a growing legion of half-known women who had rejected him (or in the rare case, vice versa), and yet whose faces were burned into his memory all the same. He wished he could forget all the failed online dates he'd been on as soon as they were over. From talking to other guys, especially

Ian, it seemed like they were able to do just that. He constantly got advice that it was "a numbers game", and to take a "shotgun approach." He even knew a few coding colleagues who treated dating apps like another system to conquer, creating spreadsheets and elaborate calendars to go on as many dates as possible per week, sometimes even twice in one day. But for Rami, every date felt like it cost him a piece of himself, even if it'd only been two hours of conversation over coffee on a Wednesday afternoon. Every date left a mark. Maybe he was just broken.

He'd met his first serious girlfriend in coding boot camp, and they'd stayed together amicably for nearly three years. Their end hadn't been traumatic. They simply realized that they'd transitioned into being friends instead of lovers at some point, and while he may have been more than slightly inclined to just go with that, she had wanted to keep looking for a great, fiery love. Then she'd moved to Austin, and by the look of her socials, found exactly that within barely a month. He'd even sent them a pressure cooker for their wedding, no symbolism intended. After taking time to lick his wounds and get his bearings, Rami had figured it was time for him to go searching for his other half, too. Everyone was on the apps, so he'd joined BeTwo, which was supposed to be for serious relationships, not just hookups. A little over two years and many disastrous quasi-relationships later, his heart felt worn out like a tattered shoe. Not just because he'd been disappointed, but because he'd been ghosted, breadcrumbed, zombied, roached, friend-zoned, stood up, lied to, and cheated on by just about every single woman he'd met online. Over and over. For years.

He sighed and twisted the lollipop in his mouth. Blue raspberry never disappointed. Rami had tried a hookup just once, after being warmed to the concept by a neighbor who'd preached its virtues over pitchers of fruity vodka drinks on his balcony. So, one IRL meetup, after two quick rounds of surprisingly strong cocktails and some pleasant if inane banter, Rami had gone home with a woman on the first date. He'd been a little drunk, and she'd been exceptionally pretty in the way that made words evaporate from his mind, and he honestly hadn't needed to try too hard for her to pull him close and suggest that they get out of there. He'd felt mildly queasy in the ride-share on the way to her apartment, but chalked it up to the booze. Inside her studio apartment, she'd handed him a glass of water and wordlessly made up the sofa into a bed by throwing the cushions onto the floor and pulling a second pillow from the kitchen cupboard that was, essentially, her nightstand.

The digital clock on the microwave had lit them in a clinical glow as Rami tried to play the role of the dashing sexual rogue. But he didn't know anything about this woman. She was beautiful, and her skin was impossibly soft, and the alcohol buzzed pleasantly in his head when they kissed, but when he opened his eyes, the evidence of her life was all around him. Posters for modern art shows that he'd never heard of. Framed photos of smiling strangers. A string of fairy lights nestled in a souvenir glass shaped like a Buddha next to a clutch of dried flowers. How was it right that he could know what her breasts looked like, but not why there was a note that read *POLAR BEARS!* tacked to the wall above the sofa bed?

She'd pulled off her underwear and reached into his boxers. He still remembered the way she'd knelt naked in front of him on the bed in the blue glow, one hand rubbing her pert, dark nipples and looking hungrily into his eyes. Her other hand worked between his legs as he'd willed himself to perform. "Come on, baby," she'd cooed in his ear. "Get hard for me."

But he couldn't. His nakedness had felt ridiculous, as phony as if he'd tried to don an accent or rev the engine of a family sedan. He'd only had sex with two women at that point in his life, and the difference between what he'd done with them and what he was trying to do now felt like trying to cook a meal in a tiny toy kitchen. The faucet was solid plastic. The burners were stickers that peeled off with a fingernail scratch. There was no heat. It was all pretend. And it made his heart ache for the real thing.

"Whiskey dick?" she'd said, already rolling away and reaching toward her phone. "It happens."

It had seemed less embarrassing to just go with that, and he'd quickly called a ride-share and left. Every so often, Rami made sure that he still remembered her name — Michaela.

The bus lurched to a stop, and the riders stumbled into each other with a chorus of groans and grunts. The doors opened with a sick mechanical wheeze. The man next to Rami shuffled out with a few others, and suddenly there was a parting in the aisle. A filthy man in a thick, crusted-over coat stumbled down the bus. People covered their mouths and noses and scooted away as the doors closed and the bus rattled forward. The man muttered to himself, eyeing every passenger with a burning scorn as he moved down the aisle. The bus took on a tense quiet as the riders watched him.

Then he started screaming.

"Skin lice! Skin lice!" He shoved his ruddy, bandaged hands between the riders, now frantically pulling the cord for a stop. People squashed toward the back to give him as much room as possible as he yelled.

Rami watched in horror as the man zeroed in on him with a devilish smile. His matted hair and tattered coat pushed toward him as people practically climbed on top of each other to get out of the way. Rami looked around, heart racing in his chest, but he was trapped.

The man stopped in front of him. His eyes were glassy and nestled in a thick grove of wrinkles. "Skin lice!" he cried, and fell onto Rami's lap. He writhed for a second against his thighs as

Rami's mouth fell open in shock. Then the man grabbed the lolli-pop from Rami's mouth, popped it into his own, and shoved off.

The bus jerked to an emergency stop as people cried out in the pain from smashed toes and elbowed ribs. The doors screeched open, and the man and his new lollipop jumped off. Rami's mouth was still open as he watched him shuffle off into the dark night, looking until it was just his own dumb reflection staring back at him. It was a familiar image. Because no matter what happened, it seemed like his nights always ended just like this. And maybe now he had skin lice? Rami pulled out his phone to google the possibility as the bus rolled on.

* * *

Nat sat alone in the flickering fluorescent light of the BART train. Her head throbbed with the sparkling wine and recent crying, and Jo and Eric and of it all. Thankfully, the car was mostly empty, except for a couple of teenagers making out in the accessible seats. The hum of the train through the tunnel was almost enough to cover the sounds of their smacking. Her headphones were in her other, larger, non-date-appropriate purse, of course.

Her phone buzzed. It was a text from Jo in their BeTwo group thread.

Jo: *How'd it go, boss? We win this thing?*

Nat scoffed as Jo sent a GIF of a woman anxiously chomp-ing gum, as if Jo were actually worried about her. Justin "loved" the message, and Nat closed the thread. She was definitely not responding to that.

Instead, she opened a new message to Sara.

Nat: *Whatcha doing?*

Sara: *Working on my résumé.*

So fun!!!

How was the date?

Nat: *EPIC FAIL!!!*

Meet at the spot?

Sara: 😖 *I was gonna try and finish this tonight . . .*

I suck at proofreading even without a martini in me

Nat: *Send it to me! I'll polish it up for you*

The train eased to a stop with a shrill squeak, and the doors opened with their pneumatic hiss. A loud group of yet more teens entered the car. Fantastic. One of them produced a portable speaker and began blaring an upbeat disco-inspired jam that made frequent use of an air horn sound. Even better.

Sara's text buzzed back.

Sara: *You're the best!!!*

OMW

See you there 🍸

Nat sighed and regarded the glass and metal rectangle glowing in her hand. *Et tu?* she wanted to ask. She opened her app. There was a crop of new messages and a bouncing heart in the menu bar, which meant that she had secret admirers to unlock, a feature that was available instantly behind a paywall or for free every twenty-four hours. But Nat knew her own algorithm, and so she knew that she had to swipe on as many profiles as possible in that crucial first forty-eight hours of creating an account in order to keep from getting buried in the daily crop of new users, and also feed the algorithm enough data to get the most matches. She started swiping right on profiles, barely even taking in the pictures, let alone their names and pithy twenty-word bios, before the screen filled with a green *YES* heart and flipped to the next man in the queue. Why not? The more the merrier.

She'd initially based BeTwo on a system called collaborative filtering, which was basically the same system that streaming services used to suggest what movies or music someone might like based on what they've already watched or listened to. If Bob liked smooth jazz, it showed Bob songs that other people who also like smooth jazz had listened to, thus making Bob feel satisfied and deeply understood by the magic of lifeless code.

Most dating apps lifted that model and stopped there. They sorted users based on broad categories like race, gender, job/income, educational level, age, and once someone matched with enough people of a certain type, it showed them that subset of profiles pretty much exclusively.

Of course, Nat had decided to honor the revolutionary insight that people usually liked more than one type of music, and so her version of collaborative filtering ended up being a lot more nuanced. Years-of-her-life-level nuanced, but it meant that BeTwo's match suggestions were based on more factors than any other app that she knew of.

The teens kept blasting their jams. Nat kept blindly swiping right.

Something that had always bothered Nat was the fact that most dating apps' collaborative filtering didn't just group users based on the demographic categories, it also ranked them based on the majority preferences for each category — or in other words, it ranked users by popularity. Each and every user was given a score based on how likely they were to get right swipes compared to every other user on the app. So, when a user inputted their age, it was compared to data on how many "yes" swipes a user of a similar age had received from their potential matches. That meant that if the user pool skewed young, which they naturally tended to do, users over thirty-five were automatically ranked lower in the dating pool — even before taking other factors like ageism into account. Nat had felt that an algorithm reflecting that Bob likes smooth jazz, and so probably isn't into heavy metal, was one thing. An algorithm reflecting that Bob likes twenty-five-year-olds and not thirty-five-year-olds, never mind the fact that Bob himself is forty-three years old, and then punishing those thirty-five-year-olds because of Bob's preferences, was entirely different.

She'd labored to create a novel algorithmic approach because, as she'd learned through her many betas, most algorithms didn't surface their low-ranking users nearly as often for matches, because most dating apps had a vested interest in making users feel that their match pool was brimming with the hottest singles around. In fact, many apps didn't show low-rank users to higher-rank users at all. They just disappeared into the dregs of the user pool, and matched only with users that the system had deemed on-or-below their level of swipe-ability. In other words, it was a likeability contest where not coming in first place would essentially banish you to Siberia.

Nat had thought that approach was not only a moral outrage, but it was also lazy. It didn't take a genius to see how this could do more than just perpetuate the worst biases of society — it would literally codify those biases with every single swipe. It was part of what she'd been trying to say when Tracy had brought up breaking toxic social tendencies in the panel discussion. That was exactly why her algorithm was so special. It was why it was worth protecting. It was why she had to beat Rami.

The teens with the speaker were now standing in the aisle. One of them lay down a flattened cardboard box. A young man in baggy jeans and an all-black San Francisco Giants cap started breakdancing. The kissing teens stopped kissing, and clapped and whooped at the kid's moves. The song bopped with lyrics about feeling yourself and owning the moment — no haters!

Nat shrank down in her seat, all the better to hide her hater tendencies, and kept swiping. At least someone out there was having a good night.

* * *

Nat pushed open the red pleather swing doors to her favorite bar, and felt the atmosphere greet her like a sigh of relief. Bathed in moody red light, the place was intimate and dive-y, with jazz standards on the jukebox and no-nonsense bartenders who served up stiff, classic cocktails in front of a hand-painted mural of forest creatures cavorting with elegant, robed figures. It was a little slice of the city that time and the tourists had never touched. It was perfect.

It didn't look like Sara was there yet, so she pulled herself onto a stool by the door. She set her phone on the tarnished brass bar top and kept swiping. As if by magic, a gin martini appeared in front of her with a wink from the server. She took a sip and let it course through her body, unraveling her nerves like unzipping a zipper.

"No way, this place is off-limits for dates."

She turned to the voice at her shoulder. It was Rami, standing like a sentry with a bourbon in his hand, and glowering at her.

"It's definitely off-limits," she snapped. "And I've definitely been coming here longer than you have, so, sorry."

Rami eased up his glare by an iota. "So, you're not here for a date?"

Nat sipped her martini. "Never. This place is sacred."

Rami's entire body softened with relief as he said, "Tell me about it. Did you know they'll kick you out if you order a cosmo?"

Nat tossed her hair. "Was that embarrassing for you?" she asked.

"You're hilarious," said Rami, flatly. He gestured to her phone. "You should put that on your profile!"

Nat blushed and stashed her phone as Rami pulled himself onto the seat she'd been saving for Sara. He let out a theatrical sigh and looked at her sadly. "One night of the BeTwo hellscape and you're already hitting the sauce." He sipped his bourbon with a smirk. "Sounds about right."

"How do you know that this isn't a celebratory drink?"

"Because you're drinking it alone."

Nat shrugged. She looked into his amused brown eyes with what she hoped was utter confidence. "The date was great, actually. He was really nice."

Rami frowned. "It'll wear off on the second date."

"Oh good, another cynical insight!"

"It's not cynical if it's true."

At that line, a smile twisted on Nat's face. She couldn't help it.

Rami's left eyebrow perked up, and his eyes narrowed with interest. "Trust me, there's a weird thing that happens when you meet up with someone you've been talking to online. First online dates are notoriously unreliable."

Nerves suddenly crept into Nat's stomach. "You know we're not supposed to be in contact, right?" she said.

Rami waved his hand in defiance and continued. "First of all, you have the huge relief that your date is not, in fact, criminally insane, which is a low bar that makes you overlook a lot of other perfectly valid red flags."

Nat rolled her eyes at him. "Should I be writing this down?"

"Then there's the fact that you've already formed this whole idea of them in your head from their messages. You think, 'Oh, she's a nurse. She must be kind!' or 'She wrote 'lol' to my *Hobbit* reference and went to a good school, she must be smart—'"

Nat almost choked on her martini. "Please don't tell me you're a sapiosexual."

Rami grimaced. "God, no. That's just code for 'asshole.'"

"Right?" she cried, raising a hand in righteous validation. "Who says that?"

Rami lifted his nose in the air and took on a pompous tone as if reciting from a profile. "Hello, I want you to know that I think I'm smart in the most entitled way possible."

Nat scoffed in appreciation. They both took sips of their cocktails.

He ran a hand through his curls and faced her. "Basically, the whole premise is flawed. In your head, you'll always be dating the person you first imagined when you read their profile."

"So? What's the difference?"

"Just wait until you get to a second date with a promising guy. You walk in to meet him, all excited. You totally feel like you know him." He sighed and smiled, and his dimples winked at her in his olive cheeks. "Then before the first round of drinks even comes, surprise! You can't stand each other!" His smile dropped. "You're horribly mismatched."

Nat frowned. "'Mismatched' seems like a strong word. No algorithm is going to be perfect."

Rami leaned in toward her. He still smelled like sandalwood and, weirdly, also gummy bears. "Oh, but you were feeling so good about him that you agreed to a full-on dinner, and now you have to suffer through the next two hours making conversation about whatever it was you did have in common, like some 80s teen movie." His face scrunched up in a mock grin. "Isn't that quirky?"

Nat shook her head as her algorithm swirled in her mind. "Liking the same movies is a factor of compatibility."

He scoffed through his drink. "Please. Most people's pop culture taste just shows that you both live in America in the year 2025. It means nothing romantically."

Nat drank her martini and considered this. She looked at Rami, his shoulders sagging from some clear weight as he eyed the intricate flora and fauna in the mural. His guard was down. He wasn't trying to intimidate her or insult her. He was telling her about his experience with her app. She leaned her elbow closer to him. "So how often did BeTwo match you with people that you didn't like?"

He looked at her with bright eyes. He opened his mouth to speak, and Nat noticed his full lips were tinged a faint blue color that somewhere in her mind she wanted to lick off — when Sara burst through the door.

"Sorry, late bus!" she wheezed, out of breath. She eyed Nat and Rami for a beat. "Ready to go?"

"Yes, definitely!" Nat downed the last of her martini as she watched Rami straighten his posture away from where he'd been leaning toward her. "I was thinking about the place with The Smiths cover band?"

Sara crossed her arms, mean-mugging Rami, as she said, "Fauxrissey. Yeah, I already got us on the list, so get ready for some feels."

"Amazing!" Nat hopped down and reached for her purse. Rami held out his hand.

"It's on me."

She froze. "Really?"

He fixed her with a sad smile, but his puppy dog brown eyes danced with mischief. "It's the least I can do now that you're in the BeTwo trenches of despair."

"You make it kind of hard to thank you."

He shrugged with a satisfied glow. "Well, you're welcome."

Nat took Sara's arm. She pulled her scarf tighter around her neck, but something felt off. She made sure she had her phone in her purse. Then she turned back to Rami. "Take it easy," she said.

He raised his glass to her with a tiny smile. "You too."

Warmth rushed up through her, and she smiled. It was the best she'd felt all night. Then she pushed open the red pleather doors and left.

* * *

Sara and Nat clutched their jackets closed as they walked down the sidewalk. The fog blurred the streetlights into fuzzy halos around them, and the tops of the pastel Victorians that lined the street disappeared into gray mist.

Sara let out a whoop and smacked Nat on the shoulder. "Holy hell, that was the weather app guy who's out to destroy you?"

"Yeah, so?"

"So? He's totally cute!"

Nat thumbed her phone on. "He's a pill," she said.

"Yeah, he is. Yum."

"No, like a bad pill. Not a fun pill." Nat sniffled away the last of her earlier tears.

"Are you OK?" Sara asked. She rubbed a few brisk circles on Nat's shoulders like she was prepping her for another round in the ring. "Wanna talk about your terrible-no good-very-bad date?"

"Definitely not." Nat shot Sara a quick smile to signal that she really was feeling surprisingly okay after her awful night. The best martini in the city must've done the trick. Then she opened

BeTwo. After all her swiping, she'd earned a red number 18 emblazoned on her inbox. Goodie.

Sara peered at the screen. "Oh, more messages! Let me?"

Nat happily handed over the phone, which had begun to feel like an albatross. "Be my guest."

Sara silently read as they walked, but her commentary was out loud. "No . . . Weird! . . . No . . . Oh, yikes!"

"Yikes?"

Sara shook her head. "Just a classic neg, moving on."

Disgust curled into Nat's face. "Negs are classic now? Are they that common?"

"Totally. I once had a guy send me three full paragraphs of his pros and cons for dating a woman with short hair." She gestured to her jaw-length undercut curls. "It ended with a line about how I would probably think I was too good for him, but he was, and I quote, 'just being honest.'"

"Seriously?" Anger made Nat's footsteps fall harder. "I'm so sorry."

Sara shrugged. "Happens all the time, and way worse. It's whatever, and also part of why I'm focusing on the ladies right now." She stopped walking and held out the phone. "Here, what about this guy? Coder, but not douchey. Cute in a 'you' kinda way. His message was obviously written about your profile, and his profile says he's looking for commitment."

Nat peered at the man smiling out at her. His name was Nick. Close-cropped beard, shaggy salt-and-pepper hair, kind eyes, lanky frame under a charmingly dorky sweater. He was definitely cute. Eighty-five percent match. That was really, really high.

"Nah," she said.

Sara was shocked. "What? Come on! We've got to beat the hot weather guy!" She laughed at her own pun. "Hot weather."

"Just nah, OK?" Nat started to walk again.

Sara matched her stride and slipped the phone back into Nat's purse. "I'm just saying, you might have to step up your game to win this thing." She put an arm around her friend's tight, tense shoulders. "But that is a concern for tomorrow. For tonight," she continued in a dramatic tone, "all that matters is the dance."

Nat laughed as Sara struck a pose in the fog. She hooked her arm around her friend's elbow. "I love you," she said. "Let's see if we can get Faux-rissey to give us his orthodontics business card again."

* * *

Hours later, Nat stumbled into her room and drunkenly kicked off Sara's beautiful red shoes. Her throbbing feet were absolutely wrecked. Now that it was nighttime, her cat, Pixel, had emerged and was curled up on her pillows. He stood and arched his back for her arrival. She collapsed onto the bed beside him and pushed her face into his warm belly.

"Baby boy," she cooed as he purred and writhed around in the affection. She knew she had a small window between him happily wrapping his paws around her hands and him turning those same paws into razor-sharp weapons that would grab hold of her hands so as to bite the shit out of them. It was a risk she was willing to take.

The alcohol made the room wobble. However, her memories of the night, particularly the humiliating date and pocket dial from Jo, remained frustratingly steady. The bass of the dance music echoed in her ears, and the cheap alcohol flip-flopped in her stomach.

She pulled her purse off and poured its contents onto the bed. Pixel darted off as his paws knocked a few mints to the floor. Her phone. That's what she needed. She pulled up BeTwo and the message from Nick, her eighty-five percent likely Prince Charming, and tapped open a response window. She stared into the white void of the text box. The cursor blinked.

"Hey, there he is," she said to herself. "P.S. Your haircut sucks. Let's get married."

She groaned and rolled over and looked at the line-up of other messages in her inbox. She could see that some of the matches were ranked below sixty percent, so she wasn't even going to bother opening those. No other user came close to Nick's eighty-five, but a few were in the respectable high-sixties and low-seventies range.

Seeing that his message contained only the word *hey*, Nat opened the profile of a guy who went by "B," and immediately recoiled. B was in his fifties, at least, and seemed to only have pics of himself where the camera had been placed directly underneath his large, orange-tanned nostrils. Flash, very unfortunately, on. B also listed himself as unemployed, and had written a long and poorly spelled paragraph on all the things he didn't want in a woman, including a warning that he *was not looking to rush into a relationship right away*, which didn't seem like a problem a guy like B would actually encounter all that much. Were there that many women rabid to lock down a middle-aged man with no job, no hair, no discernible waistline, and no problem writing the words *don't be uptight about condoms* in his digital introduction?

Nat shuddered and blocked B, but his profile lingered like a bad taste in her mind. Surely this was just the product of her manic swiping earlier that night, not the fault of her algorithm — plus her profile was just an assortment of high-performing traits, so this didn't reflect on the accuracy of the match. The more disturbing truth was, a man like him had thought he had a chance with a woman like her — twenty years younger, successfully employed (she'd just put that she worked in tech), and in full command of grammar and common etiquette. Did he really think they were on the same level? Even as her logical mind recoiled in indignation, she felt the dent in her self-confidence all the same.

Nat thought about how Jo was horrified at the prospect of being like her, how Eric hadn't even thought she was worth treating kindly, and now some gross guy thought he had a chance with her. The scientist in Nat couldn't deny three consecutive data points, no matter how much she wanted to. So, what was it about her that was so rotten?

She closed out of the messages and went back to swiping. She raced her finger over the screen, looping into faster and faster swipes.

"Swipe right one, two . . . ten! There! Are you happy now, *Algorithm that I designed?*"

She sat up with a cold sloshing in her stomach. She knew she should go get herself a glass of water, but she also knew that would be an impossible feat at this point.

She thumbed open the message from Jo. No further response. The overheard call seeped into her thoughts like spilled ink.

She lay back down on her bed, opened her email, and found the contest contract from BuzzFill. She did a quick copy and paste and opened a text message to Rami. He seemed to hate her. Maybe she could get answers on her loathsomeness from him. She knew from experience that he certainly didn't sugarcoat his words.

> Nat: *Hey, thanks again for the drink. I still wanna know if my app mismatched you a lot*

She hesitated before pressing send. That was no way to address her enemy. She erased it and tried again.

> Nat: *It's Nat. Here's a question for all your BeTwo wisdom. What's the best opening message to send a guy?*

Three typing dots appeared right away. She sat up straighter. The room wobbled.

> Rami: *You're asking me to help YOU? AKA The Enemy?*

She scoffed.

> Nat: *Don't you have all the answers?*

> Rami: *📽 Just be yourself!* 📽 ♥ 🦄 ✦

Nat cackled.

> Nat: *That's beautiful. You should sell T-shirts*

> Rami: *IDK I just ask about something in their profile.*
>
> *Smth like*
>
> *Hey I love that band too! Did you ever see them live?*
>
> *You like to cook! What's your favorite dish to make?*
>
> *Is that a llama in your profile pic?*

> Nat: *Can the llama come on our date?*

Rami: *If I become emotionally attached to
the llama, is that going to be a problem?*

Nat: *No prob-llama at all!*

Nat laughed and stretched. Her phone buzzed again.

Rami: *See? You're a natural.*

She watched the typing dots wiggle.

Rami: *But I'm still gonna kick your ass . . .*

In a totally figurative way

 *Llamaste*

She stared at the phone for a beat, but couldn't think of anything else to say. Besides, she had her information.

She opened BeTwo again and started writing her response to Nick.

CHAPTER 10

Later that week, she was on the office rooftop for lunch with Justin and Jo, meant to be enjoying another crisp and sunny San Francisco afternoon. Instead, she was absorbed in her phone, silent and reacting only to the pings of Nick's incoming BeTwo messages. Her salad lay forgotten in the sun.

> Nick: *No way really????*

> Nat: *OMG totally. The kids called me Not-alie. I was that unpopular.*

So far, Nat had been pretending like nothing had changed between her and Jo, which was much easier to do when she had a screen to stare at.

The twins carried on their conversation around the random bursts of laughter from their boss.

"OK, but a face is only one part of how you recognize someone," said Jo, spearing a chunk of ahi tuna. "Wouldn't she notice that her husband's entire body is different?"

"Maybe it was different in a good way," said Justin. He wiped some mustard from his purple corduroy joggers. "Let's ask our elder millennial for the social context."

Nat picked up her fork and blinked at them. She still didn't trust herself to speak non-work-related sentences to Jo.

"You still with us, boss?" asked Justin.

Nat's phone pinged. She hunched over.

Nick: *Aww, I hate those kids!*

"Nope," said Jo. "And you know our jobs kind of depend on this thing not turning into a dumpster fire live on BuzzFill, right?"

Justin sighed. "You've mentioned it."

They watched a seagull glide past. Nat giggled at the message, hand still clutching her fork mid-bite. It was even easier to avoid thinking about how Jo secretly hated her when this guy was so clearly into her.

Nick: *And you're totally hot now, so joke's on them.*

Jo squinted in thought and brushed a crumb off her white button-down. "So, you're saying the wife was like, 'Finally! The love of my life has transformed from the neck down.'" She waved her napkin in dismissal at her brother. "Nat, are you hearing this trash?"

Nat glanced at the twins as a blush crept across her cheeks. She supposed she could say just one thing to them to keep up appearances. "Yeah, airplane prison. Funny!"

Justin reeled as if he'd been punched. "Whoa! That's apples and oranges."

Jo got up and scooted close to Nat on the picnic bench. She gestured to the phone. "Catching some good ones today?"

Nat felt her body tense up and pull away from Jo. "Oh yeah . . . this guy . . ." She trailed off.

> Nat: *Hbu? Were you super popular or something?*

Jo smiled and adopted her perkiest tone. "Ooh, so a guy is texting you?"

At this, Nat saw an opportunity to flaunt. "Texting me for three days. Like, all the time!"

Jo brought her hands in front of her chest in a miniature clap. "Yay! That's awesome."

"It *is* awesome! We talk about really deep stuff. Things it took me months to tell most people. And Nick just totally gets it." Nat took a bite of sun-softened avocado. "We're an eight-five percent match, you know. Which feels spot-on."

Jo tilted her head. "Well, he's an eighty-five percent match to the person represented by your profile, but do we even know who that person is?" she teased.

"That person is me," said Nat, an edge flaring into her voice in spite of herself.

Jo's eyes narrowed with playful mischief. "Is it, though?"

It was a tone of banter with Jo that Nat usually loved, but it seemed a lot less fun now. "Well, I'm the one messaging him, right? So, he must like something about me!" she snapped.

Jo blinked in surprise. "Sorry!" She searched Nat's face for an explanation. "I mean, it's cool that he likes you."

Nat rolled her eyes.

Justin frowned and leaned protectively toward his sister.

"Sorry, I'm just distracted," Nat mumbled, feeling small. She should have known this would be the downside of hiring siblings. It'd always be two against one. She sighed, trying to radiate self-actualized contentment. "Isn't it just completely gorgeous out here today?"

Her phone pinged.

Nick: *tbh I was kinda popular. Prom king
means you're popular, right? Or that you
had the money for a very large bribe?*

Nat smiled brightly at Jo. "And he's so funny! Oh my God."
She went back to typing.

Jo nodded like a cruise activities director who had just been
told the pool was contaminated. "Great! That's super great, but
like, you're gonna actually meet up with him, right?"

Nat nodded as darkness dripped back into her mind. Of course,
Jo didn't think someone would actually enjoy talking to her. She
managed a quick, affirmative hum, but kept typing to Nick.

Jo tucked a loose strand behind her ears and nodded. "Cool,
cool."

Nat: *OMG I didn't even go to prom! I just
watched old BBC DVDs all night with
the other weird kids.*

Nick: *OK you would've destroyed me in
high school. I secretly wanted to date the
cool smart chicks like you.*

Justin cleared his throat. "So, boss, when's the date?" he asked,
his whisper-soft voice pushed to top volume.

Nick: *I bet you do that whole sexy librar-
ian thing . . .*

"When?" said Nat. "I don't know. Soon."

Justin frowned and stood with his empty lunch wrappers. "Hasn't come up yet, though? And it's been three days of
messaging?"

"Not yet. Relax, geez!"

Nat: *Shhh. No talking!*

Nat giggled.

Jo turned to Justin. "Catfish?" she stage-whispered to her twin. "Lurker? What do we think?"

Justin shook his head sadly. He tossed the wrappers in the trash. "She's fish bait."

Anger flared in Nat's chest. That was too much. She looked Jo right in the eyes. "Excuse me? Is it so impossible to believe that someone would actually enjoy talking to me?"

Jo blinked in shock. "What? No! You're great!"

Nat crossed her arms and frowned. "Gee, thanks. Your words mean *a lot.*"

Jo's face crumpled in confusion. "OK . . . did I do something? What's going on right now?"

Justin took up the space next to his sister like her shadow, and Nat felt her aloneness echo at the sight of it.

She shook her head. "Look, we're just doing our jobs. It doesn't need to be anything more than that."

"Yeah, we know," said Justin. "The contest is just for the publicity, not to find, like, your soulmate."

Jo chirped a nervous laugh. "Totally get it!"

Nat stood. "Actually, you two wouldn't know this because you weren't here when I created the app, but I *did* start it to find a partner. I know sometimes people like me seem weird or lame, or . . ." Nat took a breath, but she was too fired up not to say it. "Or maybe we seem like *a lot.* But I don't need you to like me. I just need you to help me win this contest and then we can all get on with our lives, OK?"

Justin had lowered his eyes to the ground, and Jo was staring at Nat with a queasy expression. "OK," she said in a meek voice as Justin nodded in agreement.

Nat took a deep breath and dumped her mostly uneaten salad in the trash. "Good. Let's get back to work."

* * *

Rami wasn't proud of the things he'd been saying into his phone that afternoon. Things like, "Your sister got married? No, come on!" and "Did she have any cute bridesmaids?" and "What about on the groom's side?"

It had been humiliating. And fruitless.

He sat perched on the end of his bed, drumming a pen against the notepad on his lap. Every name on the list was crossed out — every cousin, second-cousin, semi-aunt, and old childhood friend searched and found devoid of leads for someone he could date. He even would have asked his little sister, Sana, to set him up with one of her giggly friends — a task that would have thrilled her to no end had she not moved away last year for a fresh start after an epic breakup. He didn't want to risk opening any old wounds. There was one last name on the list. It read: *Amma?*

He ripped off the paper, crumpled it, and threw it against the wall with a groan. There were depths to which he would not sink. Yet. Besides, one of his cousins had probably alerted his mom to his little quest by now, anyway. Usually, he was grateful to have grown up in the Bay Area, but there were days he wished he had flown a little farther from the nest.

A sharp knock sounded on his door, and Ian popped his head in. "Sounds like someone needs a little help?"

"Were you just standing right outside my door?"

Ian breezed in. "The shaman sends his own invitation." He made for Rami's closet and began rifling through the clothes. "We're going to start small, little polliwog. If you want to catch a fish, you have to go to the fullest pond."

Rami frowned. "OK, that is a very mixed metaphor, and I think a frog might be a poor choice given the negative romantic connotations of frogs—"

Ian pulled off the shirt he was wearing and tossed it to Rami. "Wear this. Let's go."

Rami watched the massive, coiled snake tattoo on Ian's back ripple as he walked out of the room. He held up the weird, silvery button-down pooled in his lap. At least Ian's plan probably wouldn't involve any more phone calls.

* * *

Ian and Rami pushed their dark green grocery carts through the cavernous produce section of the grocery co-op. Rami could smell the cedar and ylang-ylang notes of Ian's cologne in his shimmery borrowed shirt. He had to admit it was a nice scent. Ian, himself, was wearing a somber navy-blue hoodie for a reason that had something to do with peacocks. Rami hadn't tried to understand it.

He leaned his elbows on his cart. "Why would you ever want to meet someone at the grocery store? It's too much pressure." He watched the millennials and Gen Xers in yoga pants and fair-trade organic kaftans mill around them, with the occasional aging punk and muscle bro thrown into the mix of urban hippies. "Sometimes you need to buy toilet paper and canned chili, and you can't impress a girl with that in your cart."

Ian cocked his head. "Can't you?"

"Gross."

Ian placed an enormous bushel of kale into his cart. "Relax, everyone knows the co-op is the hookup store. This food is not for eating."

"OK, but it is also, like, criminally overpriced," Rami grumbled and picked up a nearby artichoke. A woman with blonde dreadlocks and a shibori-dyed sarong sauntered toward them holding a towering stalk of Brussels sprouts like it was her wedding bouquet. She glanced at the artichoke and wrinkled her nose. She neared Ian, clocked his kale, and batted her lashes as she stepped behind a pyramid of mangoes.

"What is happening?" said Rami, holding out the artichoke like a vegan Hamlet.

Ian snatched it. "Produce is too advanced for you, polliwog. Too symbolically loaded, like an art form." He nestled the artichoke delicately back into place on the shelf. "You need to go to the meat market."

Rami scoffed. "Do they even sell meat here?"

"No, buddy. Bulk foods. If you go there, you're practically begging for a phone number." Ian smiled at the dreadlocked woman with the Brussels sprouts. "Everyone knows that," he said, and patted Rami on the back as he sauntered toward his cruciferous conquest.

Rami watched as she playfully tapped Ian with the stalk. "Everyone knows that," he muttered, and pushed his cart toward the bulk foods.

* * *

Rami had been watching the "meat market" scene for the length of two Mumford & Sons songs and one Grateful Dead jam on the store speakers. So, for him, an eternity. He'd seen an indie rock girl with bleached bangs and a nose ring fumble to fill a baggie with banana chips, and an indie rock guy with a bright orange bob and pink hoodie, swoop in to hold the bag for her with a winning smile. They'd left together. He'd watched a slight young man in a gray cardigan scoop up a bag of unsalted almonds, twist on the tag and then stand there, pretending to browse, until a tall shopper in a sequined skirt filled their own bag of all-natural fruit juice gummies, and then Unsalted Almonds asked Gummies for the pen to write the SKU number. They'd left together.

It was all really just a lot of pressure. But he was here in this ridiculous, melted-Terminator-looking shirt, and how else was he going to find a date before the BuzzFill deadline? He took a deep breath and waded into the aisle lined with little plastic bins.

"Need any help?" he offered to a freckled redhead in front of the yogurt raisins. She smiled wordlessly and poured a waterfall of raisins into a reusable cloth bag like modeling for a marble fountain of the Platonic ideal produce shopper. "Yeah, OK, you seem good," he mumbled.

He kept walking, slowly down the aisle. He put his hands behind his back so he felt more like he was strolling and less like he was creeping.

A dark-skinned woman with cropped curls gingerly dropped dried pineapple rings into a bag with plastic tongs. "Don't want to accidentally get too many!" he said. "Expensive." She ran her eyes over him, head to toe, then went back to the pineapple.

He was sweating. The flame-out with Lynn shadowed his mind. How could he know if someone was interested in dating a straight, monogamous, cis man without some way of seeing that information spelled out? How could he know their pronouns, availability, or if they believed in some heinous, immoral stance like *meal prepping*? It was so much more complicated than looking for a wedding ring.

He neared the end of the aisle, where the candies taunted him with their luxurious confidence. Everyone wanted a miniature chocolate-covered pretzel drizzled in caramel. Must be nice. A petite woman with a burgundy bob, intricate leg tattoos, and a black denim overall dress dropped pieces of white chocolate cranberry bark into a small box. She looked up and smiled at him. Her eyes were dark and witty and lined in black. "I'm addicted to this shit," she said. "Too bad it's expensive as fuck."

Rami tried to give her a rueful, knowing laugh. His mouth was suddenly very dry. Somewhere in his brain, his neurons pumped out a normal potential response along the lines of, *It's ridiculously overpriced but also most places mess up white chocolate so egregiously that it's worth the extra dollars if you ask me, Rami, a normal and affable man.* But all he said was "Hmm", as the rest of his mind flashed vivid images of the woman screeching at him to leave her alone, and stop being a creep, and can't a woman go shopping without getting hit on?

He heard her sigh as he hurried away. Another failure in his race against Nat. But at least he'd remembered that they were out of almond milk at home.

* * *

Outside, Ian's bushel of kale poked out of the bag, covering his sharp, stubbly chin as he carried his groceries up the steep hill away from the co-op. Rami juggled two equally full bags against his ribs as he tried to keep up with Ian's long uphill strides.

"What if I actually like cashew cheese?" he asked Ian, between huffing breaths. "It'd change everything I know about myself."

Ian chuckled sagely. "Better luck next time, pal."

Rami squinted up the hill. It seemed to stretch endlessly above them, leading straight into the sun. "Whatever, I can't imagine being happy with someone who would make me pretend to like," he glanced into one of his bags, "Kool-with-a-K Ranch Kale Chips." He grimaced. "Gross."

"Look out!" a panicked female voice cried out. "Oh no!" she wailed, as Rami heard a terrible metallic thunder rumbling toward them. He peeked up over his bags. A stray shopping cart was zooming down the massive hill, straight for him. Rami lunged for it. He felt the wire frame scrape into his arms as he tossed his bags into it. The extra weight slowed it, and he caught the handle just in time to stop it from careening down the rest of the hill. The wheels twisted over his toes, and he grimaced in pain as a woman with bright pink braids and a long, flowing skirt ran down to him and the cart.

"Oh my God, thank you!" she cried and wrapped her tattooed arms around him. "I swear, I had visions of it taking out a baby stroller or something." She pulled back and fixed him with light hazel eyes and an impish, crooked smile.

Ian cleared his throat. "Don't worry, he's saved all the babies in the vicinity."

The woman giggled and looked at Rami's groceries, spilled all over her once wayward cart. "Kool Ranch!" she said. "Those are like my crack."

Rami's heart was still racing with the adrenaline of the murderous shopping cart. "Me too!" he said, very loudly. "I love them!" He looked at Ian, whose eyes were closed and his face as serene as if in prayer. "But . . . I guess I can share?" He offered her the bag.

She giggled again and took the chips. "Thanks," she said, tucking a cotton candy-colored braid behind an ear clustered with silver hoops. "I'm Gemma. Nice to meet you."

* * *

Nat was curled up on the living room sofa with a blanket and Pixel snoozing at her feet. The room had gone dark with sunset, but she was too absorbed in messaging Nick to notice. She watched his typing dots blink as she waited for his latest reply.

> Nick: *You'll have to tell me more about that tonight, beautiful*

She giggled, warmth winking in her chest like glitter.

> Nat: 😊 *One more thing to look forward to . . .*

Things had been tense at the BeTwo offices since the lunch confrontation with the twins. A frostiness had settled between her and Jo, which Nat took as a silent admission of the dislike she'd clearly harbored all along. Justin reverted to being spacey and ensconced by clamshell headphones at all times, which Nat took as a silent admission of his unwillingness to stand up for her.

But it was fine. It hadn't been healthy for Nat to think of her employees as part of her social life. Even if the twins had been lying about their affection for her, as they apparently had, Nat could understand it. It was their job, and Nat had been naive to the power imbalance. Just one more thing not really covered in the hashtag-girlboss discourse.

So that was also just one more reason why Nat was so excited about Nick.

He hadn't been the only guy she'd messaged, but it seemed like after a few exchanges, most of the chats just simply, inexplicably, cut out. She currently had six separate threads where the last thing she'd written was, "And how about you?" followed by days of silence and/or being suddenly unmatched.

Of course, she'd reviewed these abandoned conversations to see where it was that she'd gone wrong, but she'd never expressed an opinion more controversial than mentioning that she liked pineapple on pizza, which seemed to be a hot question given how often it was asked of her. Ever the good scientist, she'd of course tried the opposite approach and lied that she didn't like pineapple on her pizza, just to see if that would result in less sudden silences. It hadn't. She'd even scoured Reddit forums to see if liking pineapple was actually some kind of slang for a disgusting sex act or, God forbid, a right-wing dog whistle of some kind, but it was not.

It was all very confusing, and it made Nat think and rethink, and then rethink one more time, every word before she typed it into a BeTwo message. She felt like there surely must be some internal logic to the pattern of sudden silences that she just wasn't seeing, but the nagging conclusion was that something about her messages was wrong.

Luckily, Nick seemed to want to communicate with her, both in the app and in real life.

It'd been nearly a week of messaging, but their first date was finally happening in a few hours. Aligning their schedules for a meetup had been a challenge, plus she'd honestly appreciated the time to warm up her rusty flirtation game through the safe distance of BeTwo messages. And she had to say, they'd gotten quite flirty, indeed.

Sara stumbled in through the door with their stack of mail. Her curls stuck to her forehead with sweat, and her whole body seemed to droop. "Why is mail still a thing?" she sighed, dropping a few heavy bags on the floor.

Nat perked up. "Hey, can I borrow your shoes again tonight? Is that cool?"

"Yeah, fine." Sara eyed her roommate with a weary caution. "So, it's the big meetup! How are we feeling?"

"Technically we're just meeting tonight, but I feel like I already know him, you know?" Nat blinked her sharp green eyes. "Meeting in person just feels like a formality at this point." She stretched and cracked her neck. "We've got so much in common!"

"Cool, yeah, good luck!" Sara fidgeted by the sofa. "Hey, so did you get a chance to look at my résumé that I gave you the other day? My apprenticeship is almost over and I've got to submit a formal job app before the salon will let me wield scissors around the public."

Nat winced and covered her face. The text exchange where Sara had asked for her help resurfaced in her mind like a phantom. "Oh shit! I'm sorry. This whole BeTwo thing is just . . ." She looked at Sara with guilt. "They're totally gonna hire you! You don't need help from some coder who's never had a real job."

Sara nodded to downplay her disappointment. "It's fine." She slipped some envelopes into her tote bag as she pulled out a bottle of wine and shot Nat a guilty look. "I'm probably just gonna send it in. It's due tonight."

Nat wasn't sure what the envelope thing was about, but she didn't want to ask while still feeling the tension from the forgotten résumé. "List me as a reference though, if you want?" she offered. "Or, like, the pics of my hair if that's a thing?"

Sara nodded and grabbed a wine opener from the kitchen. "Cool, I will."

Nat hopped up. "Yes, go get it!" She clapped her hands. "OK, now I'm gonna go grab the shoes, get dressed and go on my date." She gave Sara a quick squeeze. "Wish me luck!"

* * *

Rami stared at his eyebrows in the bathroom mirror. Were they OK? As far as eyebrows go? It was like saying a word so many times that it lost all meaning and sounded like gibberish. He had two hairy clumps of gibberish on his face. Should he do something about that?

Tonight was his second date with Gemma. They'd exchanged numbers after the whole shopping cart incident, and already met up once for a beer (for him) and a kombucha (for her). It'd gone surprisingly well. He'd confessed his situation of being in a livestreaming dating competition as soon as they'd sat down. He made sure to paint Nat as not just his competitor, but an ideological scourge on society with her capitalist faith in algorithms and, if you asked him, all the technology that was supposed to bring us together and yet only pushed us farther apart.

He might have been playing to his audience a little bit.

But it worked. Gemma had nodded enthusiastically to his screed against dating apps. She, too, felt they were capitalistic and she, too, had an innate mistrust of technology. (Rami had left out the part about him being a coder for his own app. It hadn't seemed like the right time to bring it up.) In fact, Gemma was a self-proclaimed Luddite, and even if she hadn't gotten Rami's joke about smashing cotton mills on their next date, she hadn't balked at the prospect of a second date, either. She tried to live as analog of a life as possible, having been converted after a profound experience with mushrooms and a pyrotechnic statue of a giant hog at Burning Man. Rami had never been to Burning Man, because Rami had never wanted to do anything less in his life than go to Burning Man.

But Gemma had pretty eyes and full lips, and seemed to think Rami was, against all prior evidence to the contrary from other women, absolutely amazing.

Ian's phone blared its aggressively long ringtone for what seemed like the millionth time. Still, it broke the spell of staring at his eyebrows, and Rami headed to the source of the sound in the living room.

"That's, like, the seventh alarm, Ian," he said to his roommate, who was stretched out on the sofa with his head on a stack of folded towels.

"It's not an alarm," said Ian without opening his eyes.

"Is someone actually calling you? On the phone?"

"Looks like it." Ian sighed.

"A voice call is rarely a good sign, man. You should answer it."

Ian rolled over and fixed Rami with a bleary gaze. "Deflecting anxiety about your date onto others is like . . ." He trailed off and closed his eyes. "Cutting the same bird twice in the mirror," he mumbled.

Rami frowned and poked his roommate's shoulder. "Hmm, even weirder metaphor than usual. And I'm not nervous to go out with Gemma, at all, actually. Why would I be?"

Ian sat up and relit the glass pipe lying on the coffee table. He took a huge inhale and gestured at Rami while holding in the smoke, as if to say, *Because of you.*

Rami got the idea. "Did it strike me as odd that she carries a flip phone from the mid-2000s? Or that she literally told me what time it was when I asked if she was on TikTok?" He began to pace. "Yes. Yes, it did."

Ian nodded through another cloud of smoke as his phone blasted them with another robotic siren.

Rami stopped pacing. "Seriously, man. Do you want me to just answer it for you?"

"It's the Green Party. They're relentless in all the wrong ways." Ian grabbed the phone and silenced it. "It's their tragedy, and also mine for voting my principles." He gestured with the smoldering pipe for Rami to continue. "You were saying?"

"OK, well, yes, I did think some things about Gemma were odd." Rami resumed his pace around the room. "Then I realized that 'odd' is just another word for 'uncommon,' which is just another word for 'special.' And that is what she is."

Ian opened his mouth to speak, but sputtered into a wracking cough.

"What *this* is, I mean," Rami corrected himself. "A special opportunity to connect with someone totally outside of our digital conditioning. Sociologists would kill for this!" He stroked his freshly shaven chin. "I could do a post on Medium about it, maybe."

Ian set down the pipe and curled up around the towels on the sofa again. "Yeah. Go get 'em, analog tiger."

Rami watched him for a beat. "That's it?" He peered at Ian's scruffy face. "Weren't you going to that Oakland art thing tonight?"

"Didn't feel like it."

Rami went to the kitchen and filled a glass of water for Ian. "So, you're just going back to sleep? At seven o'clock? On the clean laundry?"

Ian waved a limp hand in the air to shoo the water away. "You still have *your* phone, right? Call me if she tries anything funny."

"Of course, but that's not the point." Rami put the water on a coaster on the table.

Ian's tanned surfer facade showed the rare glint of actual anger. "Then what *is* the point?"

"Of you not melding into one being with the sofa while I'm gone, or of my date with Gemma?"

"The second one."

"Obviously beating Nat Lane by partnering with someone who is a modern-day Luddite would be a symbolically loaded victory." He put Ian's pipe onto the brass tray in the center of the table and moved away the precariously high stack of old *New Yorker* magazines. "I mean, it might even turn this whole stunt into something more meaningful. It might inspire people to, how did Gemma put it, 'engage with technology with intention.' It could be a movement! The spark that created sea change."

Rami pulled on his coat and checked his reflection in the hallway mirror. Now he thought his eyebrows had never looked better.

"Cool, send me the link," said Ian, voice muffled by the towels.

"I definitely will," he said, and headed out.

* * *

Nat again found herself in the packed lobby of a downtown hot spot. Nick had suggested this place, a tapas bar where Nat had never been able to get a table despite many attempts and Sara's pull with the restaurant community from her time as a bartender. She checked her phone. He was late. Only fourteen and a half minutes, but still. And he hadn't texted to let her know. The supermodel-thin hostess with long hair like shining glass gave her yet another dirty look. Nat shrugged, feeling like a different species entirely from this sublime human woman.

The hostess rolled her eyes and approached. "You've been waiting a while. Reservation?"

"I'm meeting," she hesitated in front of the woman's symmetrical, poreless face, "I'm meeting a friend."

"We can't seat you until the entire party is present, and parking the car doesn't count." Her glossed lips turned down like she'd whiffed a bad egg, but somehow it seemed like a smile. A frown-smile. "I'm gonna have to move you to the lounge area, thank you."

She gestured with pastel, almond-shaped nails to a small armless chair and end table shoved into an alcove next to the bathrooms. A couple with identical hangdog expressions was squeezed butt-to-butt on the chair.

Nat squatted next to them and checked her phone. Nothing from Nick. And now it was approaching the twenty-minute mark. Her feet already hurt. She fiddled with her phone as she felt the panic rising in her chest. She opened up a text to Rami.

> Nat: *Have you ever been stood up for a BeTwo date?*

No typing dots appeared. The clock ticked forward. She turned to the couple on the chair. "Twenty minutes late isn't bad, right? I'm sure you two are late for dates all the time!" She tried a breezy laugh.

"I won the punctuality award in fifth grade," said the one in a blue blazer. "So . . ."

The one in the green sweater shrugged. "I guess it's better than thirty?"

The Hostess Goddess breezed toward them. With a flick of her long fingers, the couple leapt up as if they'd won a prize. The punctual one patted the seat for Nat to sit and gave her a sympathetic smile before practically skipping away to their table.

"I'm sure he's on his way," said Nat, to the empty alcove.

Her phone buzzed. It was Rami.

> Rami: *I've only been stood up once.*
>
> *Twice if you count the second time.*

Nat laughed in spite of the tears building like storm clouds behind her eyes.

> Nat: *Haha*

> Rami: *Oh no did Nat Lane get stood up???*

She watched his dots, and not just because it made not-crying easier when she had something to look at.

> Rami: *And on the eve of my own very promising date with a lovely woman, no less?*

She gasped in spite of herself. The text landed like a punch in the gut. Then anger took its place. Who actually talked like that? Let alone texted like that? This was all his fault, anyway. She typed in a reply.

> Nat: *Nope. Just curious*

She scanned the room yet again. No Nick. Her phone buzzed.

> Rami: *OK good cuz that would've sounded really insensitive. Sorry* 😄

Nat shook the heavy sadness from her shoulders.

Nat: *Gotta go. Ordering another round*

Rami: *Ooh la la*

She put her phone in her purse. Should she just go home? She had a vision of herself laughing fabulously at the bar as she enjoyed a solo meal. It would be the strong, feminist move to make, surely. But who has tapas alone?

The hostess approached with clicking heels. "Are you waiting for an online date?" she asked.

"That's personal."

She cocked her perfect head. "Is it? You're in a public place of business."

Suddenly, Nat hated this woman, and deeply. "Well maybe it's none of *your* business."

"It's literally my job." She produced another frown-smile. "Anyway, some sad guy has been at a table in the back for the last thirty minutes and, I don't know, something tells me you two are a match."

Suddenly, Nat loved this woman. "Where? Is his name Nick?"

The hostess rolled her fake-lashed eyes. "Don't know. But he has Big Nick Energy."

"Look, I know you're making fun of me, but I *am* here on an online date, OK?" Nat balled her fists as she felt the rant swelling inside her. "And he's super late, and he hasn't texted, and I was all excited to meet him because we've been talking for days, and so I'm embarrassed enough right now, OK? And please tell me the brand of foundation that you use!"

The hostess put her hands on Nat's shoulders and twisted her to see into the restaurant. She pointed to a table nearly hidden behind a concrete pillar. "He's really hot, OK?" she said. "So even if he's not your date, so what? Go have fun."

Nat squinted through the low light. There, slumped at a table by himself, was Nick.

And he was, indeed, really hot.

"That's him!" she cried, jumping up and down. "That's totally Nick!"

"Nailed it," said the hostess without expression.

Nat turned to her savior. "Do I look OK?"

"Sure, yes. Go."

"Good, yes, but come with me? I'm too nervous." Nat stopped. "No, you're too pretty, stay here." She stopped again. "No, come with me. Please?"

The hostess sighed and curled a long, manicured finger. "Right this way."

Nat giggled as they neared the table. She felt like it was Christmas morning and she'd just seen the Barbie Dream House-shaped package under the tree.

"Nick?" she said.

He looked up at her. Round sapphire eyes, high cheekbones shadowed in a dashing hint of stubble, and a megawatt smile that practically made her see rainbows beaming around him.

"Nat," he said.

"*Yayyyyyyyy*," the hostess drawled as she dropped a thick menu onto the table with a loud *thump*.

CHAPTER 11

Rami sat on a blanket in Dolores Park, gazing at the lavender clouds that glowed with orange haloes in the early evening sky. He loved this idea for a date. Watching the sunset! How wholesome and environmentally conscious of them, and not at all boring or aggravating to his allergies!

Gemma approached him through the immaculate golden hour light, her long white skirt shining like an angel's robes.

"There you are!" he said. "You're, like, the third person with pink hair that I've waved to."

She sat down and handed him one of two mason jars full of what looked to Rami like green sludge.

"And you brought . . ." he trailed off, peering into the dark concoction.

"Probiotic green super smoothies! My own recipe," she said with a bright smile. "To say thanks for the kombucha the other night."

Rami was genuinely touched. "Aww. Thank you!" he cried. But he hesitated as he brought the glass to his lips. "So, you just carried these here? On the bus? Open like this?"

Gemma held out her jar. "Yeah. Cheers!"

Rami wiped the rim of the jar with his shirt and took a sip. It tasted like sucking on a rusty nail and had the consistency of toothpaste.

Gemma dropped some crystals onto the blanket around them. "Do you like it?" she asked.

"Super good," he croaked. He thought she'd been joking when she mentioned bringing her crystals for him. "What are we doing with the rocks again?"

"An energy cleansing."

She pushed his shoulders and gestured for him to lie flat on the blanket. He gratefully put down the jar of vegetal goop and nestled against the cool ground. Gemma lit a sage smudge stick.

"No thanks," said Rami. "Makes me paranoid."

She giggled and shushed him. "No joking!" She waved the smudge stick at his feet. "Just try and surrender to the moment."

Rami took a deep, fragrant breath. "Surrender . . ." he said, wondering what that should feel like, exactly. He closed his eyes. The fading sunlight made shadows flicker across his eyelids. He could sense Gemma moving the smudge stick over him, waving her hands inches away from his body. He liked that image. He felt her warmth leaning over his chest. Her long braids dragged up from his belly button. He liked that feeling.

Then, suddenly, she was on top of him.

"Whoa!" he cried, opening his eyes. She was straddling him, skirt hiked up around her thighs. The sunset lit her from behind, and all he could see were her sultry eyes and glistening lips as she leaned in. She pinned him to the ground with a deep, delicious kiss. Rami's hands flew to her soft hips before he could stop himself. They were in public!

Gemma leaned back with a smug and satisfied expression. She put her hands on his chest.

"Wow," he said. "Was that part of the cleansing?"

"No." She winked and waved the smoking smudge over his head. "I just really wanted to."

* * *

Nick held the door open for Nat as they left the tapas restaurant.

"Well," he said in the no-nonsense tone of a father at a road trip rest stop. "We finally met."

Nat willed herself to smile. "That was fun!" she said. "How long were we in there?"

He nodded with a polite chuckle. "A while." He put his hands in his pockets and rocked on his heels. "Well," he nodded again, "that was good."

For Nat, asking how long they'd been talking had not been a rhetorical question. She knew it had been nearly three hours because when she had excused herself to go text Sara from the bathroom while the second round of drinks arrived, she'd seen that they'd already been talking for ninety minutes. She'd groaned — actually groaned out loud — because ninety minutes was a very decent amount of time to know if she liked someone, and her heart was definitely, tragically, not excited in the least about the IRL version of Nick.

And yet she'd agreed to the second round of drinks. That was on its way! Because it didn't make any sense! Nick was even more handsome than his pictures, and was clearly as kind and intelligent as he'd been in their messages. She'd touched on the hobbies mentioned in her profile, even making a deeply googled joke about goats eating her yoga mat, which had gone over well. They agreed on pretty much everything they'd talked about. He even had a blind rescue dog! The man was a saint. An angel.

And, to her, a total bore.

It eased her conscience to know that he clearly felt the same way about her. Yet here they were, just standing and smiling at each other outside the restaurant like two utterly happy and polite people, when there was a figurative sign blinking *NOT A MATCH* between them in neon letters.

"We finally met!" Nat said again, nonsensically.

Nick extended his arms for a hug. "Should I?" He hesitated. "Um, here."

He leaned in with his deep blue eyes and perfectly salt-and-pepper stubble and gave Nat a dry, motionless kiss.

"Wow, thank you!" She grinned at him. All she could think to do was keep grinning.

"Well." He nodded, back in Vacation Dad mode. "I'll call you."

"Rad, yep!" said Nat, waving and still smiling as he walked away. She watched until he was out of earshot, then let her face fall. "What. The. Fuck was that?" she said out loud and kicked at an empty can on the sidewalk. She checked her phone. No new messages, BeTwo or otherwise. She knew in her heart that she would never hear from Nick again, but she also didn't want to. She just wanted to understand what the hell had happened to make such a promising date, and an eighty-five percent match that was so statistically very high for her or any app, fall so epically flat. Yes, her profile was just some cobbled-together Dream Girl of popular traits, but she had taken those traits from her own data. They were the traits men wanted, and she hadn't deviated from the script. Although now with some field research under her belt, she had to admit that she was surprised by how little what she'd put on that profile ever came up in any conversations with her dates, Nick included. Plus, their messaging had been honest and genuinely fun. Nick should have liked her, but that wasn't what happened, and she didn't quite know why not.

Worst of all, it reminded her of Rami's warning that IRL meetups were often much different than what was promised by profiles and DMs. But why would that be?

She decided to think about it over the best gin martini in the city.

* * *

Rami took in the scene around him on the patio of the vegan restaurant where Gemma had brought him. Twinkle lights dotted the tall jasmine bushes like stars, and colorful glass orbs gleamed in macramé nests from the trees. Wind chimes tinkled in the breeze. Everyone spoke at a low, companionable volume.

"I legitimately feel amazing," he said. "When can I cleanse again?"

Gemma laughed over her bowl of tofu pad thai. "Whenever you want."

"Really? Hey, do you think there's sage in my salad? Does that count?"

Gemma giggled again, and the sound made Rami's heart swell. He was funny. He could make a woman laugh.

"You know, I couldn't stop thinking about you," she said, leaning in over the flickering tea light on their table. "I know it's not chill to say that right away, but I believe in radical honesty."

"Me too!" Rami noticed how the candlelight sparkled in her gemstone nose piercing when she smiled. "I mean, I couldn't stop thinking about you either." Emboldened by the profound sense of peace all around him, he offered her his open hand to hold.

She nestled her palm in his with a shy smile. "I think what you're doing is amazing, you know? Taking a stand for real life." She squeezed his hand. "Real-life Rami. You could take down the whole online dating system if you win."

"That's what I said!" He shook his head at the overwhelming luck of it all. "I knew you would understand."

Gemma moved her hand to his leg and scooted closer.

The excitement flew straight to Rami's head. "When you think about it, why do we even need computers to introduce us?" he continued, on a roll. "Is there anything more natural than one person just going up to another person because they think, 'Hey, you look interesting and I want to say hello?'"

"Totally." She scooted even closer. "Now people get all freaked out when you talk to them in public, like they feel safer staring at a screen than a human face. It's so messed up."

He liked the way Gemma's voice pitched a little lower when she was expressing a big thought. He really liked the way her hand felt on his thigh.

"Totally," he said. "You should see the looks I got when I tried. I'm pretty sure some of those women thought I was trying to recruit them for ISIS."

Gemma's face lit up. "Oh, is that your band?" she asked. "I'm down to join."

Rami laughed. "Good one." Gemma beamed, clearly waiting for him to explain. A sinking feeling crept into his gut. "ISIS . . . the terrorist group?" he said as she blinked at him. "Because I'm brown?"

Gemma frowned sadly. "Oh, see, that's just awful. That kind of negativity is why I don't read the news."

"You don't?"

She sat up straight and shook her head, her earrings jangling like tiny church bells. "No way. Not for years." She took a sip of ice water from her metal cup. "I limit myself to consuming one hundred words a day or else it can really lower my vibration."

"One hundred?" he echoed. The sinking feeling grew heavier. "But that's like one email."

"Oh, not even! Pixels count in triplicate." Gemma delicately slurped up a noodle. "Really, it's like a recipe, a letter from my pen pal in Gothenburg, my bank accounts statements — yuck," she paused to roll her eyes. "Then maybe a poem if I have room."

"And that's it?"

"Yep!" She twirled some noodles onto her chopsticks with a proud smile. "The universe has a way of guiding any information I need into my reality. Like what are rules made on some hill, even?"

"Capitol Hill?" Rami let a limp piece of arugula fall from his fork. "I'm pretty sure those are laws, but it's whatever."

"Right? Who cares! It's just like voting. None of it is real. Why bother?" She smiled, unaware of the dramatic increase in blood pressure she was causing Rami with her mellow statements. "I'm just about the reality I can touch." She moved her hand higher up his thigh for emphasis. "Here and now."

Rami swallowed hard. "Definitely." His mind raced. He really, really wanted this to work. It would be so easy and simple and beautiful if this could just work. But a dark part of his mind twinged. Even if it was just so he could win the contest.

Gemma leaned toward him and tucked one of his curls behind his ear in a tender, sensual gesture. "Now I wanna know more about you, Real-life Rami. What is it that you do for work, again?"

"Nothing!" Rami blurted. "I mean, nothing really. More of a side gig."

"Cool, like gigs on those awful apps?" Her lips puckered in a sassy smile. "Maybe you brought me my UberEats one time and I've had a crush on you ever since . . ."

Rami laughed nervously. His conscience was not mixing well with the green goddess salad dressing or Gemma's wide-eyed sincerity. "No, but funny you mention that because I actually built and run a successful app."

Now it seemed like Gemma finally knew what ISIS was. Her face clouded over in an instant, hazel eyes hardened. "You're kidding, right?"

He shook his head, setting down his fork.

She scoffed. "So, I'm on a date with a coder right now?"

"Well, I'm an entrepreneur and that's pretty uncommon," he offered in a higher-pitched voice than he'd intended. He cleared his throat and continued. "And yes, it is a digital product, but it's about the weather!" He thought of Ian and took a wild leap. "The forces of the Mother Earth Goddess?"

"That's so much worse!" Gemma's eyes seared into him with outrage. "You take the natural world and you butcher it into an information stream. Can you 'like' sunny days, or something?"

"Liking is just one part of the functionality," he said meekly. "But really, I can explain—"

She held up her hand. "I'm gonna stop you there. My truth is that I feel like I cannot take on the emotional labor of your energy right now, or ever, and I just really need you to hear me when I say that."

He wasn't sure how to respond to, or even parse, her words. "I do hear you," he said. "Because I'm right next to you . . . on an otherwise lovely date, right?"

Gemma took a deep breath and closed her eyes. She sat silently while Rami watched, thinking she would open her eyes and start speaking again any minute now. She didn't, and it gave him more than enough time to notice, again, the adorable bump in her button nose, her smooth, round cheeks, and the pouty lips that had been kissing him just hours before. "Gemma," he started.

"No." She opened her eyes. "It's just that you completely misrepresented who you are. Your whole life is fed by the digital umbilical cord."

She pulled a glass food saver from her bag and dumped in her pad thai.

"You just had that in there this whole time? With the jars?" he marveled, and then remembered himself. "And no, my life is not like that! I mean, it is, but it's not that big of a deal that I work in tech, right?"

She stood, and her pink braids swayed sadly. "It is to me." She put her hands in a prayer position at her chest and sighed. "Enjoy your journey, Rami."

As she walked away, Rami felt his phone buzz. It was Nat.

Nat: *Date was great.*

He scoffed as he watched her typing dots dance in their little gray bubble.

Nat: *I could still meet up for a postmortem drink if you wanted tho. Gotta keep this guy wanting more.*

He let the Gemma-shaped hole fill with annoyance. Nat. This was all her fault.

Rami: *Yeah best to limit exposure*

Nat: *Is your date mad that you're texting in front of her or did she already bail?*

Rami looked around the moonlit patio. This place smelled funny, and it had flies, and a meatless salad had cost him thirty dollars, and he needed a stiff drink.

Rami: *Ha. See you at the place.*

CHAPTER 12

Nat was nearing the end of her gin martini when Rami slid onto the barstool next to her. A hot flush up her chest and swirl of excitement told her he'd arrived, even before his elbow brushed against hers.

"Don't worry," he said, as Nat caught the strong scent of mint gum. "There's plenty of fish in the sea."

A denial flashed in her head, but she recognized the defeated look in his eyes all too well. "No bites for you, either?"

Rami signaled for his usual bourbon and smoothed his wind-blown curls. "I don't know, there's almost something more pure about being rejected in person instead of in pixels."

Nat considered this. "Less digital evidence?"

Rami closed his eyes as he savored his fresh drink. "I mean, at least I got tossed back for something I actually did or said in the moment." He shook his head ruefully. "It's almost refreshing."

Nat arched an eyebrow. She couldn't resist taking the bait as she said, "Refreshing? That would imply that it's been a while since you've been rejected, and is that really the case?"

Rami shot her an amused smirk. "You've been listening. Yes, rejection has been my constant dating experience thanks to your app."

Nat smirked back. "Sure, buddy."

Rami traced a long finger around the rim of his glass. Nat's eyes watched the slow circle and felt a small sigh slip past her lips. "What I mean is that, unlike when an online date mysteriously bails out of nowhere, I experienced this crash-and-burn in real time, as a direct result of my own conscious actions. So, I know exactly why she bailed, and now I can think about that cold, hard fact instead of torturing myself for weeks wondering if I listed the wrong band on my profile or, Heaven forbid, had an emoji misinterpreted." He sighed and sipped his drink. "It's a gift, really."

"Well, you seem thrilled about it."

"I am," he said into his bourbon.

Nat downed the rest of her martini and signaled for another. Rami was clearly in a pontificating mood, and she was beginning to suspect that it was his default setting, which suited her just fine. Why else spend time consorting with her competitor? It was true that Rami was literally the only other person who could understand the pressures of the contest, and it was nice to commiserate — and monitor his progress to make sure he wasn't winning. But he was also the only person she knew who seemed to think as much as she did, or overthink, depending on who you asked. That meant that he was a valuable cache of user feedback. Time to see if she could mine his experiences for data. "Let me ask you this about online dates, then . . ." She twirled the olive in her teeth for a bit as she thought of how to frame her question, but the whiplash of her dud of a date with Nick was too fresh for nuanced wording. "What if their texts are perfect? Then you meet up, and whoops! There's one giant thing missing."

Rami grunted with a knowing laugh. "No chemistry."

"Nothing! Like a mayonnaise sandwich on white bread, served on a CD of Christian pop music."

"Been there. That's why you have to go for the in-person meeting right away."

She met his eyes. "How quickly?"

He knit his brows in thought, the way he had when they'd been on the floral sofa backstage. Nat felt the alcohol buzz a little in her temples. She smoothed her hair and sat up straighter.

"I once texted with a girl for six whole weeks," he said, swirling his bourbon in the glass. "Long, thumb-cramping texts about real stuff."

"You were pen pals."

He put down his drink and looked at Nat with tender eyes. "I was completely falling in love with her."

His candor hit her like a wave. Suddenly, she could see it — the too-soft underbelly behind his prickly, just-the-facts exterior. He was a softie, a crab holding a knife. "Is that all it takes for you to fall in love?" she asked.

"Fine, I was smitten." Rami did a little self-deprecating shrug with the admission. "But we texted about so much. I could write all about politics, past relationships, what I ate for dinner, and I'd always get the same great things back. And then she'd write to me all about her life."

Nat didn't need to search too far in her memory to know what he meant — it'd been the same with Nick. "Like she understood you."

"Exactly." He raked his knuckles against the dimple in his chin. "She was traveling a lot, and I didn't want to ask her out too soon and scare her off. So, this went on and on until, finally, we met up."

"And she was totally different?"

He shook his head. "No, she was smart and cute and we had lots in common." He sighed. "There just wasn't that *thing*."

"A spark," Nat said, as Nick's handsome face and utterly lifeless kiss flashed in her mind.

"A hook," he agreed.

"But then it's almost like you feel that you *have* to like them."

"Even though you don't like them. And it doesn't make sense that you don't!"

"Because you've invested all this time!" said Nat, raising her hands for emphasis. "But you still don't."

Rami nodded in knowing sadness.

Nat sipped her martini. She liked how the red glow of the bar lit his deep-set eyes and Roman nose — an elegant profile. She felt ease spreading in her chest like she was breathing sweet, cool air. Maybe it was the martinis. But she knew her drinks and herself too well to go with that explanation. It was a feeling she'd noticed before whenever she talked to Rami. No matter what he said to her, she responded from some deep, reflexive place in her mind — no debating words, no clench of anxiety, no ringing in her ears that made her voice sound hollow and shrill. Even when he was frustrating her so much that she wanted to scream, it was an authentic scream. With other people, she usually felt like there were two versions of her at all times, one saying the words and making the moves, and another one hovering like a commentator to score and strategize on every step. It was hard to remember a time when she hadn't felt that way. In fact, maybe she'd never noticed it was just a feeling and not a permanent state of being until, like now, it was just suddenly, beautifully, gone.

Rami shot her a glance through his thick lashes. "Let me guess, how long did your date with this guy last tonight? Two hours?"

"Three!" she blurted. "Why didn't I just leave after one drink?"

"The sunk cost fallacy." He rubbed his hands together like he was about to dive into a good meal. "This is something I've thought about a lot, actually." He leaned closer to her, eyes dancing in the low light. "At a certain point, it becomes harder to walk away from something even though you know it's going nowhere. You keep trying to tell yourself that you can save it . . ."

"Yes!" Nat touched his arm, charged up to hear her terrible evening narrated in a logical way that she could make sense of. "Your brain is like, 'Oh, remember that really smart thing he said about politics? He's not *un*interesting. And he's objectively really hot!'"

Rami laughed and picked up the thread. "One more drink and you'll click." He rubbed a hand over where she had touched his arm. "And then another hour goes by, and another . . ."

"Until suddenly, you're a little drunk and not even listening to him because you realize that you can't remember a single person who actually enjoys your company!"

Rami raised his eyebrows. Nat bit her lip. The echo of her confession flamed hot on her cheeks. Her eyes darted at him with a sheepish glance.

He lifted his glass to her. "Or you find your girlfriend kissing Hot Patrick from the mailroom, and you have no idea what just happened to your life."

Nat's hand flew to her chest in surprise. "Ouch. Really?"

Rami slumped over his glass but gave her a sad, knowing smile.

Nat picked up her glass with a shaky hand and clinked a toast before they both drained their cocktails in unison.

Rami signaled for another round. "And you're not so bad." He gave her a shy glance. "Don't let the turkeys get you down."

Nat snorted a laugh. "Turkeys?"

"Yeah. I say, anyone who doesn't treat me with respect is a turkey, because clearly those things are dumb."

Nat felt her eyes crinkle. "Is it really that easy for you to brush it off?"

Rami sighed. "No." He raked long fingers over his face, like wiping cobwebs from his eyes. "Therapy helps, and anxiety meds, but really, it's laziness. So many people don't like me already, so to argue with them all would be truly . . ." He trailed off as he eyed his drink.

"Exhausting," finished Nat. "Easier to just stick with the people who are able to stand you, even if that's literally only one person."

Rami raised his glass in a silent salute. "You get it."

"Yeah," Nat said softly, feeling suddenly morose. The reality of being no closer to winning the contest washed over her. She took the last swallow of her martini. "Anyway, now I get to go on long and disappointing dates, so it's fine."

Rami motioned for the check. "Did you get any food on this long and disappointing date?"

"Not enough," she said, memories of the tiny tapas plates taunting her mind.

"Pizza?"

Nat threw her head back. "Yes," she practically moaned.

Her stomach flipped as he raised his left eyebrow with an approving smile. Nat saw his eyes flicker down her body, and she silently thanked herself for wearing a mini skirt as she shifted her long legs and pretended not to notice his gaze.

"I know a place," he said.

***

Nat and Rami perched on cracked leather stools at a crooked silver table. They held their huge slices of pizza in front of their faces and took big, unembarrassed, cheese-oozing bites.

"Oh my God," said Nat, mouth full of pepperoni. "There's nothing called a 'pizza fallacy' is there?"

Rami shook some more crushed pepper onto his mushroom and spinach slice. "Not that I know of."

"Right, and you know why?" she said, taking his offered pepper jar and adding more to her slice. "Because it's always delicious. Pizza is my rock."

Rami laughed. "Put that in your BeTwo profile."

"Well, I've definitely seen worse." She pulled more napkins out of the dispenser for the grease puddles forming in the corners of her mouth.

"My favorite profiles are the ones that have thousand-word screeds all about who the person doesn't want," said Rami, taking some of Nat's offered napkins.

Nat quoted a medley of profiles from recent memory. "No smokers, no kids, no games, no stupid small talk. I just want someone real and hot." She paused. "And again, you really have to be hot."

"Gotta be looking for something real, not just shallow hookups!" He dropped his voice. "And don't message me if you're under six foot, thanks."

They chewed in happy silence as aggressive punk music blared from the speakers. Nat let her gaze wander to Rami. He was watching the late-night crowd teeter into the pizza shop in a constant, overdressed stream. He looked, as always, deep in thought.

"What kind of thing did you put in your profile?" she asked.

He hit her with a doubtful look. "Oh, come on. You must have it cached somewhere. You can just look it up."

"Absolutely I can," she said. "But I haven't."

He reeled back with genuine surprise. "Wait, really? Why not? Opposition research, Nat!"

She gave him an amused nod as she mulled the question and a gooey bite of cheese. It truly hadn't occurred to her to look up Rami's old profile, which now seemed like an egregious oversight. It wasn't like her to make oversights. Was she afraid of what she might find in his profile? But why? She glanced at Rami, his boyish face looking as relaxed as she'd ever seen it. Contentment looked damn good on him, even in the fluorescent lights of a pizza dive.

"I don't know, but tell me what your profile said, anyway."

He sat up a little straighter and a small smile warmed his face. "Fine. It was dumb." He wiped his shiny fingers on a napkin. "I wrote about how I was just out of a relationship, and wanting to take things slow but not looking for hookups, either."

"What's wrong with that?"

He kept his eyes fixed on his hands and shrugged. "Well, I may have actually used the words, 'My heart is a little tender.'"

"Aww!" cried Nat, feeling something deep inside her melt like a chocolate drop. "But it was!"

"Yes," he said, meeting her gaze with his signature look of quiet mischief. "Which is exactly the time *not* to be on the internet."

Nat had to concede that point. She bit her lip in thought as he stood and gathered their empty plates and balled up napkins. The force of habit to rifle through her knowledge of profile search terms and metrics kicked in, but her mind seemed to be somewhere else. She was too distracted to think about data and sharpening her algorithm. It felt unfamiliar, but it also felt a lot like having fun.

"Ready?" he asked, gesturing to the door.

* * *

It seemed like the number of people on the street had doubled in the time they were in the pizza shop. Nat squeezed close to Rami to avoid getting elbowed by drunken groups taking up the sidewalk in their crooked march to the next bar. He leaned his body back toward hers in response and guided them through the chaos as a little unit.

They managed to walk a few blocks, and the crowd thinned out. Nat realized that she didn't know where they were going, and that she also didn't want to ask and have the answer possibly be "nowhere." She also noticed that he hadn't moved away from her, even though the sidewalk was now wide open.

Rami cleared his throat. "Shall we get a nightcap? We could probably make last call."

Before Nat could answer with her definite *Yes*, she felt her phone buzz just as she heard Rami's buzz in unison.

They pulled out their phones.

"Oh shit," said Nat, reading.

"Shit-shit," said Rami, also reading.

It was an email from Tracy Goodwin-King at BuzzFill. She was reminding them of their pre-arranged midpoint check-in interview in the morning. It seemed that neither of them had accepted the calendar invite, or maybe her intern had forgotten to send it — an idea to which she had added a smiley face. Either way, the date was in the contract, so she expected to see them bright and early, and ready to give updates on their contest progress — on camera, obviously.

"More like BuzzKill," Rami grumbled.

"It really is." Nat sighed. She eyed Rami's figure standing next to her in the hazy street light. "Unless . . ."

"Unless you don't want to give the interview, for some reason," he said, voice turning up into a taunt as he finished her sentence.

She balked. "I have no reason not to! Everything is going fine for me."

"Good. Me too."

"Good." Nat shifted her weight and straightened her coat. "So then we can both just report on our respective dating success tomorrow."

"Absolutely."

The idea of this same voice deriding her app, *her work*, was all too real, no matter how sweet it sounded to her now. After all, she'd heard him do it before. She stuck out her chin in defiance. "I've been meeting great guys through BeTwo. I haven't found the right one yet, but I will."

Rami nodded and tucked a few of his glossy curls behind his ear. "Yeah, and I just had a great night with a cute girl I met totally organically . . ." He hesitated, biting his pouty bottom lip. "I met her at a tech convention."

Instinctively, Nat nodded with a tight smile. Then his meaning hit her. The city street seemed to hush around her. All she could see was his face — his doe eyes under expressive brows, and strong, stubbled jawline offset with a shy smile. For the first time with him, her mind went blank. She just stared.

"Sorry, bad joke," he said, as cars and sirens and other people's conversations swirled back into her awareness. He rubbed his hands together with an awkward laugh. "I should probably call it a night."

But she didn't want to call it a night. "No," she said, stepping forward and taking his hand. She let the warmth of his body fill her with courage. "I had a nice time with you, too."

Rami drew close to her, and his soft fingers curled around hers. Chemistry, that thing she had been chasing all night, practically sparked in the gap between them like electricity. His eyes searched hers, and she nodded silent permission. Slowly, so slowly, Nat could *feel* her shaky breath.

He leaned in, and their lips touched.

And it worked. His lips moved with hers, and she felt his broad chest pressing against her. She wrapped her arms around his steady shoulders. He pulled her close with a deeper kiss. The city was hushed for her again, and the only sound she heard was their breath.

She felt his hands rest on her hips as she leaned away. "That was nice, too," she whispered. But it had been so much more than nice.

"You're nice, too," he echoed back to her.

* * *

Rami opened the door to his apartment in between their kisses.

"I don't understand anything about you," she said, barely taking a breath.

"I don't understand anything about you," he said, flicking on the lights and pulling her into the hallway toward his room.

"And yet you want to punish me," she said.

She felt him smile through her kiss as he closed the bedroom door behind them. "I really, really do."

She smiled back and pulled off his jacket. "Yes," she moaned. The thud of his jacket on the floor brought her briefly back to her senses. "I mean, no! My app. You want to punish my app."

Rami pulled off his shirt and leaned his bare chest against her. "What's an app?"

She kicked off her shoes and lay back on his bed, pulling him down with her. *Rami*. She let his name fill her mind. His arms were golden brown and muscled as he leaned his weight into her body. He had a dark thatch of hair on his chest, leading a trail into his waistband, a trail she wanted very badly to follow with her tongue. Rami. He was also going to publicly attack her app in approximately eight hours. Her body and brain had very different agendas going on right now.

"So, bad dates? That's why you hate BeTwo?" She arched her back so he could slip a hand under her blouse.

"Can I tell you later?"

Nat shook her head and so genuinely wished she could lie. "I'm just gonna be distracted until I know what it is."

He nestled hungry kisses into her neck, and she sighed with pleasure. He whispered in her ear, "Your app isn't perfect. No one's is."

"Yeah." She panted, rubbing her hands across the smooth skin of his back. "Yeah, but did they also spend the best years of their life on their apps, and now it's somehow being turned against them?"

He raised his face and hovered above her. "Are you sure this is about the app?"

"Just tell me," she urged. "Should I make it ultra exclusive, maybe?"

He shook his head, sinking into thought as he nibbled down the line of her shirt buttons. "Honestly, I don't know if that would fix it."

"I agree," said Nat, unbuttoning them. She started to wriggle out of her blouse. "It's because of the users—"

"No, the flaw is in the design," he said. "Not the users."

Nat froze and stiffened. Rami looked up from nuzzling her belly button.

"I'm sorry." He shook his head, his eyes dark pools of regret. "But you asked."

"It's fine." Nat sat up and tugged her shirt closed.

"It's obviously not fine." He slumped over on the bed. "Look, my app has flaws, too!"

"Well, then how about I go on a rant about them for the entire world to see?" She stood and buttoned up her shirt.

"I'd rather you didn't."

"So, it's OK to drag my app through the mud, but not yours?" She scoffed as he buried his head in his hands. "Yeah, that seems really fair."

"My app is just about predicting the weather!" He stood and started looking for his abandoned shirt. "The stakes aren't nearly as high."

"Hmm, I guess I didn't realize that I had to make the world's most emotionally intelligent algorithm."

"Why didn't you?" He pulled on his shirt and looked at her with rumpled hair. "BeTwo is about the search for lifelong companionship. Is there anything more sensitive than that?"

"Come on, it's not that big of a deal," said Nat, putting on her shoes. "It sucks when you don't connect, but it's not personal." She could practically feel the cameras on them already. She gritted her teeth. "It's just a numbers game."

"Do you really believe that?"

"Yes," she lied.

He shook his head in disbelief. "Right, so when you find yourself with a stomach condition because no one has responded to your profile for weeks, or people actually harm themselves because of the rejection they feel from your little algorithm, it's all just a silly game that has no bearing on human emotion?"

"You're exaggerating."

"Am I? Have you checked in with your users about that?"

Nat waved his words away. "There will always be bad actors. I can't be responsible for every time someone acts like a jerk on the internet."

Rami stood his ground. "And yet you know that now there's all sorts of ghosting and toxic messaging and abuse and general people-treating-each-other-like-shit that's happening because of platforms like BeTwo, and on a scale that it never did before."

She shrugged, hoping he wouldn't see the doubt in her eyes. She'd always known those things were happening, of course, and on every app, not just BeTwo. But for the first time, she was a victim of the bad behavior herself, instead of just an outside observer. She had to admit that it hit differently.

"So, then it comes down to this," he said. "Either you think something about the technology is encouraging people to act like assholes, or you think all of humanity is just, innately, a bunch of assholes." He crossed his arms. "Personally, I can't be that cynical."

"You take it too seriously."

"You don't take it seriously enough!"

Fully clothed, from opposite sides of the room, they glared at each other.

Anger and exhaustion and bubbling tears throbbed in Nat's chest. How had she gotten here? Not just the ruined night with Rami, or the ruined night with Nick, or the one with Eric, or even the years of ruined camaraderie with Jo. But how had the one thing that had always been the antidote to all the ups and downs of her personal life — her steady, successful work — led her to this? Burned out and humiliated from some disastrous stunt that put every single aspect of her life on the line. And she wasn't even close to winning.

She should never have pivoted from sorting fishing lures to trying to match people. Then the conversation about her app would have focused on the quality of her work instead of being a referendum on her love life. Then she could have at least kept her dignity. And maybe a boyfriend, too.

"I just think . . . ." Rami trailed off and blinked away the tears of frustration forming in his eyes. "People are getting hurt."

"I'm fine," said Nat.

She watched his face harden. He gave her a cold nod. "You sure about that?"

She picked up her purse. "See you tomorrow."

Rami sank onto his bed. "Sure, have a good night."

Nat's feet stayed put. She didn't want to leave. "Good luck finding your next date."

"You know what? I hope that you find a really good date, too," he said. "I really mean that." He held her eyes with a look of genuine tenderness before it flashed into defiance. "Then you might remember what actual human feelings are like."

Suddenly, Nat couldn't leave fast enough. "You have no idea what my feelings are like," she said, and left before he could see her tears fall.

CHAPTER 13

The next morning, Nat watched as Tracy Goodwin-King and the BuzzFill crew set up lights, mics, and an unbelievable amount of cables as they readied the BeTwo office rooftop for the interview. Whither, Weather didn't have an office, and apparently, Rami had felt that being outdoors was an adequate gesture toward neutral territory. At least the BeTwo billboard wasn't in view, even if part of Nat wished that it were.

Justin and Jo rushed around making notes on the instructions and taking pictures for the BeTwo socials. They seemed to be avoiding her on some instinctive, animal level, and Nat had noticed that they were leaving her out of any of the shots. She could guess why they weren't speaking to her, and as for making sure she wasn't in the pics — that was probably because she couldn't stop pacing and because she was wearing every hour of her sleepless night under her eyes.

Tracy and V, the green-haired producer from Tech-Talk, approached Nat with a clip-on microphone.

"So glad we're doing this outside," said V, squinting into the bright sunlight. "A lot of these tech offices have glass walls everywhere, which, hello? San Andreas Fault?"

Nat's stomach gurgled loudly. Had she eaten since the pizza with Rami? She didn't think so. V eyed her with what looked to Nat like fear.

Tracy struck a confident pose and hit Nat with a glowing smile. "So, this is just a natural, friendly chat today, OK? Our audience wants to know how you're doing, how the dates are going, and if you've met anyone promising." She nudged Nat with a playful elbow. "Have you?"

Nat stayed quiet, staring at the microphone clipped to her shirt.

"Have you met anyone promising?" Tracy repeated, her smile starting to crack into a more aggressive, manic energy.

Nat's eyes searched Tracy's flawless skin as she wondered how to even answer that question. Yes, she had met men who had seemed promising. But then, pretty much the moment she'd met them, all of the promise had gone down in flames faster than someone posting a nuanced opinion on the internet.

So, where did the problem lie? Her profile had been specifically engineered to get the most matches from the top users on the app. She had basically fed her app's data back to itself — it should have been a perfect closed loop of victory. Yet her dates had been disasters and almost all of her messaging had gone nowhere. Rami's words rose in her mind in spite of her best efforts to push them away. Either her user pool was really just that bad, or there was something wrong with the approach, aka her app. Now she stared down the barrel of two options for an existential crisis — A) an entire segment of the human population, namely cis-het men, were irrevocably inept, or B) her entire career was.

But of course, there was a third option for what the problem could be — the problem could be her. Even a city full of desirable men and a complex and high-performing algorithm would be utterly thwarted by someone who was, essentially, unlikeable even when she was hiding behind the veneer of proven crowd-pleasers. Maybe she was the wrench in her own machine. Maybe she was the design flaw.

So, which theory was she going to posit for this live interview?

Tracy's gaze sharpened into a cold calculation of Nat's silence, even as she maintained her megawatt smile. "You good, Nat?"

Jo hurried over, yanking Justin along by his hand. His leather slides slapped against the ground like distortions of his sister's heel clicks. "Ow," he said, ever so gently.

"She's just taking her time sorting through everyone!" said Jo, matching Tracy's perky urgency note-for-note. She gave an open-mouthed laugh. "There's just so many guys!"

Tracy rolled her eyes. "Oh girl, tell me about it. Every time I open up my messages, it's just—" She waved her long brown hands in her face like slapping away a swarm of flies — "so many *dicks*."

Justin raised his eyebrows in approval. Jo laughed again, loudly, and kicked the toe of Nat's shoe. "Right, boss?"

"Totally!" cried Nat, springing to life. "Tell me about it!" She clapped her palms in a single loud smack in front of her chest with a smile. "What am I gonna do with all these dicks?"

Jo's eyes sparkled at her, and Nat couldn't help but feel a twinge of their old connection. She shook it off. Jo was just doing her job because their fates were intertwined at the moment.

Tracy's laugh faded, and her symmetrical face grew serious. "Listen, Nat, I like you and I like your app." She smiled again. "And my bosses like the sponsorship opportunity at play here. So, let's be real for a second, OK?"

"Sure?" Nat swallowed her rising panic. She met Jo's eyes again with a silent plea for help. Despite everything, leaning on her was an instinct, plus she didn't have anyone else to turn to.

Tracy shooed V away and wrapped Nat in a hug that was more like a huddle. "Are you on something right now? Microdosing without the 'micro' part? Because I can work with that."

Jo wedged the shoulder of her navy blazer into the huddle. "She's just excited!" She gestured to Justin for assistance.

"Yeah," he said. Stretching his arm around Nat as his stack of beaded bracelets rattled in her ear. "Who wouldn't be excited to share intimate details of their personal life on the internet?"

"Right." Tracy beamed, but her eyes were sharp. "It's an amazing opportunity, for sure."

Nat grinned too, which didn't seem to soothe anyone's nerves inside the huddle. The silence seemed to thicken around her like a wool sweater. She felt a drip of sweat slide down the small of her back.

"Well, maybe have a cup of coffee or something before Rami gets here," said Tracy with a sigh. "I'm gonna be honest, our numbers are showing that he's way more likeable."

At that, Nat gasped. Now the wool sweater was wrapped around her neck, and something was pulling it tighter.

"Yeah, our audience is misogynist trash," said Tracy, in the tone of a barista announcing she's all out of croissants for the day. "The internet, right?" She sighed. "The list of requirements to simply be allowed to exist as a woman are just . . ." She trailed off and blinked her eyes wide. "So much."

Nat muttered in agreement while her mind raced ahead of Tracy's words — *the list of requirements*. Maybe all this experiment would prove was that she was a hateable ogre, some doomed monster knocking down condos with her tail while she was just trying to walk across the street for an iced coffee — but if Nat knew nothing else, she knew about running data experiments, and there was one variable she hadn't yet tried.

She eyed the door back into her office and checked the giant digital clock ticking down by the cameras. Yes, she had only one option left to save herself in this ridiculous stunt, but she also still had time to pull it off. "I'll be right back!" she called over her shoulder as she ran inside.

* * *

Nat's fingers banged on her laptop keys so loudly that she didn't hear Justin and Jo follow her into the office. First, she went into BeTwo's God Mode, the all-access portal she used to change the code — or look at every user and run them through her own personal set of finely-tuned filters every night on her couch. But now she wasn't just observing from her wine-laden, pajamaed perch; she was churning around in the app like everyone else.

She copied the filters from her last couch search, the digital embodiment of her wish list, and clicked into her user account. Within seconds, she applied every last filter to her profile. Now the wish list was live. Now she would only see men who matched it.

Then she opened her profile and started editing.

Justin cleared his throat.

"Hey, lady," said Jo in the kind of whisper one might use when coddling a Jenga block. "Whatcha doin'?"

"I'm fixing it," said Nat, not looking up from her screen. "Or burning it down. I guess we'll find out."

"Not super jazzed to hear that," said Jo with barely restrained panic in her voice.

Justin sat down next to Nat. "Fixing what?"

"My profile." Nat leaned back and cracked her neck before going back to her keyboard. "All my info was fake, so of course I wasn't meeting anyone that I'd be compatible with." She shook her head in the electronic glow. "I mean, it's so obvious! If I put in real answers to these questions, and search based on the things I'm actually looking for, then I'll meet someone who I actually like." She laughed and pried her eyes from her screen to glance at the twins. "I mean, what was I thinking?"

"It kinda seemed like maybe you wanted to make sure that you wouldn't meet anyone who would really be a viable match," said Justin in his breathy monotone. "Classic self-sabotage."

"What? No!" Jo laughed, her manic energy back in full force. "That's *not* what happened!"

Nat clicked around on her screen, unfazed. "It was smart to try and give the algorithm what it wants to win this thing, but I forgot that I was the one who designed the algorithm!"

"You did?" asked Jo.

"I'm not following," Justin added.

Nat scowled. "Obviously I didn't actually forget. What I mean is that I was too worried about the turkeys."

"Should we cancel this, maybe?" squeaked Jo.

"Absolutely not!" Nat snapped her laptop shut and stood. "No one likes me, right? The guys on my app, the BuzzFill audience, my—" She bit her words back as she met Jo's wide eyes. "No one. But you know who does like me?" Nat shook her curls. "Me. *I* like me. And I have to trust myself, or the algorithm I built, to be able to handle me."

Justin raised his thick eyebrows. "That's kinda beautiful, boss."

Jo bit her manicured nails. "I don't know if we should change strategies this late in the game."

Nat scoffed. The fact that Jo thought her profile was doomed if it was accurate was all the more reason to do it and prove her wrong. "Well, it's too late and it's my call."

Both twins nodded in silence.

"We're on board," said Jo, stoically. "But at the risk of you hating me, can I give you some advice for this interview that's happening in, like, ten seconds?"

Nat swallowed a dry laugh. As if Jo cared about Nat hating her. "Of course," she said, coolly.

Justin winced as Jo pushed ahead with her thought. "OK, so, I know this is bullshit, and you're way smarter than this—"

Nat stifled an eye roll. Flattery, fine.

"But just be positive? Like channel the most annoying Instagram influencer you follow, OK?" Jo was practically pleading. "Project confidence that we're gonna win this."

Through the open door, she saw an obviously Rami-shaped figure heading toward the roof. "I *am* going to win this," said Nat, narrowing her eyes. "So, yeah, I'll be perky, or whatever."

"Gucci." Jo nodded and went back to biting her nails.

Justin held out his palms. "You wanna do a quick grounding meditation?"

Nat shook her head. "Can't say that I do, thanks." She rolled her neck and stretched. "Let's just get this over with."

* * *

V crouched in front of the cameras and held out their fingers in a countdown. "We're live in ten . . . nine . . . eight . . ."

Rami shifted in the folding chair next to Nat. He smelled good in a new way, like expensive flowers and mountain springs and cuddling with a book of crossword puzzles. It was infuriating. "Did you make it home OK last night?" he whispered to her.

"No, I'm dead in a gutter somewhere, thanks for checking." She snuck a glance at him through the glaring stage lights. "Are you OK?"

He stared straight ahead with a blank expression. "Never better."

V waved their hand wildly and pointed to Tracy, whose posture seemed to leap out of her body with sudden poise.

"Hey you, guys, thanks for tuning into this BuzzFill BuzzCheck Exclusive interview with our very own dating lab rats, Nat Lane and Rami Zamir!" Tracy gestured to her subjects as the spotlights glinted on her creamy manicure and gold rings.

Nat raised her bare hand in a timid wave. With all of the stage lighting, she could only see about three feet around her in any direction. It appeared as though she, Rami, and Tracy were simply levitating in a cloud of blinding white, which was jarringly heavenly imagery for what felt very much like hell.

She blinked into the glare as two shadowy blobs began to form at the edge of her vision. The twins — her angels and her demons. They gave her matching thumbs-up signs.

Tracy continued. "We're just about halfway into this little experiment, so let's see how the competition is shaping up!" She turned to face Nat and Rami with a dazzling smile. "Rami, let's start with you. How is the analog dating life?"

Now it was Rami's turn to generate a sudden burst of poise. His face lit with a grin. "Even better than I'd hoped, Tracy!" He raised an index finger to his chin as if in spontaneous brilliance. "You know, it's incredible how much richer our connections are when we don't have all the digital spoilers laid out for us." He nodded and crossed his legs, the glowing picture of a cosmopolitan man with interesting opinions. *Dammit.*

Nat's heart raced as Tracy turned to her. She felt her palms go clammy.

"And Nat? How is it using BeTwo for the first time?"

Nat scoffed. "Well, I wouldn't say it's the 'first time' since I literally built it . . ." She trailed off as the twins gestured wildly off-camera. Jo sliced a hand across her throat. Justin smiled and pointed at his huge grin. Nat smiled and rolled her shoulders back. *So positive!* "But I guess I just never realized just how much fun it can be!"

Justin brought his hands into a prayer position at his chest, and Jo pumped her small fists in victory.

"I'm connecting with guys who I would've never met in daily life, and it's really expanding my perspective!" Nat chirped.

Rami shifted in his seat.

"Amazing," said Tracy. She turned to Rami and narrowed her eyes. "Rami, since you and Nat have been forbidden to be in contact, how does it feel to hear that she's been successful so far?"

Motes of panic shimmered in Nat's vision as she watched Rami give a thoughtful frown. Of course, they had been very much "in contact" less than twelve hours ago, and of course, he also knew just how very unsuccessful her dates had been. She wondered if his mind was also flashing to the scenes in his bed, and she drove her fingernails into her palm to push the memories away.

Rami cleared his throat. "I wish Nat nothing but happiness," he said. "It's what we all deserve."

Nat felt her mouth go dry. How was she supposed to take that? Was he being kind, or was this a subtle nod to his accusation that she was essentially heartless? She snuck a glance at him, but his eyes were downcast and his face was dark.

Tracy commandeered the silence. "Couldn't agree more!" she trilled, crossing her long legs. "And, Nat, how is it for you to hear about Rami's app-less romantic adventures?"

"I haven't seen him, so it's news to me!" Nat blurted, heat flaring into her face. *Radiate calm*, her brain reminded her. *Be an influencer*. She forced a grin and fixed her eyes on the camera. "I mean, I just really love that journey for him."

Rami's mouth twisted in a suppressed laugh, and his eyes twinkled at Nat. Of course, he would see the dark hilarity in her saying something so inane. Of course, he would get it.

Tracy, however, nodded with the deep understanding of an acolyte. "Totally. So, then it sounds like you're both really enjoying yourselves in this little social experiment?"

"Absolutely!" said Nat, visualizing herself wearing a linen kimono and holding a jar of three-hundred-dollar face cream.

"One hundred percent," chimed Rami.

"And what about our big deadline?" Tracy tilted her head and leaned in with a frown as if they were all discussing a tense political negotiation. "Are either of you feeling confident that you'll be bringing a *real date* to the BuzzFill BuzzForce Expo opening party in two weeks?"

Nat's stomach gurgled. "One hundred percent," she cooed, hearing vocal fry creep into her own voice for the first time in her life.

"Absolutely," said Rami.

"How fun!" Tracy beamed and turned back to the camera. "Well, I know that I'm not the only one who can't wait to see how this plays out!"

* * *

Nat took stock of the last twenty-four hours as she looked at her reflection in the communal bathroom mirror of the BeTwo offices. There'd been so many firsts. The first date with Nick, when he'd given her the first kiss she'd had in two years — and it hadn't even been good. Her first BuzzFill BuzzCheck Exclusive interview, which she had apparently "crushed." It was the first time that she had gone viral — #BeTwoChallenge. The first time she had lied to Justin and Jo, when she'd told them that nothing strange had happened the night before. The first time the ache in her chest was not about missing some abstract notion of the perfect partner, but instead it was about missing someone specific, even if that someone had been sitting next to her in a folding chair the whole time.

No wonder she looked so exhausted.

She splashed some water on her face and massaged the dark circles under her eyes. Still, now her profile reflected her actual desires and personality, not just the data on what got the most swipes. Now her fate was truly in the hands of her own algorithm, and there was nothing else she trusted more. Right?

She pushed the swinging door back into the hall. It hit Rami on the shoulder.

"Sorry!" She tried not to look at the way the muscles of his arms rippled as he gestured.

"Nice office," he said, rubbing his arm. Sunlight streamed in through the hallway's floor-to-ceiling windows, lighting his skin with a warm golden glow. "If I had this view, I wouldn't need to make a weather app."

"The view from our actual office isn't like this, believe me." She forced herself not to look at the way he filled out the jeans he was wearing, and met his coffee brown eyes. "You do have a really great app, though."

His face softened. "Thanks." He nodded. "You did good out there."

Nat felt her body slump in relief. "Oh God, I have no idea what I even said."

Rami let out a huge breath. "Me neither! Like, I know my mouth was moving, but my brain just kept screaming at me with all the words I absolutely should not say."

"Same!" she cried. "What the fuck, brain?"

Rami gave a thoughtful frown with an amused tilt of his eyebrows. "Someone should look into fixing that design flaw."

Nat winced with a gasp at his words. *Design flaw.* Suddenly, she was back in Rami's bedroom, buttoning her shirt over her naked chest and trying not to cry.

"Shit, that's not what I meant!" He grimaced.

Nat shook her head and dug her palms into her aching eyes. She was way too tired to stop any tears this time. "It's fine."

"Last night or just now, I didn't mean whatever it is that's making you make that face, because you also made that face last night and that face is killing me."

"It's fine." She took a deep breath and fixed her gaze behind him. "See you in two weeks."

"See you in two weeks," she heard him say as she walked away.

* * *

Nat ducked behind the BeTwo office door like it was a shield. She pressed her back against it and closed her eyes. A few hot tears rolled down her cheeks. She really did have almost no idea what she'd actually said in the interview, except the lies about not having seen Rami. It felt like a blur, like a smear of goo across her memory that made her stomach sick to think about.

The only thing that soothed her was remembering Rami's dimpled smile from the night before. But that comfort only lasted so long before reality, and memories of the rest of the night, set in. She might never see him smile like that at her again.

"Good job, boss," said Jo.

Nat cracked an eye open.

Jo stood before her, holding out an iced coffee like the patron saint of elder millennials. "Justin is out for the rest of the day, and also I thought you could use this."

Nat briefly considered waving it away, but even her wounded ego was only so strong. She wiped her face with her palm and reached for the coffee.

"But really . . . are you, like, OK?" Jo's face was drawn with concern. "I know this whole thing is bananas."

"B-A-N-A-N-A-S," Nat and Jo immediately sang in unison.

Jo giggled.

Nat felt relief melt into her heart. Their old inside joke, still going strong enough to push past Nat's recent defenses, and however Jo really felt about her. Maybe the butt dial had all been a misunderstanding, somehow? Would you still sing a cheesy song from twenty years ago with someone you hated? Nat felt the iced coffee bringing her back to life. Should she just ask Jo about it? That was the obvious and mature solution, not that she had the energy to possibly bring it up now. Still, the madness of the contest must have clouded her mind from seeing it before. She really couldn't wait for this ordeal to be over. Nat nodded. "I'm good, thank you, Jo."

"Thought so. Just checking."

Jo's heels clacked behind her as Nat shuffled to her desk with the coffee.

"So, I know it's early, but the discourse is definitely going our way," Jo reported as she tapped on her phone. "The main reaction to Rami seems to be very much *cringe*, so nice work!"

Nat paused. "What do you mean? It's not like I told people to hate him."

"You didn't have to!" Jo rolled her eyes and shot Nat a knowing look. "He's cute but he's kind of *a lot*, don't you think?"

The words snapped like rubber bands against Nat's nerves. Her mind swung wildly back to her previous hurt. She knew that the exhaustion crackling through her body was dangerous, unpredictable, even *unhinged* — and she was helpless to stop its trajectory. She scoffed. "I don't want people to hate Rami."

"Sure, but . . . it's kinda good for us if they do."

"I'm a good person, Jo! Why would I want people to hate Rami?"

Jo raised her hands in mock surrender. "That's not what I was saying!" She shook her glossy ponytail and fixed Nat with a concerned look over her crossed arms.

With the pink Breton sweater Jo was wearing, the clashing stripes hit Nat's senses like a primal warning of danger. Her frazzled emotions and drained adrenaline from the interview made every word rattle like kindling in the tinderbox of her mind.

Nat downed more iced coffee. "Oh, so you were saying that even though I'm a disaster, I still, somehow, managed to come off as better than him?"

Jo let her mouth fall open in shock. It might have been the only time Nat had seen her perfect composure crack in all the years they'd worked together. "Seriously, are you OK?" she squeaked.

Nat set her glass down on her desk with a loud *smack* and glared at Jo. "Do you *seriously* care?"

"Of course I do," she said. "What's going on? It feels like you just totally hate me now, actually it's felt that way for weeks, and I don't know what I did, but I'm sorry, OK?"

Nat scoffed. Even through her haze of wounded pride, caffeine on an empty stomach, and exhaustion, she knew that she didn't hate Jo, but she did hate that she knew Jo well enough that she could read her face. "Jo, you don't need to apologize to me, and I don't need you to be my friend. We're just here to do a job."

For example, Nat knew how the tiny, dark mole underneath her left eye disappeared when she scrunched up her eyes with a good laugh or a good cry. She saw a shiny glare fill Jo's dark brown gaze and knew she wasn't finding anything funny right now.

"I thought it was both?" Jo's shoulders drooped underneath their pink stripes, making her whole posture look like a frown. "Yes, this is my job, but you're also my friend."

Nat couldn't hold back a sharp laugh. She couldn't hold anything back anymore. She felt like she was sitting in a movie theater watching another version of herself crash out, and all she could do was wince as the scene played. "Really? Well let me ask you a question, then. Do you look up to me? Would you want to be like me someday?"

"Of course I look up to you! You created one of the best apps in the market." Jo gestured around to the silent office as if to support her claim.

Now it was Nat who crossed her arms. "Not my work," she said. "Me. As a person." Nat glared into Jo's confused, searching look. "Tell me I'm not just some cautionary tale to you."

Jo's eyes darted around. "Like right now? You seem . . . not in a good place, but I know this is all really stressful for you, and as your friend, I want to help you through it."

Nat shook her head. The thought of a heart-to-heart was a smoldering ruin, and she was still holding the match. Might as well burn it all down. "Well let me give you some friendly advice, then!" She pointed a finger at Jo's quivering face. "If you don't want to end up like me, don't try to look for friendship at work. It's pathetic."

At that, the tears spilled from Jo's eyes, and she covered her face as she hurried out of the office.

"Have a good weekend!" Nat called. She heard the front door close.

Nat took her coffee glass into the kitchenette and covered it in enough dish soap to clean fifty glasses. She let the soapy hot water scald and sting her hands as she scrubbed the glass over and over again.

Logically, she thought that all she had done was cut the strings of false friendship from someone who didn't even really like her. She knew what she had overheard on the pocket dial, and since then, all she could see were confirmations of Jo's patronizing fake camaraderie.

Emotionally, she felt like she was drifting farther and farther out into a dark sea, becoming some untouchable island. But maybe that was just how she was meant to be all along, alone and unreachable, for the good of everyone else who was back on the mainland.

* * *

The weekend passed in relative peace, and Nat could see that Jo's assessment of the online discourse had been right. Downloads of BeTwo were through the roof, and the general consensus seemed to be that Rami was on a fool's errand to try and meet anyone without a digital go-between.

Languishing in bed, Nat would scan her feeds with a mix of dread and excitement for mentions of her own name. The inevitable fringe takes aside, no one seemed to believe that Nat was a pathetic mess, or doomed to be rejected by the unsuspecting men who would fall prey to her embarrassing advances.

And yet, she kept refreshing her feeds to make sure. Because, even if she never found the indictment she dreaded so much that she could practically taste it in her darkest heart, her new, accurate profile also wasn't generating any attention. The only invitation that had been extended her way all weekend had been to help Sara make Sunday dinner.

So, Nat sat slumped at the kitchen counter with one eye on her phone and one eye on Sara bouncing between simmering pots on the stove. Nat's job had been to chop the vegetables, and they were all arranged in neat piles of nearly identical squares. It had felt good to focus on something other than the competition for a while. And now, she had wine. She took a sip and relaxed with the comforting spicy smell of her friend's cooking.

"I'm sorry, but I have to just say it again," said Sara. She turned around, her face blotched pink from the heat. "You killed it in that interview." She waved a wooden spoon around for emphasis. "You were all, 'my app is the shit and this guy here ain't shit, so date me, bitches!'"

Nat forced a thin laugh. "Good, glad you liked it." She took a sip of wine. Had she truly been mean to Rami in the interview? Was her callousness part of the whole reason why she seemed to push people away?

But then, there had been their last kiss, long and full of genuine want. It was true that a lot had happened since that moment, namely her storming out of his bedroom, but she could still feel it on her lips. She still got butterflies when she remembered the shy way his tongue had darted into her mouth. How she had brushed her hands over his chest and felt the little alert bumps of his nipples. The way she had wanted to bite them once they'd been in his bed . . .

Anxiety seeped into her reverie — her brain's bad habits were as inevitable as a shadow. She realized that it was also true that they had both been drinking all night before they'd fallen into his bed. So that meant the kisses weren't exactly the most reliable gauge of his intentions. Maybe he'd regretted everything the moment he was sober.

Her phone pinged with a text.

It was Rami.

As a person who was old enough to remember the time before smartphones were a constant tether, her nerves would probably never get used to the idea that the lines of communication with someone were just constantly open and following you around. Gone were the days when you could step away from your computer and live in ignorance of anyone sending you messages. Now, every waking second could bring any number of soul-crushing horrors with just a digital chime of the relationship reaper's bell. Of course, that was the cynical take — she supposed it was theoretically also true that any second could also bring a sweet and lovely message. But either way, how did anyone ever relax?

She opened Rami's text right away.

Rami: *So are we gonna talk about it?*

The kissing, I mean.

A strange mix of excitement to hear from him and fear that he had seemingly been psychically summoned by her thoughts clutched in Nat's heart. Sara was humming to herself in happy concentration, and Nat honestly didn't want to bring Rami's name into their conversation again — that would only make it harder to pretend that she wasn't thinking about him pretty much all the time.

She called on her scant forays into watching romantic comedies and dating shows. Wasn't there advice to play it cool, to pretend to be uninterested or hard to get? She had vague but persuasive memories of a no-nonsense redhead in a power suit saying dialogue to that effect. It seemed like the best strategy, or at least the best one at hand, as she clutched the phone and stared at Rami's name next to the word *kissing*.

Nat: *It was no big deal.*

And we were drunk.

She watched the typing dots wiggle by his name. Then vanish. Then appear again.

Rami: *Yeah.*

OK glad we're on the same page.

Sara refilled their wine glasses. "So . . . the interview went well. Check. Then why are you looking so sad right now?"

Nat put her phone down. "It's nothing. Just not that many bites on my profile."

"Since when?" Sara set down two plates of steaming larb and sticky rice with papaya salad. The smell alone made Nat's whole body buzz with happiness. "Last I heard you were getting, like, twenty messages a day."

"Guess I'm old news now. Someone should really talk to the person who designed this app!" Nat gave Sara her best, casual hair toss. But the truth was, she really hadn't gotten any "bites" since she'd rewritten her profile to reflect her actual personality and applied her entire catalog of desired traits as a search filter. If this was her last trial run in the experiment to see whether she was, in fact, remotely dateable, the results were not looking good.

She took a larger-than-polite gulp of wine and tried to focus on Sara. "So, what'd you want to talk about? You made dinner so I am definitely thinking that it's something bad."

"I'm dying."

"Fuck off."

Sara's voice took on a musical patter. "Dying . . . to tell you . . . I . . ." She trailed off, and her humor deflated. "No, there's not a cute way to spin this, I'm sorry."

Nat frowned with concern. "Did you poison this totally delicious rice?" She watched Sara manage a small smile. "And, to be clear, you're totally healthy, right?"

Sara laughed. "Yes, ship-shape."

"Then tell me the news! I can take it," Nat said, even though she wasn't so sure that she could.

Sara looked at her with sad eyes. "I found a new apartment. A room in a house, actually." She took a breath. "It's a little commune-y, but the people are super chill and the house is this gorgeous old Victorian, and I got a great deal as long as I cook family dinners every other weekday. I just . . ." She went quiet as she studied Nat's face. "I can't afford this place anymore."

Nat sighed with relief. "Oh, oh my God, is that it?"

Sara blinked, confused. "I mean, I love living with you and I'm gonna be really sad to leave."

"And I love living with you!" Nat's appetite rushed back as she scooped up a bite of rice. "Listen, just pay what you can and I'll cover the difference. It's no big deal."

Sara balked. "No way, I can't let you do that."

"Um, and I can't let you actually pay rent to sleep in a twin bed and cook for, like, ten random hippies every night," said Nat. "Forget it."

Sara hesitated and put down her fork. "Nat, that's really generous, but it's actually fine. It might be a good thing! I just don't want this to change anything between us . . ."

"It totally won't!" Nat said, much louder than she'd intended. Sara looked at her with alarm. Nat bit her lip and looked around their home. Panic thudded in her ears. She couldn't lose Sara, too. Not now. "Listen, my *fucking app* can't get me a date, but at least it can help me keep my best friend around, OK?"

Sara fixed her a heavy look. Quiet filled the space between them. "I don't know what to say."

Nat raised her wine glass. "Say cheers!"

Sara shifted uncomfortably across the table.

Nat's phone pinged. The screen flashed a new BeTwo message — her first since making her profile honest. It was a ninety-nine percent match. "Holy shit," she said.

"A new match?" asked Sara, eager for a change in subject. "See, you still got it."

Nat opened the app, saw the message in her inbox, and felt the blood drain from her face. "Yeah . . . a match," she muttered as the man's name swirled in her vision — Thom.

Someone named Thom was a ninety-nine percent match for her actual self.

Someone named Thom was a ninety-nine percent match for her entire wish list.

And the little green dot next to his name showed that he was online at that very moment.

Nat shoved back from the table with a screech of the chair legs. "Sorry, I've gotta . . ." She looked up, but Sara had also grabbed her phone and was scrolling. Nat grabbed her wine glass. "Be right back," she said and ran into her room.

CHAPTER 14

Nat tapped open the message from Thom with shaky hands. After reading it no less than seven times, she felt confident in saying that his message was original, witty, and sincere — and he'd asked if she wanted to meet up for a drink right off the bat.

She clicked on his profile.

He was English, an interior architect for a prestigious firm that had brought him to San Francisco, six foot three, looking for marriage, a non-smoker, tanned in a way that seemed healthy without seeming vain, a cat lover, religiously and politically aligned with Nat, strawberry blond, capable of referencing literature without getting it wrong or coming off as an elitist, lean with a long, swimmer's body . . . the list went on, and so did Thom's perfection.

But Nat didn't really need to verify that Thom had all the qualities on the list — her algorithm had already done that for her.

Nat looked at Pixel with wide eyes. "Holy shit," she said.

The cat blinked back at her and yawned.

The glowing green dot by Thom's username shone at her like a shot of adrenaline to her heart. She took another swallow of her wine and perched on the bed. Obviously, it would be better to write him back now, while he was still online. That way, she was more likely to get a response back right away and not have to spend the night in a kind of sleepless torture, writing and rewriting messages in her mind.

She sat down and opened up a reply message. If he were online and watching his messages, then he would be seeing her typing bubbles. No going back now.

> Nat: *Hey Thom, nice to meet you! Sure a drink sometime would be good!*

She hit SEND and immediately stood back up. She shrugged to her own reflection. Was that good? Was that bad? If this was her ninety-nine percent soulmate, could anything she say ever really be bad?

Her phone pinged with his reply.

> Thom: *Brilliant. How about Saturday?*

She sat back down. Pixel gave her a dirty look and jumped off the bed. That was practically a week away, but she couldn't exactly suggest an earlier meetup, right? She didn't want to seem desperate.

She typed her reply.

> Nat: *Perfect!*

> Thom: *So glad to hear it. I'll send you some options tomorrow.*

Sweet dreams

Thom's green dot vanished beside his name, and she felt herself exhale as if every cell of her body had been holding its breath. She thumbed over to his profile pictures. If he was her perfect match, shouldn't she be seeing sparkles in her vision or hearing angelic choirs in her head as she gazed at the image of him leaning against a bookshelf in a lavender hoodie? She scrolled through the picture of him wearing wayfarers and laughing into the sun in front of the Golden Gate Bridge. She paused on the picture of him in a soccer jersey — or "football" to him, she realized — his face flushed and his blond hair flattened into sweaty curls around his high cheek-bones. He was undeniably hot, but she felt about as many sparkles as she did during a Google Image search.

The ninety-nine percent match number blinked and twirled inside its heart icon in the corner of her screen. She had allowed Justin to indulge himself on this animation because she knew that achieving this high of a match was very unlikely to happen, so if this was the one corner of BeTwo that sparkled and gyrated out-side of her preferred clean aesthetic, it was also a corner very few people would ever see.

Except she was seeing it now. With Thom. And her actual self.

Ninety-nine percent.

Maybe a finely-tuned algorithmic output was the new seeing sparkles. Maybe her lizard brain just hadn't caught up with her coding brain to feel the dopamine rush of a genuine connection delivered on the wings of a hundred data points.

Maybe Thom would actually like her.

Nat looked at herself again in the mirror. She saw a very tired and terrified woman staring back at her, who also desperately needed to go shopping.

* * *

It was a store Nat had walked past many times, but never been brave enough to venture inside. Marked by black-and-white polka dot awnings and a telltale crowd of variably patient male part-ners waiting outside, Milieu was the best boutique in the city, packed to the gills with everything from the trendiest new denim silhouettes to timeless knits, cocktail dresses, gemstone rings, and almost literally everything in between.

As soon as Nat stood in the entryway, she felt claustrophobic. Circular racks of clothes were jammed with so many hangers that it seemed to defy the laws of physics. How much weight could a metal tripod possibly support? Every inch of wall space was lined with racks of tops, bottoms, and dresses, all arranged by a logic that Nat could not discern but was deeply intimidated by. Women squeezed themselves around the stuffed racks and towering piles of denim and shoeboxes. By their defensive postures and intense focus, Nat got the sense that every woman in the store was locked in battle against each other. She could see that more than a few of them were sweating. A thirty-something in athleisure approached a teeming display of dresses and actually stretched her biceps for mobility, and also maybe violence, before pushing apart the frilly fabrics to clear a browsing space with an audible grunt and a pterodactyl-like screech of the metal hangers.

With rising horror, Nat realized that this was only the downstairs portion of the store.

She scooted toward a rack of what appeared to be regular, cotton long-sleeve tops in a full rainbow of colors — a non-terrifying starting place! Another woman was already flipping through the shirts, snapping the hangers aside with daunting speed as she looked through heavily mascaraed eyes. As Nat reached for a pale blue popover, the woman's face shot up, and she glared at Nat with distinctly territorial vibes. The woman shifted her oversized tote purse toward Nat, twisting her back to take up more space and hunching over her spot on the rack like a student covering up their test answers. It was the shopping equivalent of a cat hissing.

Nat stepped away and moved to the denim wall. Suddenly, she felt self-conscious of her current leggings and chunky sweater outfit, even though she'd worn it at least once a week for years.

Although she had no idea what she wanted to wear on her date with Thom, she was deeply sure that nothing she already owned would be right for it. She couldn't remember the last time she had bought an outfit for a social event of any kind, let alone for a date. She knew that, as far as bodies went, hers was decently OK-looking, and she could always fall back on the reality that she did, in fact, have breasts. But she'd always relied on her friends to help her pick out clothes, or at the very least, she had simply bought things that she thought had looked good on Sara or Jo.

Now, though, she had to do this alone. Sara had never confirmed an answer on Nat's offer to help her with rent, and she'd gone to her room by the time Nat emerged from messaging Thom that night. Nat wasn't eager to rock the boat when it seemed like her friendship with Sara was the one relatively normal thing in her life at the moment, so she hadn't brought it up again, either. With a pang, she realized that she'd never heard whether Sara had gotten the job at her salon or not. That meant Sara hadn't bothered to tell her, and also that Nat hadn't bothered to ask. Both were bad signs. This contest was sucking away her soul . . . which was why she had to win it.

She ran her fingers over a stack of dark jeans that were folded with origami-like precision. She did at least know that jeans were probably not what she should go with for a cute date, but she also figured maybe she could start in her comfort zone and work her way into trying on clothes with patterns and pleats and maybe even ruffles, if those were a thing?

A lanky and lean woman, also in running clothes, strode up beside her at the denim wall. Nat tried to stand taller and make herself appear even larger than her five-foot-eight height. *Welcome to the jungle, baby. You're gonna die if you take my ten percent off, size M, high-waisted flares.*

Without so much as a glance at Nat, the runner grabbed a single pair of white, wide-leg crops in one rapid motion and headed toward the staircase. Nat balked. She hadn't even looked at the stack of off-white crops right next to the white stack, or even glanced at a size tag! And yet this woman had somehow already found an item and was heading up to take on the next level of this sartorial Tetris?

Nat grabbed the same pair of jeans, no matter that the prospect of white denim terrified her and the pants were three sizes too small for her. If there was some kind of hack going on here, she needed to know what it was. She followed the runner up the paisley-carpeted steps.

Upstairs, there was a long line of about a dozen women waiting for one of the velvet-curtained dressing stalls. All of them heaved colorful piles of clothes to try on, battle-weary expressions drooping under their beachy waves — and yet the runner held a single item as she smacked gum and scrolled blithely on her phone.

What was her secret? Store employees, all in their twenties and in impeccably original combinations of clothing, hairstyles, and makeup, buzzed around the dressing stalls like gorgeous bee-butterfly hybrids.

Nat tapped the tall runner on the shoulder and gestured to the white jeans they were both holding. "Excuse me, um, nice choice!"

The woman blinked clear brown eyes at Nat and then swept them over her from head to toe. "Oh, I'm not gonna buy these." She smacked her gum. "But I bet they'll be cute on you!"

Now, Nat simply had to know what was going on. "So, either you enjoy waiting in long and chaotic lines, or you have maybe cracked some kind of code to this place?"

The woman's face broke into a broad smile. "Oh yeah, you just gotta get the Milieu gals to shop for you," she said. She held up her white pants. "I grab something, anything, just to get in line for the dressing rooms. Then, once you're in there, you tell them your sizes and they'll pull stuff for you." Her Texan drawl made this foreign concept feel folksy and natural to Nat. She gestured downstairs. "I don't have time to sort through all that crap."

Gratitude flooded Nat. Maybe angels were real?

An attendant in an oversized floral blouse, neon blue overalls, and patent leather Mary Janes buzzed up to Nat.

"What's your name, hon, and are you shopping for anything special?"

The runner winked at Nat.

Nat smiled at the attendant. "Hey, I'm Nat, and yes, I'm shopping for a date!"

* * *

That night, Nat bumped open the door to her and Sara's apartment with her hip as she wrangled the large Milieu shopping bag inside. She'd ended up going for a V-neck midi dress with a line of tortoise shell buttons along the side. It was the kind of care-free but curve-hugging shape she'd never even thought to attempt before, and in a soft coral color that was, apparently, in her "seasonal palette." She had to admit that she'd savored the warm glow of excitement as she'd watched the sales attendant stuff reams of tissue paper around the single item, swaddling it like a three-hundred-dollar organic cotton baby before gingerly slipping it into a bag at least two sizes too big.

Nat had carried it home like a trophy.

For the first time in maybe ever, Sara had beaten her home and sat cross-legged on the couch, eating from a takeout box as she scrolled on her phone. She shot Nat a guilty glance over her raised chopsticks. Nat wasn't sure what the look was for, but Sara never did have much of a poker face.

Then Nat saw the reason — leaned up along the walls were stacks of unassembled boxes, towers of packing tape, and a package of fresh markers. Moving supplies. Her shopping-induced euphoria popped like so much bubble wrap. She guessed that now she had Sara's official answer to her offer.

Nat set her shopping bag on the floor. "Wow, look at all this," she said, pointedly.

Sara cleared her throat. "It's a crime what they charge you for stuff that's going to be literal garbage after one use," she said, forcing a smile.

"Uh huh." Nat bit the inside of her lip as a cold surge of panic splashed into her stomach. This was it. Sara was leaving. The realization screamed into her mind, and all she wanted to do was scream right back for it not to be true. "Well, if money is what you're worried about, then I don't see why you don't just stay here."

Sara sighed and put down her chopsticks. "Because I can't afford this place anymore. I told you that."

"And I told you that I would pay for you, so you don't have to move into some weird commune!" Nat stomped her foot. She knew she was turning the volume up on this argument right away, but something deep and dark within her was forcing her hand. Logically, she knew she was talking to Sara, her best friend of many years, but shadowing Sara's shape on the couch was a rogue's gallery of all the other so-called friends and outright bullies who had suddenly stopped including her in lunches and parties, or left her to sit alone on the school bus every day like she was radioactive, or burst into laughter whenever she walked by — all for reasons she never knew and so always wondered about.

Of course, she did know now that she was an adult woman with a successful career who had every reason to embrace herself as a #badassbitch. And yet, she'd also thought she'd been pretty good, or at least OK, when she'd also been the kid getting pelted with wadded up paper in the cafeteria, or called gross and weird to her face, or left alone weekend after weekend because hanging out with her just wasn't a desirable option for anyone. So how could she trust her own judgment? She had a lifetime of evidence that there was something deeply wrong with her — something that everyone else could see except her. With Sara, she'd thought that maybe she'd shaken it, or Sara hadn't seen it, but now her so-called bestie would rather leave her than accept free rent, so clearly, Nat's truth had finally caught up with her.

Sara's eyes were stony as she stood up from the couch. "It's not a commune," she said flatly. "And I can't let you pay for me to live here, Nat. That *actually* would feel like a commune and that doesn't feel good to me."

"Right, because living with me is so awful that I literally couldn't pay you to do it?"

Frustration made Sara's light olive skin blotchy as she turned to Nat. "It has nothing to do with you! It's a rent problem in San Francisco, for fuck's sake!" She gritted her teeth. "And thanks for being sensitive to how it might embarrass me to admit that I can't afford this place anymore, by the way."

Nat waved her hand in dismissal. "Now you're the one taking it personally. This city is unaffordable to everyone who lives here, Sara!"

Sara rolled her eyes. "Not for you, it isn't!"

Nat staggered back with a laugh. "Is that what this is about? I'm being punished for my success now?"

"That's what you don't get!" Sara said, pointing a finger at Nat with every word. "Your roommate moving out because everything in this city costs a million dollars is not your punishment! It has nothing to do with you, at all!"

Nat scoffed and rolled her eyes, but Sara kept talking.

"It's not like I wanted to leave. I had no choice!" Sara shook her head and took a deep breath. "But now that you're acting like this, I actually don't want to live here anymore. Now I don't want to tell you about my day, or what my new roommates are like — even though you also haven't even asked me anything about it — and that sucks, because I thought you were my best friend."

"I know the feeling." Nat swallowed hard against the tears forming in her throat. The truth was, she did want to hear about the new roommates, and she deeply missed the constant back-and-forth updates on each other's lives that sweetened the air when you were living with someone you loved. No matter what happened in her day, good or bad, it didn't quite feel real until she had told Sara about it. But now it was going to take a series of texts, planning some future date and time, and an equidistant cocktail-or-brunch spot before Nat could tell her anything, when it used to be as easy as just walking into the living room. Now, who would be her confidant, her cheerleader, her co-pilot, and quite simply, who would care about what happened to her? On some level, she knew that Sara was leaving the apartment, not leaving her life, but as she faced her sudden future of hundreds of silent hours alone and no one to share them with, it didn't feel like there was much of a difference.

And yet, here she was, pushing Sara away instead of taking advantage of one of their last few nights together as roommates. Nat hadn't even told her about Thom, and she had no idea what had happened, or not, with Sara's new résumé and job search. That was definitely something an unlikeable monster who couldn't keep friends would do. Nat took a deep breath and tried to focus on Sara, not the shadows in the room. "Listen, it's been a long day," she said, letting her voice soften. "Why don't I open a bottle of wine and we can put everything on pause and just chill?"

But Sara shook her head with a frown. "I'm sorry, but no." She gathered her dinner and gave Nat a teary-eyed look. "I need some space."

Nat's heart clutched in her chest as she watched her friend pad down the hallway away from her and close her bedroom door. She was shut out. She was alone. And it seemed like she would have to get used to it.

CHAPTER 15

The week was off to a rainy start, and Nat couldn't help but check to see if Whither, Weather had called the prediction correctly as she rode the bus to the office. It had — or rather, Rami had. For days-long stretches of rain like this, the mascot, Fun Sun, would be shown wearing a fuzzy gray cardigan and crying little blue tears. Some of Fun Sun's characteristic pointy rays would droop over his head, giving the effect of swooping bangs. Nat had seen more than a few tattoos of Emo Sun on limbs around the hipster-y Mission District of San Francisco. She stared at the cartoon on her phone and felt the now-familiar mix of being impressed with Rami and also infuriated by him. His app inspired people to permanently ink it onto their bodies. If she listened to Rami, all her app left on its users were scars.

Several soggy blocks later, she shook the rain off her umbrella as she dashed into the building. In just the few days since she'd last been here, she'd made both Jo and Sara cry and storm away from her, but she had also secured a date with a man who was apparently perfect for her. Was that a wash, maybe? Nat sighed and flipped on the lights inside the BeTwo office. At least she was the first one here, so she could hole up in a corner and avoid the twins for as long as possible.

Opening her work email, she saw that Sara had replied *YES* to the calendar invite to attend the BuzzFill opening event, where she and Rami would declare the results of their ridiculous stunt to the entire internet. Her heart fluttered — Sara couldn't be that mad if she was agreeing to come see the interview. Then she noticed the timestamp — Saturday morning, which was before their fight and ensuing weekend of icy silence. Still, she hadn't changed the RSVP, so maybe there was still hope that she would show. Considering that Nat still didn't officially have a date for the event — which was kind of the whole purpose of the event that was less than two weeks away — she was very much hoping to have at least a semi-friendly face somewhere in the audience.

Nat heard the office doors open, followed by the sounds of the twins grunting and squabbling.

"I said you should push and I would carry it!" Jo whined.

"Why would I let you carry it when you're the one wearing heels?" came Justin's exasperated reply.

Then there was a very loud *thud*, and both twins groaned.

Nat rushed out. "Are you OK?" she cried, taking in the sight of the twins rubbing their necks and looking at a very large, wet box on the floor.

Jo nodded but wouldn't meet Nat's eyes. She gave the enormous box a little shove with the toe of her kitten heels. "The swag arrived," she mumbled.

"What swag?" Nat asked. She hadn't ordered any new BeTwo merch and forgotten about it in all the contest chaos, had she?

"It was gonna be a surprise," said Justin with a sigh. He was at least making eye contact with Nat, but his usual sweet tone was definitely missing.

"OK, well I don't have to see what it is," said Nat, trying to seem nonchalant. "I was gonna be heads-down on stuff all day, anyway."

"No, it's fine," Jo snapped. She pulled her keys from her purse and sliced through the box's tape with a loud rip. Like the angriest kid on Christmas morning, she yanked open the flaps and pulled out a BeTwo-pink T-shirt emblazoned with the words *Team Nat!* in loopy cursive. She held out the tee with an expressionless face. "We were all gonna wear them for the final interview," she said flatly.

Nat's mouth opened, but she was speechless. She stepped up to the box gingerly, as if it might vanish if she got too close. No one had ever made her T-shirts before. She picked one up and ran her fingers over the lettering. No one had ever voluntarily been on anything like "her team".

Jo sighed. "Anyway, it was a stupid idea, but here they are. We can burn them if you hate them. It's whatever."

"No!" Nat cried, clutching the shirt to her chest. "Don't burn them!"

Justin picked up a shirt. "I told you the hemp blend was gonna be sick," he said, rubbing it against his cheek like he was nuzzling a baby bird. "Soft on face. Soft on planet," he cooed.

Jo let a smile flicker across her face. "OK, well we already paid for them so if we don't wear them it would wreck our marketing budget for the quarter." She held one up to her chest. "Ugh, people really need to align on what they call 'ballet pink' these days."

Seeing Jo modeling a shirt with her name on it made Nat's chest twinge with regret. Even despite everything Nat had heard her say in the phone call, Jo had done this for her. The shirts didn't say *Team BeTwo*, they said *Team Nat*. Why had she made them specifically to support Nat if she didn't even like her? Knowing Jo, she had definitely considered all options and implications before making a final choice, and there was probably even a spreadsheet somewhere listing it all out. And yet she had gone with the personal support of Nat, and planned to publicly wear a shirt with her name on it, even though she'd also clearly said she thought of Nat as a cautionary tale.

It made no sense, but the millennial pink baseball tee in her hands insisted otherwise.

All Nat could think was that the shirts proved one of two things. The first possible explanation was that Jo was so dedicated to doing a good job that she was willing to publicly support someone she disliked. But Jo could have easily just gone with their usual BeTwo merch. The choice to make it a personal gesture toward Nat was totally, as Justin would say, extra.

So, then the only other possibility was that Jo had actually really meant it when she'd typed out *Team Nat* into the order form for an entire box of baseball tees. Even though it would have been after the overheard pocket dial. Even though it would have been after at least one full day of Nat suddenly acting cold and tense around her and Justin. Even though Jo thought she was "a lot" and her own worst enemy . . . Jo was still on her team.

Which meant that Nat had truly, deeply screwed things up with her.

Nat swallowed hard and tossed the shirt over her shoulder. "Super great work," she said, feeling the urge to shoot a thumbs-up rise in her body like a curse. "Amazing stuff! I love—" She stopped herself before she blurted "you" and raised her clenched fists. "I love them!" She grinned as the twins eyed her suspiciously.

"Really?" said Jo. "We were fifty-fifty on whether this would totally embarrass you."

Justin nodded somberly. "We know how you feel about personal space, and we want you to know that we respect your boundaries."

Jo nodded, too, and her voice took on a practiced tone. "We absolutely respect your boundaries."

Nat gave a laugh that she hoped sounded delighted and amused, instead of mildly frantic. "Boundaries-shmoundaries!" she cried, waving a hand like in a GIF she'd seen of Katherine Hepburn. The twins just blinked at her, and she wasn't sure where to go after that incredibly insightful bon mot, so she just laughed again.

Jo's face crinkled with concern, and she opened her mouth to say something. But then she shook her head and dug into the box of shirts. "We'll let you get back to being heads-down, but just one thing." She pulled out a tee from the bottom. "Here, catch," she said, tossing it to Nat. "For Sara. I figure it's easier for you to just give it to her tonight instead of mailing it out with the other kits, right?"

Nat managed to catch the shirt before it flopped to the floor. Her heart, however, was fully on the ground. "Right," she managed to say. "Sara. Definitely." Then she tossed the shirt over her shoulder and went back to her desk.

Maybe she would just send that one to her mom, instead.

* * *

Nat's ride-share pulled up to the address Thom had given for their meetup. It was a full-on winery in Napa. Now she understood why he'd informed her that he would be wearing attire he'd defined as "elevated casual."

She walked up the gravel path to the rustic-modern cabin perched on top of a grassy hill. Her low heels crunched on the white pebbles, and the skirt of her coral midi dress swirled around her legs in a way that felt choreographed. The afternoon sun lit the oak trees with golden halos. The breeze was cool with the scent of lavender and multiple income streams. A hostess dressed in white coastal linens met her at the door.

"There you are, Ms. Lane," she said with a serene smile. "I'm Alana. The VIP Lounge is right this way."

Nat hesitated. "Are you sure? I mean, I know you just said my name." Alana gave her a happy nod and beckoned. They took a leafy path around the side of the building. Gleaming hills of grapes unfurled in all directions around her. Nat gathered her skirt as they climbed an open staircase to a loft space. Alana seemed to be humming a soft, melodic song, or else music just generated from her pores, which also seemed possible. Nat tried to focus on the tune to calm her racing nerves, but all she could think about was how bad she was at carrying a melody herself.

Alana stopped in front of a curtained doorway. She swept it open with a long, tanned arm.

"Wait, how do I look?" Nat asked. She gestured to the dress and resisted the urge to also point directly at her own face.

"Beautiful," Alana said with a makeup-free wink, "and deserving, so enjoy."

Nat took a deep breath and ducked under the curtain.

Sunlight streamed in through a full-wall picture window with sweeping views of the valley. Bud vases and orbs of soft candlelight dotted the airy space. Thom stood in silhouette, gazing out of the window with his hands behind his back.

Nat swallowed and took a shaky breath. "Hey, stranger . . ."

He turned, and there he was — light glinting in his soft blond waves, eyebrows raised in angles over thoughtful eyes, and a hint of pale stubble across his high, angular cheekbones and sharp jawline. "Nat. You're here."

Ripples of heat shot through her body. His rich, musical baritone melted like warm honey into her mind. There were the sparkles.

He stepped toward her. "Thank you so much for agreeing to meet."

"I thought we were having a drink," she said as her voice echoed a bit in the loft space. "This? Is a vineyard."

"And so technically it's within the parameters." He gave her a sly smile. "You look as stunning as your pictures."

Words left Nat's brain and instead seemed to fly around her ears in dizzying waves. She stammered as a trio of waiters entered, each carrying a loaded tray of plates and glasses. They descended

upon a low, knotty hardwood table. The sounds of clinking silver-
ware and porcelain plates, gurgles of pouring waters, and dutifully
shuffling feet filled the room. Nat dared only darting glances to
meet Thom's steady gaze. She kept thinking the waiters' set-up
was almost done, and she would be alone with him, but they kept
producing more items from the trays. Nat shifted on her feet,
unsure of what to do with her hands.

Finally, the waiters stilled with a hush and broke their formation around the table. One of them gestured as the others pulled
out the chairs. "The first tasting course, sir."

"Brilliant, thank you," said Thom, breezing to the table.

"I think I need that drink," said Nat.

Thom called after the waiter. "Send in the sommelier, would
you?" He turned to Nat, deep blue eyes shining. "You're going to
love this."

Nat willed her shaky legs to sit at the table as a man in a waxed
apron and full sleeves of dark tattoos swept into the room.

"I understand this is a special occasion," he said in a library
voice. "So today I've arranged a tasting flight based on the theme
of hope."

Yet more waiters rolled in a brass cocktail cart filled with
wine bottles and an army's worth of tiny glasses. They set rows of
glasses on the table and began to pour. Thom watched them, rapt,
and as comfortable as if he were watching a crackling fireplace
in his own home. Nat folded her hands in her lap and spent several moments hoping that her posture was acceptable while the
sommelier went into great detail about each of the wines, using
many words that she had read but never heard pronounced. Time
seemed to stand still.

Finally, the staff shuffled out with knowing nods. Nat watched
with confusion as the sommelier remained. He hovered next to
them with an expectant silence.

"Well," said Thom, arching an eyebrow at her, "let's start with the flight and let them know what we might like in a bottle."

"This is lovely, but . . ." Nat lowered her voice.

"Oh, it's absurdly over the top, I know!" Thom arranged his napkin in his lap and gave her a bashful smile. "This place is one of my projects, and they are preparing for a debut, so it's good practice for them and it's all on the house."

"Oh, thank God," sighed Nat.

The sommelier rocked back and forth on his heels; his eyes discreetly fixed on the exposed-beam ceiling.

"Being honest, I just couldn't stand another non-descript outing at a non-descript bar that's not too divey but also not too nice." Thom leaned forward conspiratorially, and the sunlight lit his angular jaw. "One must always maintain the illusion of not caring too much. Can't show actual emotion!"

Nat felt her nerves unclench, and she drew a deeper breath than she had since walking in the room. If he was interested in showing genuine emotion, that seemed to signal that he was trustworthy, right?

"So, this is all for me as much as it is for you," he said. "Besides, it's not every day that one gets to go on a date with the brilliant mind behind BeTwo." He winked and offered her a tiny goblet of rosé.

She took it. "You . . . know me?"

Thom nodded. "I know how this might sound, but I've followed your work. BeTwo is the only app I've ever used for longer than a fortnight. It's different from the others." He frowned, but his round eyes shone. "I mean that it's far better than the others, and every time I've read about the mind behind it, I could see why."

"Why?" she asked.

"Because of you," said Thom, blue eyes wide and genuine, as if he were stating the most obvious thing in the world. "In my work, the strength of the individual's perspective is what makes a site special or ordinary. I imagine it's the same if you're an architect of an app."

Nat blushed and managed a nod. She sipped the rosé, and a splash of summer fruit and brown sugar swirled in her mouth. *He knew her and wanted to be here.* The ninety-nine percent match figure hummed in her mind.

"*A votre santé*, Nat Lane." Thom winked and met her glass with a crisp clink.

* * *

Rami leaned against a bike rack on the sidewalk. His feet hurt in his sneakers because he'd been standing just that long. He craned his neck to scan the long line ahead of him, grumbling to himself at all the snuggling couples and frazzled parents and rowdy groups — the typical brunch crowd, and him, a single man alone. Not weird at all! But Rami did have a book — *Walden, or Life in the Woods* by Henry David Thoreau, in a hunter green leather hardback edition he'd swiped from Ian's library on his way out. It had seemed like reading about a man's escape from modernity inside a tiny New England cottage would provide some like-minded solace. But now he was dealing with the reality of hefting around over three hundred pages of that like-mindedness. He shifted the book to his other hand to give his wrist a break.

A couple approached him. "Hey, man, how much do you charge?" the man asked in a brisk, businesslike tone.

Rami took in the man's grunge rock bob and all-black outfit of cargo culottes, leather shirt jacket, and platform boots. "Excuse me?" he said.

"To wait in line for us? You're one of those taskers, right?" His eyes darted over Rami's lone figure. "My phone's dead, so I have to book this old school."

"You pay people to wait in brunch lines for you?"

"Yeah. What is it today, like two hours? Three?"

Rami snapped his book closed. "Where's my cabin?" he muttered. The couple gave each other confused looks as he leaned off the bike rack to literally take his stand. "Well, as much as I would love to make a few bucks—"

"Fifty bucks," said the fashionable man.

Rami blinked. "Seriously?"

The man produced a turquoise-studded money clip from a leather belt bag and counted out the bills. Rami watched and debated whether accepting the task would weigh on his dignity for the rest of his life, or just for a few weeks.

"Remy!" a voice called down the line. "Ray-mi? Party of one!"

"Sorry, that's me." Rami waved the cash away. "Kind of."

The man shrugged and squinted down the line.

"Live long and pancakes," he said as he maneuvered toward the door.

* * *

Rami followed the host as they scream-spoke over the din of chatter in the restaurant.

"Had to put you with another solo," they called over their shoulder. "Can't justify a whole table for just one, you know?"

Rami rolled his eyes. He'd brought the book specifically to ward off awkward small talk. Even if this was his favorite brunch in the city, and even if he'd stood outside for over an hour, a man had to take a stand sometimes. He clutched *Walden* and trudged behind the host, his mind forming his eloquent refusal to accept this modern compromise. "Sharing is not acceptable!" he yelled over the din.

Then he saw his potential tablemate.

She sat nervously in front of an open paperback. Loose coppery curls framed her round face, creamy fair skin, upturned nose, and watermelon-pink lips.

"Sharing is totally fine!" said Rami, as the host dropped a menu on the table. Rami smiled and took the seat across from the beautiful stranger. "Hi, I'm Rami!"

She looked up at him with a shy smile. "Allison. Nice to meet you."

* * *

Nat followed Thom with slightly tipsy steps on the trail out into the vineyard. Seeing his lean frame moving in front of her, with his rumbly baritone voice dancing in her ears and the wine buzzing in her temples — it all felt natural, like everything she had waited for was finally falling into place. She held out her hand, letting the tips of the leaves kiss her fingertips.

"God, this view beats the hell out of London." Thom threw her a lidded glance over his shoulder. "For a few reasons."

"Napa is adult Disneyland." Nat sighed.

"Bang on, it is." He stopped in front of a rusted iron gate and turned to her. "Except now, instead of being full of sugar, we're full of fermented sugar." He flashed a grin. "Full circle, that."

Nat laughed. "I like the way you think."

"Same."

"Really?"

His face grew serious. It was like he had the ability to open secret doors in his deep blue eyes. They drew her right in. "What's not to like?"

Nat broke his warm gaze to look around. Her tipsy mind fuzzed out the dark reaction to his question — wasn't there literally *so much* not to like about her? — and instead she blinked into the Napa splendor. The sun was fading into a cotton candy sky. She ran her eyes over the way Thom's flannel shirt jacket fell across his broad shoulders, how his chambray button-down was open enough to show the curls of caramel blond hair on his chest, how his dark jeans wrapped around the muscles of his thighs, and how his sapphire eyes tracked hers. She stepped closer.

"Oh!" he said with a start. "We've got another appointment to keep!"

"There's more?"

"Oh, darling," his voice purred like an engine. "We're not done, yet." He held out his hand.

She looked at his open palm and sucked in her breath in spite of herself. Butterflies fluttered into her chest as her desires rolled over her fears like mounting waves. She slipped her fingers into his smooth grip.

He smiled and pulled her back toward the winery.

She let him guide her as she used her other hand to pull out her phone and text Rami.

> Nat: *Just thought you should know, I've found a date to the BuzzFill party.*

She watched for a bit, but no response bubble appeared.

> Nat: *Just didn't want you to be too embarrassed.*

She slipped her phone back into her purse and followed Thom through the dappled California sunlight.

* * *

Both Rami's and Allison's books were pushed to the side of the table, completely abandoned.

Allison let her laughter from his latest joke fade into a shy smile. "I have to say, you've really cheered me up." She raised a syrupy bite of waffle. "I thought this was going to be the saddest brunch ever."

"Is your book that bad?"

Allison laughed again and shook her head. "No, it's not that." She hesitated. "It's embarrassing."

"More embarrassing than the fact that I took three buses by myself just so I could eat something called 'miracle pancakes?'" Rami gestured to the half-eaten lemony cakes on his plate.

Allison gave a serious nod. "True, that might be worse."

"See? And I don't even have any special healing powers now!"

She gestured to Rami's pancakes with her fork. "May I?"

"Oh, please."

She grabbed a bite and chewed in thoughtful silence. She turned her bright green eyes to him. "So, it's my birthday."

"What? Happy birthday!" Rami felt his heart swell. "Why is that embarrassing?"

"Because I'm here by myself!" Allison's smile drooped, and she poked her fork around her breakfast. "Because I don't have any other plans besides sitting in my apartment and sticking a candle in this leftover waffle."

"Oh."

She sat up and looked at him with a pleading expression. "I'm not crazy or anything!" She shrugged and looked down into her empty coffee cup. "I just moved here. I don't know many people yet." She tucked a coppery curl behind her small ears. "Actually, I don't know anyone here besides my boss." She looked up at him with a desperate smile. "But she seems totally nice!"

Rami's heart twinged in the way that it might for a wayward puppy.

The waiter appeared and set down two checks. "Whenever you're ready," he said.

Rami grabbed them. "My treat. For your birthday!"

Allison winced. "No! You don't have to."

"Please." Rami suddenly never wanted anything more in his whole life than to pay for this adorable woman's brunch. He placed his hands on the table. "Please let me perform this miracle."

Her face twisted with a suppressed grin. "Well, thank you." She gave his hand a quick, shy touch. "I hope all San Francisco people are like you."

"Well, I don't like to brag, but I've actually celebrated almost all of my birthdays in the city." He dropped his voice to sound serious. "I'm something of an expert on what to do."

Allison matched his businesslike tone. "Is that so?"

"I'm sensing that you don't believe me."

She crumpled instantly. "No, I do!" She laughed.

Rami shook his head and raised his hands in surrender. "Fine, if you insist on being skeptical, then I guess I'll just have to show you how to have an awesome birthday in the Bay."

Her face was pink with excitement. "Really?"

He rubbed his chin solemnly. "It's my civic duty."

Allison clapped her hands in front of her chest so quickly that she rattled the dishes on the table. "OK, yes! Let's go do some birthday things . . ."

CHAPTER 16

Nat pulled the plush, velvety robe around her neck as she stepped into the open-air hot tub suite. Thom was perched on the edge of the natural stone bench in the same cream-colored robe.

"This is officially too much," she said as she padded toward him with bare feet on the cool stone.

"Well, you'll notice that I'm partaking in everything, too," he said, standing as his robe winked open against his body, and she clocked the toned *V* leading into his swim shorts.

"I noticed," she breathed.

"So, it's hardly a sacrifice for me."

Nat sighed and craned her neck to take in the burnt orange sky of dusk above them. Gray-blue clouds drifted across the open-air roof as the first stars twinkled into sight.

"Shall we?" said Thom. "They tell me it's quite important to them that we test out this part of the property, specifically."

"I mean, if they need our help . . ." Nat gestured to the steaming water. "It would be a crime not to."

In one fluid gesture, Thom shrugged his robe to the floor. His black trunks clung to him as he slowly lowered himself into the aqua water. He cupped water in his hands and slicked it back over his head. His darkened blond waves framed his high forehead. His cheeks flushed with the heat. Water droplets ran over his pink lips, and his deep eyes were on her, round and open.

Nat could barely move in her robe.

"Shall I turn around?" he asked, somehow making the question sound proper and unbearably suggestive at the same time.

"Stop, it's fine."

He gave her a devilish grin through the steam. "No, no! I insist on being a gentleman lest you think this is merely some tawdry ploy."

Nat's face scrunched with charmed delight. "No, how could getting me into a hot tub ever be a ploy?"

Thom laughed. "It's medicinal, I tell you!" But he turned around and made a show of covering his eyes with both hands.

Nat gingerly slipped out of her robe. There had been a selection of black two-piece swimsuits hanging in the spa changing room when she'd gone in. In a karmic burst of mercy, one was her size and also, in a true gift from the gods, high-waisted.

She also thanked those gods that she had done a full armpit-to-ankle shave to get her head in the game for her date with Nick. "I don't usually wear suits like this, but it's all they had." She put a toe in the bubbling water. "And thank you, by the way."

"If I could see it, I'd say it was lovely on you."

Nat sank into the warm water with a deep sigh. She peeked at Thom. He was still turned away with his eyes covered, but she could see a schoolboy blush on his face.

She giggled and flicked a splash at him. "You can look now."

He dropped his hands into the water and drew closer to her. "So," he said softly. "Are you having a nice time? I mean, I know this is a little unorthodox for a first date, and I'm realizing now that it might be a lot of pressure."

"No, I'm having a nice time," she said, bobbing closer to him. "It's a grand gesture, but I think it's romantic."

Relief washed over Thom's face. "Christ, I was really hoping you would say that. While I was waiting for you to change, I had some truly sobering thoughts about the thin line between romance and, I don't know, being too intense and scaring you away."

"I'm not scared." Nat let her lips curl into a smile as she realized how true her words actually were. She kept forgetting that it wasn't as though she was on this date without a safety net. Yes, it would have been a big ask for her to trust Thom right away, but she wasn't on this date by random chance — she was here because of her algorithm, her real profile, and her heart's full desires. They were what had brought Thom into her life at this moment, and they were what she could trust.

Thom narrowed his eyes with a theatrical wince as he gestured to their picture-perfect surroundings. "I guess it's a bit hard to hide how much I wanted you to like me, though, isn't it?"

"Yeah . . ." Nat watched him bite his plump lower lip to catch a droplet of water. "But how did you know that you were going to like me?"

"I didn't," he said. He bobbed closer to her in the water, and she felt the solid muscles of his legs graze hers. "But I do."

Nat wondered what one should be thinking when their dreams were literally coming true. She wanted to memorize every atom in front of her. She brought her hands around his broad shoulders and leaned into him. Thom softly closed his eyes and cupped a hand behind her head.

"Champagne and strawberries!" said a waiter, rapping at the door.

Thom grimaced and pulled away. "OK, now *that* was too much."

Nat giggled and watched Thom climb out of the water to fetch the tray. Her whole body buzzed with happiness in the soothing rumble of the hot tub jets. Her heart felt like it might burst. *Every single atom.*

* * *

Rami stood next to Allison on the observation deck of Coit Tower. The sweeping city views he knew so well were completely hidden by a thick gray curtain of rain. The whole deck was empty and dark. Allison shivered with a sudden chill.

"I'm sorry," he said. "It's an iconic view. Trust me!"

"It's OK." She gave him a cheerleader's smile. "How could you possibly know that it was going to rain?"

"Because the ratio of moisture saturation didn't correlate with the range of variable temperatures in this microclimate."

"What?"

Rami pulled out his phone to show her his app. He saw the text from Nat and scoffed, clearing it away. He waited until Fun Sun was loaded on the screen and showed it to Allison. "Whither, Weather, that's my app."

Unfortunately, Fun Sun was currently doing gleaming, muscle-y cartwheels across the whole week. Every single day shone yellow with his forecast for sunny perfection.

"Whoops," said Allison.

Rami brought his phone to his face and squinted at Fun Sun's grinning, flossing figure. "My Sphinx," he muttered. "The more I learn about you, the farther away you get." He slipped the phone back into his pocket as a guard approached.

"Shutting down! Let's go!" she bellowed into the empty space.

Allison shrugged politely. "Well, predicting the weather is basically like fortune-telling, right?"

"Sometimes it feels like that," Rami granted. "But my algorithm actually reads and ranks multiple feeds of raw meteorological data to improve the accuracy of our data points. It's not unlike how an app with millions of users might . . ." He trailed off. He knew Allison's glazed-eyed nod all too well. "Sorry. Sorry, you're right. I do have a lot in common with a county fair palm reader."

Her face lit back up. "Does that mean you're gonna tell that I'll meet a great love by a large body of water?" She batted her eyes and looked out at the downpour.

"Now that would just be statistics . . ."

The guard clapped her hands and circled them with a pointed stare. Rami winced again at his ruined plan.

"Actually, I'm kinda glad that it's closing." Allison took a huge step back from the domed windows. "I'm kinda afraid of heights." She swallowed with another big step backward. "Like, a lot."

"Oh my God!" he cried. Rami quickly ushered her back into the elevator lobby.

She jammed the button.

"So, I just took you to the one place that's your absolute nightmare? On your birthday?"

Allison gave a nervous laugh. "I mean, no clowns here yet, but . . . yeah."

They hopped into the antique elevator with a creak.

"Why didn't you say anything?" he asked.

The doors closed, and the tarnished iron grate slid across the car as they lurched down.

"You just seemed so excited," she said, still clutching her hands to her chest.

"I can make this up to you. I know another spot — all indoors, all ground-level."

"Is that their motto?"

"It's actually, 'We Will Not Terrify Nice Girls.'"

She relaxed a little. "I feel bad, though. I mean, you must have other stuff to do today?"

The elevator doors pinged open, and they walked into the lobby, just two more figures among Diego Rivera's colorful mural.

"Seriously, this is what I'm doing today. It's your birthday! We can't give up now." Rami knew he sounded like the overly earnest hero in a children's cartoon, but he didn't care. Cringe be damned! He was going to make this a romantic day, no matter what.

They paused at the doors, looking out at the sheets of rain cascading through the street.

He sighed. "Why let one humongous miscalculation get in the way of an adventure, right?"

She hit him with a mischievous smirk. "Now you're speaking my language." She stepped backward into the rain with a small, "Whoop!"

He watched the rain darken her red hair into tight curls as she lifted her arms and tilted her face back into the downpour. Patches of water instantly spread across her oversized athleisure pullover and streamed down her black leggings.

She grinned at him with sparkling, manic eyes. "Is this what you'd call a data point?" she yelled through the gray sheets of rain.

Rami felt his heart swell, as his mind saw a rush of invisible cartoon hearts swirl around Allison's laughing frame. He stepped out into the rain with her.

* * *

The rain reached Nat and Thom in their open-air hot tub suite as a sudden downpour. Cold drops pelted Nat's skin as she clambered out of the steamy tub. She shrieked.

Thom grabbed their robes and opened the door for her.

Nat registered anew that their suite was in the middle of a large, grassy field. It had seemed perfect on the way in, but that had been before the sky opened up.

Thom pointed to a large barn in the near distance. "There! I see a roof."

They pulled their robes over their heads and ran into the field. Nat shrieked again as they splashed through the soaking grass. The robe-tent over her head echoed the happy panting of her own breath. All she could see were her bare feet sloshing in the soft mud. She heard Thom give a high-pitched howl. She laughed between her breaths and peeked out from under the robe.

Thom had reached the barn and stood in the rain holding the door open for her. She raced inside.

He caught her with strong, soaking arms. He wrapped his slightly less soaked robe around her. They huddled in the dark, empty barn, catching their breath through racing hearts. Chairs and tables draped in white cloths lined the space. Dark strings of Edison bulbs looped through the beams. Nat could practically see the happy ghosts of the beautiful weddings that had happened here.

Nat nuzzled her face into the patch of hair on Thom's chest. She closed her eyes. Both of their heartbeats thrummed in her ears.

"I didn't plan this rainy bit," he said through panting breaths. "I promise."

"Maybe I did," she teased, cheek still pressed on his warm chest.

"I see." She felt his voice purr under her ear. "I guess I shouldn't be surprised that the woman who designed a dating app knows romance better than I do."

She met his eyes. "Sorry, not sorry."

She watched Thom's deep blue eyes flicker over her face. "I think you might actually be sweeping me off my feet." He stroked her cheek with his hand. "Honestly."

She wrapped her hand over his.

Thom laughed a quiet chuckle and looked at a faraway spot in the distance. "It's funny because the lads at the office said I should give BeTwo a go now that I was stateside. Try to have fun, whatever. I agonized and read up on the app because, I don't know, I'd had some bad experiences before. I only just signed up last month." He held her face with his palms and gazed into her eyes. "But it led me right to you." Those secret doors in his eyes welcomed her. "Your brilliant app," he whispered.

"It did."

The soft patter of the rain filled the quiet, like music. The sweet, earthy smell of the land curled around Nat and relaxed her senses even more than the fruit of its vines already had.

"It seems we might be stuck here for a while." Thom's lashes were still heavy with wet. "Can I make you more comfortable?"

"You can," she whispered and leaned into his soft kiss.

He tightened his arms around her. Her wet skin pressed against his. Her legs rubbed against the hair of his strong thighs. She tilted her throat to him and deepened their kiss.

The rain pattered on the barn roof. He ran his hands down her back, dropping the robes to the floor. He pulled off a nearby tablecloth and spread it into a kind of nest on the wood planks. He kneeled and reached for her, and she let him gently push her to lie on her back.

She braced her hands on his muscled shoulders as he nuzzled his nose between her legs. His hot breath sent waves of desire burning through her hips. His fingers slipped into her wet waistband, and he teased it taut before letting go with a soft *smack*. She gasped, then giggled and sunk her fingers into his wet curls.

He pulled off her swim bottoms.

She gasped, then moaned as his tongue explored her. Deep swells of pleasure filled the hollows all the other dates had left inside her heart. She let her body melt open as he spread her legs. Tingles coursed up her thighs and throbbed into her hard nipples. He licked her like he could never get enough, and his hands tightened around her ass, drawing her in. She let her arms fall over her head.

He slipped a finger inside her and the sensation exploded into her breath. He traced circles inside her wet pleasure. The tension trilled in her thighs. She raised her hips for him and he drew her deeper. He flicked his tongue against her, fast and slow and soft and hard all at once. Buzzing waves rolled through her body, and she released them with soft moans. He pulsed his finger in and out, slick and smooth with her. Her body tightened around him. He pulsed faster. She arched her back.

Her cries echoed in the rafters.

* * *

Rami grumbled and shifted in his moist sweater. The back of the cab smelled like wet dog. He peeled the thick collar from his neck with a damp slurp to attempt some kind of ventilation. He felt like a giant slug. Allison sat beside him, just as soaked but somehow not looking like a used dishrag. Her athleisure seemed to have dried perfectly. He sighed. The cab inched forward through the dense traffic, which he could barely see through the fog condensing on the windows.

"It was really nice of you to get us a ride," said Allison.

"Never leave your birthday to the whims of public transportation," Rami offered meekly.

They sat in steamy silence.

He rubbed a small circle into his fogged-over window. A bus rolled up, unencumbered in its special lane. Rami glared as his wheeled nemesis whizzed past them.

Allison gave a tiny sigh and subtly checked her phone.

* * *

Nat held Thom's hand as they walked down the sidewalk to her apartment in the streetlight. After the rain had let up and they'd made themselves decent, they'd left the winery and grabbed dinner at an Italian bistro in her neighborhood. Her belly was full of pasta, and her body hummed with satisfaction. Thom carried her to-go box. Walking next to him, it was easy to feel like they'd time-traveled from first date into falling in love over the last few magical hours. She could even start to imagine that the last few solitary years, and especially the last few weeks, had only been a bad dream.

An older man in stained clothes was sprawled on the sidewalk in front of them. He watched them closely as they neared.

"Lady goes on the inside!" he shouted.

"What?" Nat took in his thick gray beard and sunken eyes.

He gestured toward her with a gloved hand. "The lady goes on the inside!"

Thom switched their places, so he was walking along the curb instead of Nat. "Fair point, mate." He handed the man the box of leftovers. "Here, take care."

The man took the food and grumbled back into his squat on the sidewalk.

Nat waited until they were out of earshot. "That was nice," she said.

Thom shrugged. "I try to do whatever I can. You know, if you give those people money, who knows what they might do with it." His voice rose as another couple passed them. "But it doesn't cost anything to just give them something that was probably going to go bad in your fridge, anyway." He nodded to the couple with a pronounced, "Good evening".

They shot him weary nods.

Nat squeezed his hand with a tight smile. "Uh huh!" Something dark pinged in her mind, but she brushed it away. She checked her phone. Still no response from Rami. Her day had been perfect, and now she really wanted to rub it in his face over a martini. "That's really nice of you."

They reached the iron gate to her apartment building.

"This is you, then?" Thom rocked back on his heels like meeting an old friend. "Seems charming."

The reality of being at her home poked into Nat's wine-soaked fantasy. She felt the patterns of her old life, and her old self, tugging at her like hands shooting out of a grave. "I'd invite you in, but . . ." She trailed off.

"No, no, we need to save something to look forward to." He drew close to her and tugged her coat closed underneath her chin.

Nat blushed. "I had a really nice time today."

He nodded with a question in his eyes. "So? Shall we?"

"Kiss?" she said. "You don't have to ask every time."

He gave a low chuckle. "I meant, shall we give it a go?" His sapphire eyes searched hers. "You and me."

Nat realized that she hadn't officially asked him to the event, yet. Or told him about her ongoing public dating competition. But at the winery, he'd said that he had read up on her, right? Maybe he already knew about the BuzzFill thing and was fine with it. And maybe it was also fine if she just assumed that and didn't actually confirm it. She produced a bright, perky grin. "What if you were my date to a party next week?"

"What kind of party?"

"Oh, nothing big . . ." Nat hedged. "Just a work thing. Probably totally boring but you know . . ." She rubbed his bicep. "I just need some arm candy."

Thom lit up in spite of the joke. "Oh, I see! Well, then, by all means, sign me up."

"Really?"

"Absolutely." He leaned toward her with bedroom eyes. "As long as it means I get to spend more time with you."

Something in Nat hesitated as he nibbled at her neck.

"It's hard for me to let you go," he cooed against her skin.

Nat smiled and thought of sliding onto a bar stool at the jazz bar. "I know, but I don't want to rush this." She pulled away.

"You're right. Proper dates. Like your work party." Thom winked and nodded. "I'll be there." He raised her hand to his lips for a soft kiss. "*Bonne nuit.*"

Nat leaned in her doorway to watch his figure walk away. A few feet away, he turned around and met her eyes. Her stomach flipped. He blew her an air kiss.

She pulled out her phone. Rami still hadn't responded, but she was too wound up to sleep without a cocktail and a chance to flaunt her victory. She texted him one last time.

Nat: *See you at the postmortem.* 🍸

* * *

Rami and Allison pulled up a long driveway in their cab. Their muggy journey had finally come to an end at Rami's next birthday surprise — the California Academy of Sciences.

He hopped out of the car and opened the door for Allison, barely pausing his narration. "Anyway, I can't wait to show you these penguins. The live feed just doesn't capture it."

She gave him her hand as he led her up the steps.

"One of the penguins, Harold, I swear he can look into your soul." Rami sauntered up to the ticket booth. But it was a void of darkness. He checked his watch — it was only three o'clock.

Allison tapped on a handwritten sign taped to the glass.

"Closed early for cleaning?" he cried. "But penguins regularly preen themselves in order to stay warm and waterproof!" He sighed and fixed Allison with a sad stare. "I'm sorry. Again."

Allison bounded down the steps, trailing red curls. "Hey now, don't give up so easily." She shot him another of her sly looks. "What would Fun Sun say?"

Rami caught up with her as she poked around a construction fence on the side of the museum. "You're right," he said. "Fun Sun lives in the moment."

Allison nodded as she rattled the chain and sized up the chain link fence. "We used to do this kind of thing all the time back home."

He watched her ignore his nervous chuckle and keep exploring.

"Really gotta make your own fun in a farm town." She put a sneaker into a gap in the fence and hoisted herself up. "All right!" she cried. She grinned at him over her shoulder. "Ready for an adventure?"

Rami felt his eyes widen. "Seriously?" He waited for her to say it was a joke. She didn't. "I mean, I'd do anything for Harold, but . . ."

"No one is here. You can do this!" She climbed up the fence like it was something she did every day. "Just pretend you're Jason Bourne."

"Yeah, that's not the character who I play in that movie."

She dropped to the ground on the other side and dusted off her hands. "We'll just walk around the open areas for a bit, and if we see a guard, we can hide in the bathroom!" Her teeth flashed in a feline grin. "And who knows, maybe we'll find a golden statue and solve a mystery."

"Are you making a *From the Mixed-Up Files of Mrs. Basil E. Frankweiler* reference?"

She nodded with the same toothy smile.

Rami sighed and hoisted himself onto the fence. "I think you've discovered my data point."

Allison jumped up and down when he landed on the other side. She grabbed his hand and pulled him toward the building.

He followed for a few steps and then tugged her gently back toward him. She turned to him, her green eyes gleaming. He pulled her close and kissed her.

"Ooh, I see someone likes a little danger," she cooed.

"Mmm-hmm." Rami nodded. "I do."

"Come on." She pulled his hand again. "Let's go inside!"

"Yeah, I know the guy who designed the AI surveillance system for this place, so we're definitely not breaking in," he said. "But that's also how I know there's a blind spot in the system right about . . ." He led her toward a copse of trees.

She followed.

"Right about here."

She leaned back against a tree and reached for him.

He put his arms around her. Droplets of rain fell as the wind rustled the leaves. And they made out in a way that he imagined would be described as "furiously."

* * *

Nat tapped her fingers along the stem of her martini glass. She was at her stool in the bar, waiting to see if Rami would take his customary place at the one beside her.

She realized that she could no longer pretend that she was merely sipping her martini until he arrived — there were only about two sips left. She downed them and checked her phone for what felt like the hundredth time.

Nothing.

Even in her current, fuzzy state of having had a powerfully strong martini after a full day of wine tasting and a pasta dinner, she knew with certainty that this only meant one of two things — neither of them good. The first possibility was that Rami was having such a great time on his date that he couldn't be bothered to interrupt his romantic reverie to simply do her the courtesy of a response, or a simple emoji tossed her way, or hell, even a "liked" reaction.

Nat scowled as she swirled around the few drops of alcohol clinging to the bottom of the glass. She wondered if Rami's dream date had lush, shampoo model hair and the body shape needed to pull off puff sleeves.

The other possibility, of course, was that Rami no longer wished to speak to her. The thought landed like a lead weight in her belly, and a ripple of fear splashed through her as she imagined this being the truth.

They hadn't had any contact since establishing that they were *on the same page*, a phrase that still confounded Nat's mind despite having stared at the inert blue text message bubble every night as she tried to fall asleep.

What had become crystal clear from reviewing the texts dozens of times was how deeply she had bungled the exchange. *It was no big deal*, she'd written, followed by the factual observation, *we were drunk*. Both of these statements could be interpreted as simple statements of objective reality. People kissed all the time, right? It was an extremely commonplace occurrence, even if she had just recently ended a two-year streak without so much as a peck.

And the remark that they had both been drinking cocktails all night and so were at least somewhere between tipsy and drunk, no matter their respective metabolisms? Nat scoffed to herself. That was definitely impossible to negate.

So, her only conclusion was that when given the opportunity to discuss an event that had been replaying constantly in her mind since it happened, with the very person she'd shared it with, she had really only managed to get him to agree that they seemed to be inhabiting the same reality. No quantum jumping between timelines, here. They had indeed kissed. When they were drunk.

And now they weren't talking.

Nat scowled deeper at her empty glass. That pithy red-headed woman was a monster, and her friends were idiots.

Her phone buzzed. She sprang to attention.

It was a text from Thom.

> Thom: *Nat, please tell me that I didn't just hallucinate our day. It was too perfect.*

Nat ran a hand through her long curls and glanced around the small bar. Couples leaned in together in cozy triangles over their small tables. The empty stool next to her seemed to burn in the red light. She started typing her reply to Thom.

Nat: *Well the day's not over, right?*

* * *

A little over an hour, and one quickly downed round of drinks later, Nat and Thom stumbled into her dark apartment. She could barely bring her face away from his lips long enough to take full breaths. So, she really couldn't be bothered to turn on a light.

Until she cracked her shin on something hard that wasn't usually there.

"Mother of pearl!" she shouted, unsure why she'd opted for the PG version around Thom. Burning razors of pain radiated up her leg. She clutched her shin and hopped on one foot. When she closed her eyes, all she could see were spirals of electric hurt jolting through her body. Her brain needed another outlet. "Hats!" she cried, randomly.

Thom flicked on the light. Nat winced at the stack of moving boxes she'd knocked against.

"Good evening to you, too," said Sara. "You OK?" She was leaning against the kitchen counter in a silk kimono, passing a glass of water back and forth with a tall, muscled woman with close-cropped hair and tattoos over every inch of her body that Nat could see. Considering that she was only wearing a sports bra and small white briefs, Nat could see a lot.

"It's like a troll cave in here," said Nat, realizing that packed boxes lined the apartment. "Light a sensual candle or something, geez."

"Oh, we packed up the candles already," said Sara's companion, innocently.

"Yeah, I can see you've been working really hard," Nat grumbled. She and Sara had become ships in the night, barely speaking and certainly not sharing details of their lives and paramours. Now there was some unknown and unnamed person half-naked in her kitchen with her best friend, and Nat had no idea who they were. She felt like a stranger in her own life. So, she wrapped her hands around Thom's firm arm with a contented smile. "This is my boyfriend, Thom," she said in the tone one might use to announce the latest addition to their house — *just had this Italian marble added to the guest bath. It really matches the soaking tub and heated floors, don't you think?*

Sara arched an eyebrow and held a hand out toward Thom. "Sara, nice to meet you," she said.

"Pleasure." Thom shook her hand with a winning smile, but his eyes were helplessly fixed on the half-naked woman.

"This is Jax," Sara added, nodding to her smiling friend. "We'll give you two the space."

"No, no!" Nat sputtered, the martinis pushing her to make a scene. "Stay. Enjoy it while you can!"

Sara sighed and fixed Nat with a look she knew was a warning.

Nat didn't care. "And feel free to take any sentimental objects as mementos, you know, if you even want to remember this place at all."

Thom cleared his throat awkwardly.

Jax winced. "You said she was your 'roommate,' babe, not 'ex-girlfriend,'" she said, scowling at Sara.

"Nat's not my ex," Sara replied, coolly, wrapping an arm around Jax's waist. "She's my friend." Sara looked Nat square in the face, and her chocolatey eyes pleaded through their cat eye liner and sparkly shadow. "She's my best friend, actually, and I'd really like to keep it that way."

Sadness blurred tears into Nat's vision, and she shook her head to clear it away. Sara was her best friend, too, and she wanted more than anything to hold onto that. It was just hard to feel secure when Sara's things were packed in boxes all around her.

Nat took Thom's hand. "It's fine, we're tired." She couldn't bring herself to look at Sara, but she managed to mumble something about seeing her in the morning as she led Thom down the hallway.

* * *

In her room, Nat pulled Thom into her bed like she'd done it a hundred times before. She nestled her backside against him as he curled around her. They fit together in exactly the way she would expect from a ninety-nine percent match — perfectly.

Then her phone buzzed and slipped out of her pocket.

"Really?" She grabbed it and sat up.

It was a text from Eric, her very first BeTwo date. She blinked in shock at the picture of his blurry, purpled dick.

Eric: *U up?????*

"Everything OK, beautiful?" said Thom, pushing pillows into shape. His voice was gravelly with sleep.

Nat set her phone on the floor. "Everything is perfect."

CHAPTER 17

Rami padded into the kitchen in his pajamas. He stretched his arms over his head. The morning sun streamed into his apartment like the rays of Heaven itself. Was he whistling? He felt like he was whistling.

Ian hunched over their pour-over coffee maker. An array of tubs, jars, and bottles surrounded him, as he added spoonfuls of various powders to the coffee grounds.

"Good morning, my friend!" chirped Rami.

His tone broke Ian's concentration. He frowned and looked up from his chemistry experiment. "You got home late. Did you get lucky in the carnal and-or cosmic sense?"

"You know what? It *was* cosmic." Rami dropped a tea bag into his favorite mug. "I met this incredibly nice girl. Finally. And I met her like a normal person, just sitting down to brunch, and *poof!*"

Ian sipped his steaming dishwater-colored brew. He placed an approving hand on Rami's shoulder. "I'm proud of you, analog polliwog. What's she like?"

"As I said, she's nice." Rami poured hot water over his tea. "And she's totally perfect to bring to the BuzzFill party this week, and win Nat's stupid bet."

Ian hoisted himself onto a seat on the counter. His long legs still dangled nearly to the floor. He shook his head sadly. "Oh no, this isn't good."

216

"The fact that your ass is currently where we make our food? Yes, it is very, very wrong."

Ian was unfazed. "I was afraid this might happen."

As always, Rami couldn't help but take the bait. "What are you talking about? Everything is finally working out!"

"You spent all day with this young woman, correct?"

"Her name is Allison, and yes."

"And yet all you can tell me about Allison is that she is 'nice,' and she's a good way to beat Nat." Ian said this more like a question, when it was, in actuality, a fact.

Rami balked. "That's all I said *so far!*"

Ian raised his eyebrows in a gesture for him to please go on.

"She's an account producer or something." Rami sipped his tea and searched his memory. "In advertising!" He scratched behind his head. "She just moved to San Francisco from . . . somewhere else. She likes sushi." He gave Ian a defiant glance. "And sashimi."

Ian shook his messy bedhead and grumbled. "I was mistaken. You're not a polliwog, after all."

Rami sighed. "I'd be happy about that, but I'm so afraid of what you'll say that I am instead."

"You're a knight."

"Knights are good. That's good!"

"A knight who has become blinded by his crusade." Ian hopped off the counter. He gestured to the dozen or so bottles of tinctures and powders. "You see all of this?"

"I obviously see nothing *but* all of that."

"When my brain chemistry betrays me, I nudge it back on course." He sipped his brew. "But you? Your brain doesn't betray you with serotonin. It betrays you with ideas." He started to put the bottles back into a Tupperware. "That's all that this full and complete, entire other person, Allison, is to you, my friend — an idea."

Rami squirmed as Ian wrapped him in a sudden, somber hug.

Ian sighed. "But you'll never see any of that until you take off the bubble wrap," he intoned, turning back to the jars.

Rami looked at the amber swirls of tea in his mug. He was suddenly very, very tired. "OK," he replied. "Well, I'm gonna go to work now."

He went back into his bedroom and closed the door.

* * *

Nat stretched underneath her covers in the morning sunlight as Thom slipped into her room with two steaming mugs of coffee.

He handed hers over — just the milky tan shade she liked. "Hello, sunshine," he said in his rumbly voice.

She closed her eyes with a wave of desire. Would anything he said *not* be sexy in that posh London accent? Nat faked a frown. "Oh, hey . . . this is awkward, but what did you say your name was again?"

"Magnus."

"Pleased to meet you," she said with a smile. She sat up and sipped her coffee. It tasted like sweet justice.

Thom settled next to her on the bed. He was just wearing his black boxer briefs, and his strong chest with the blond curls of hair and smattering of freckles looked absolutely perfect nestled against her headboard. She ran her eyes over his defined legs.

"Actually, my name is Rami Zamir," he said casually. He looked at her in wide-eyed innocence. "Have you heard of me?"

"No! Yes. I mean . . ." Nat's coffee squelched in her stomach. "Listen, I was going to tell you." She searched his cool eyes. "Today! I was going to tell you today!"

"You were going to tell me that you're using me to win a bet and promote your app?" He raised his perfect jaw in a haughty angle.

"Forget it! You don't have to do it." Nat's mind was already racing to fix the situation. "I'll just call it off, no problem. It's all just a stupid publicity stunt, anyway!"

His face broke into a smile. "Are you kidding? It's genius!"

Relief flooded Nat's body. Her heart felt like it might have stopped. She searched his expression, but he looked serene as ever as he sipped his coffee.

"I just wish it were with a more serious outlet than BuzzFill," he said, scratching his stubbled chin.

"I know, it's awful. All those dumb quizzes." Nat ran a hand through his chest hair. "You're the best, though."

"And I do think that you could be a bit more aggressive with your marketing," he added in a tight voice.

"So, you'll still be my date?" Her conscience gnawed at her. "And to be clear, being my date means that you'll be giving a live interview about our relationship on one of the most popular sites on the internet."

"Of course it does, superstar." He gave her chin a soft pinch. "And yes, I'm in."

Nat wanted to go back to sleep and ravage his body all at the same time.

"I can't let this Rami character win!" he said, setting his coffee cup on the floor. He wrapped his long legs around her and pulled her in close. "Plus, I could get in a word or two about myself, right?"

* * *

Rami walked Allison along the sparkling bay at Crissy Field, as dog walkers and kite-fliers soaked up the picture-postcard day around them.

"Favorite food?" he asked her.

Her face scrunched with mock distress. "Ooh, tough one! A Denver omelet, but only at Margo's Diner back home at three in the morning after an all-night rager with the gals." She laughed at some hidden memory. "This one time at the diner, my friend Carrie . . ." She stopped and bit her lip. "Never mind. How about you?"

Rami thought he saw her eyes film over with tears, but it was also an awfully windy day. He shrugged it off. "My mother's *baingan bharta*."

"What's that?"

"Never mind. Favorite song?"

"Oh, geez, well it's kinda embarrassing but it reminds me of all my sorority gals, and then it was also the song I danced to in the Little Miss Western Minnesota pageant . . . do I have to say?"

"No, that's OK. What about pets? Pro or con?"

"Pro! We had the cutest dog growing up. Her name was Buffy! And then one year, she had puppies out in the barn, and my dad let us each keep one but he didn't tell us we could until Christmas morning . . ." She trailed off again. "Sorry, I keep talking about home. It's pretty much all I can think about, you know?"

Rami took her hand. "Well let me take your mind off it."

He kissed her, but her lips barely moved.

"Thanks, you're really sweet," she said softly.

He searched her face for the familiar, telltale sign of rejection, but didn't see any. She just seemed to be somewhere else. He tucked a long, burnt orange curl behind her ear. "Be my date to a work party this week?"

Allison startled and looked at him with uncertain eyes. "I don't know . . . meeting all your co-workers and stuff?"

"I work alone! So, it'll just be other industry people who don't matter." He smiled. "It could be good networking for you."

"But I moved here because I have a job already . . ."

"But you never know, right?" The scant forty-eight hours until the BuzzFill deadline loomed in his mind. "Come on! Be my devastatingly beautiful plus-one?"

A smile broke through her gloom. "All right, all right!" She sighed in self-recrimination. "Geez, it's just a party, after all. Sorry I'm such a downer."

He pulled her close. "You're perfect." He moved in to kiss her, but she squirmed and ducked her head for a chaste hug.

Rami's mind raced. It was technically true that he hadn't told her all of the details of the BuzzFill event, but he had a strong feeling that a livestreaming interview would scare her away. If she was upset, he would make it up to her afterward. For now, everything was going to plan.

* * *

Nat couldn't eat another bite. Thom had taken her to a French bistro pop-up with only a handful of tables inside a tiny, unmarked storefront. Even Sara had allowed herself to be impressed when Nat told her about the reservation. After cocktails, three courses, and a full bottle of wine, she was stuffed beyond thinking straight. But even fully sober, she couldn't have begun to imagine what all this would cost.

Thom took her hand over the white tablecloth. "I might be new to San Francisco, but I think I like it here."

Nat let herself drink in his boyish blond curls, his deep blue eyes shining at her, and the way the tealight flickered on the angles of his cheeks. "I'm really glad you think so."

Thom twisted one of the rings around on her finger as he spoke. "So, this BuzzFill interview tomorrow — the other guy will be there, right? Rami, is that his name?"

Hearing Rami's name in Thom's jungle cat voice sounded jarring to Nat, like clashing worlds. She shook her head. "He'll be there, but you won't have to talk to him. In fact, please don't."

Thom's eyes sparkled at her with mischief. "Oh, you really don't like him, do you?"

"It's not that!" Nat blurted. "I mean, no, I can't stand him, but I just don't want you to be stressed about it at all."

"Darling, don't worry about me," Thom purred, squeezing her hand.

Annoyance still flared in Nat's mind. "Believe me, if we could do the whole thing by Zoom call, I would."

Thom frowned. "No, no, that wouldn't work, would it?" He froze, dramatically, his fork in front of his face, mid-bite, and stared unblinking into space.

Nat laughed at his pose. "Ugh, you're right! It'd freeze right when I was sneezing or something and then that would be the image of me out there forever."

He relaxed a bit then froze up again, eyes shining at his joke. "I . . . BeTwo . . . dating," he bleated in a robotic voice.

Nat laughed, again but softer this time.

His eyes flicked to the couple at the table nearby as he froze a third time on the way to grab his wine glass. "Ehhhh-eh-eh!" he said in a loud robotic glitch, eyes darting to see if the other table was noticing his performance.

Nat felt her smile start to ache, and her cheeks burned. Her shoulders pinched in embarrassment.

The waiter returned. "Dessert? Coffee?"

Thom turned to him and then froze. He jutted his chin, and his eyes bulged. "Bad . . . connection . . ."

The waiter blinked. "I'm sorry?"

Nat forced an open-mouth laugh as she pushed Thom's rigid arm down. "Ohmygod, you're so funny. Stop!" She looked at the waiter. "Maybe just the check?"

"No, no!" Thom's face was flushed with satisfaction. "Two espressos and, what do we think about the chocolate torte?"

Nat gave an embarrassed laugh. "Well, the interview is tomorrow. I can't be up all night."

Thom's eyes took on their theatrical gleam, and he mock whisper-yelled, "Don't worry, I'll tire you out!"

Nat felt the color drain from her face as the waiter managed a polite chuckle.

He winked at the waiter. "So just those things, then the check. Thanks, mate."

She pretended to arrange her napkin on her lap. "So, tomorrow we won't be having two Manhattans before the interview . . ."

"Oh, come on. He thought it was funny!" Thom was back in his posh posture. He arched an eyebrow. "We're adults at a fancy restaurant. No one thinks we're going home to read Scripture to one another." A seductive grin curled into his face as he brought her hand to his lips. "What a waste that would be," he cooed with a kiss on her knuckles.

Nat felt her body warm to him as the espressos arrived. "Well, we can run through what to say tomorrow one more time, I guess."

* * *

An hour later, in her bed, Nat tried to summon that warmth as Thom's naked body hovered over her.

Despite having been in one hell of a dry spell, Nat loved sex, craved sex, and usually couldn't wait to have sex with her partner. But tonight, it was awkward — all she seemed to feel were elbows and apologies and re-positioning. Finally, Thom had made it inside her, and she watched the cords of his neck move as he thrust into her.

Sometimes friction felt like magic, and sometimes it felt like skin being rubbed raw. She winced.

"Am I hurting you?"

"No, sorry! Sorry, it's just my nerves about the interview."

"Totally understandable." He kept thrusting.

She watched his jaw shifting above her. "You don't think this is a huge mistake, right? Like I'm about to destroy my entire life's work?"

"Relax. Shh-shh-shh . . . I've got you . . ."

He brought a hand between her legs and kept thrusting.

"Mmm . . . OK . . . yes . . ." she tried. She closed her eyes. Time to quiet her mind and be in her body. Time to shut out every other sensation besides the one she needed to feel right now. Everything else could wait.

Her phone pinged. Nat jumped.

"Ow!" cried Thom.

"I'm sorry! So sorry!" She grabbed her phone to read the messages. It was from Justin only, no Jo on the thread.

> Justin: *I know things have been weird but I just wanted to say good luck tomorrow*
>
>
>
> *Slay queeeeeeeeeen*

"Everything OK?" Thom grumbled, rubbing his groin protectively.

"Yeah, fine. Just something about tomorrow." Nat sighed. Justin was texting on his own, late at night, and using what he called "Sad millennial speak". He was either pumping her up or patronizing her because he was just that certain of her doom. Either way, it didn't seem like a good sign. She looked at Thom's naked body sprawled across her bed.

He arched an eyebrow and rocked his hips — and his erection — toward her.

She needed to sleep. She pushed him to lie back on the bed and brought her face between his legs.

* * *

Rami stirred his simmering pots while Allison sipped wine in his kitchen.

"Well, that Gemma gal sounds Looney Tunes to me," she said, her Midwestern accent blossoming with the alcohol. "I think I read one hundred words of Kim Kardashian's Instagram before I even get out of bed in the morning."

"I know, right?" Rami muttered, worried about the new color of the sauce after his latest adjustment. He offered her a steaming spoonful. "Here, try it now. Is that better?"

Allison wrapped her rosy lips around the spoon and shot him a worried glance. "Mmm. Yeah!" She nodded and reached for her water glass. "It tastes . . . the same. I'm sorry!"

"No problem," he said, turning to the pots. "Back to the drawing board!"

"It's really OK," she said for the third time that night. "I mean, it's already kinda late, right?"

Rami glanced at the glowing microwave clock. It was ten. Maybe if he added more tomato puree to cut the spice for her? Some cream?

"I'll just eat it without the sauce!" she said gamely.

"Then it would just be rice and tofu." He shook his head. "Just give me one more try."

His conscience gnawed at him. Earlier, he had caved and told Allison about the BuzzFill interview. To his surprise, she'd been fine with it. Sure, she had lost all color in her face and her eyes had drifted apart in separate directions for a brief moment, but then she'd smiled and assured him many times that it was fine. She insisted that she was happy to help him out. She'd said, in her heartachingly pure way, she'd simply tell the truth that she'd met a total dreamboat who saved her from the saddest birthday ever.

Rami sighed as he stirred in more puree. In a rush of guilt and relief, he'd promised to make her a home-cooked meal in thanks, but foolishly choosing one of his favorite curries to serve to a white woman from smalltown Minnesota had gotten him where they now were.

He heard Allison sigh behind his back. "All right, well maybe I could practice for the interview one more time."

Rami surveyed the spices and ingredients in front of him as the sauce bubbled. He ran a hand through his sweaty hair. "What am I missing here?"

She picked up the stack of colored index cards that she'd made and started reading.

* * *

Later, Allison rolled off Rami, whom she had been straddling in bed. They lay on their backs, naked and staring up at the ceiling.

She pulled the sheet up over her breasts. "That was nice."

"Yeah, good," he said, giving her a peck on the cheek. "I'm glad."

She curled up and lay her head on his chest. "Maybe I should just stay here tonight?"

He startled. "Oh! Really?" Guilt flooded through him as soon as he said it. Was he really the guy who was going to kick a girl out after watching her choke down a meal she'd clearly thought was disgusting and then having serviceable-but-successful sex with her? Was he a *fuck boy* now?

"We're both going to the interview tomorrow, anyway." She yawned, fluffing her curls across his chest. "And if I spend the day with you, I'll know even more about you that I can tell to the whole world."

That, he realized, was exactly what he was afraid of. "Yeah, that's true . . ." he said. "It's just that sometimes I get nightmares when I'm stressed and I wouldn't want to keep you up." He eased his conscience by reminding himself that this was not, in fact, a lie.

She rolled her eyes but stuck out her lip in a sweet pout. "Oh, poor, baby!"

"I know, it's awful," he sighed. He looked sadly into her round green eyes. "I've been told that I cry." Still not a lie.

Allison recoiled. "Wait, really?" She was still smiling from her "poor baby" bit, but her eyes were full of unease. Maybe even a hint of "the ick."

Rami just shrugged and hoped the image of him silently weeping into his pillow hadn't been too over the top.

Allison stretched and swung her legs out of bed. "Well, I actually need to water my plants, anyway." She dressed with a cheerful air and then bent down to give him a peck on the cheek. "And, I'm sorry, but I am absolutely starving."

* * *

Rami walked Allison to the door as Ian watched from the sofa.

She pulled on her coat. "Are you sure that I shouldn't just stay in case you have bad dreams?" she teased.

Rami tried to shuffle her out before Ian could chime in with anything. He felt like an absolute cad. "You're so kind, no, please. See you tomorrow!"

He gave her a quick kiss, and she waved goodbye. He closed the door and leaned against it with a sigh.

Ian materialized next to him and poked his arm hard. "Pop. Pop."

"Ow! What are you doing?"

"Your bubble wrap is hurting that poor woman." He poked harder.

"Stop! I do bruise, you know!"

Ian raised to his full six-foot-six height and peered down at Rami with stony eyes. "Do you even like her? The *real* her?"

Rami stormed back into the living room. "You know, you talk all about love and finding the right person, but let me give you a little pearl of wisdom, friend."

Ian followed. "Please."

Rami started to pace. "Sometimes what you feel about somebody doesn't make any sense. Sometimes the person you like doesn't make any sense!"

Ian sank into the sofa and tucked his long legs beneath him. "Interesting theory. But it never happens."

"*Au contraire!*" Rami whirled around to Ian with a finger raised in intellectual triumph. "You think we know what we want? You think that somehow in the fucked up, garbage soup of TV shows and song lyrics and mean things someone said to us fifteen years ago that we call our minds . . ." He gathered steam. "Minds which function as a hamster wheel to distract us from what's making us miserable with new and different ways to be miserable—" He gestured wildly to Ian's numerous bongs and ashtrays and pipes strewn on the coffee table — "that in all the never-ending onslaught of messages and dopamine hits and hashtags — that we have *any* idea what to look for? What will actually make us *happy?*"

"Yes."

"Ha!" Rami barked. "Then I pity you. I pity you even more than I pity myself. At least I know that I'm in love with a woman I'll never have! At least I'm aware that I'll never be happy because I basically called her app a steaming pile of dog shit in front of the entire world, even though I really feel that it is, or it is in its current state, and yet all I want to do is see her, and kiss her again, and make my mom's recipes for her, and if she hated it I wouldn't make her seventeen different sauces. I wouldn't! I'd say, 'Too bad, sister!' Because for some reason it makes me feel better that she doesn't like parts of me. Because *I* don't like parts of me. And that somehow makes the parts that she *does* like even better!" Rami sank onto the sofa, out of breath.

Ian stood up with a slow clap.

"Fuck. Speeches are exhausting."

Ian pulled a paper crown out of his pocket, unfolded it, and placed it on Rami's head. "Congratulations. You are no longer a frog."

"Does everyone just carry the craziest shit around with them now?"

"I ordered it weeks ago. I've been waiting for this moment."

Rami had to admire his preparation. "Thank you." He straightened the crown in his hair and then slumped back onto the sofa.

Ian rubbed his shoulders like a youth soccer coach. "Go! Go get your princess!"

Rami sighed and pulled out his phone. "Well, I'm going to text her first," he said. "And I'm not going to be gender normative about it." He opened a message to Nat.

> Rami: *We need to talk. Can I buy you a drink?*
>
> *Please?*

Ian sat next to Rami and lit a packed pipe. "Is this a good time to tell you that I've been seeing Gemma?"

* * *

Nat was staring at the ceiling, wide awake, as Thom snored softly next to her. Pixel hadn't made an appearance all night. She couldn't blame him — he'd never had to deal with a new human taking up his space in the bed before. He was probably curled up with Sara in her room. She sighed and fluffed her pillow yet again. Not that he should get used to that, apparently, given the moving boxes that were still accumulating around the apartment. Why wouldn't Sara just accept her help with the rent so that things could stay the way they were? Nat rolled over again. Why wasn't the idea of not living together as upsetting for Sara as it was for her?

The sounds of a drunken conversation wafted up from the streets. She heard the high-pitched beeps of bus doors opening.

Nat imagined that maybe, eventually, Thom would move in to take Sara's place, or maybe they would find a new place together. She'd always wanted that — to share her life with someone steady, dependable, and incredibly sexy. Now her ninety-nine percent match was sleeping beside her, a living picture of the exact scenario she had been looking for night after night in all those solo BeTwo searches on her couch.

The exact scenario. Except for one big hitch. Rami. Despite the many times she'd shut him down when he'd said her app design was flawed, she still couldn't stop thinking about what he might have to say. At first, it was because she'd wanted to crush his doubt out of existence, and then because she'd wanted to prove him wrong. But now? It was because she thought that he probably had a good point, and she wanted to hear it. He could see something that she couldn't. He could man the blind spot, and she could ease up on the gas ever so slightly. Maybe even enjoy the ride a little.

She rolled over and grabbed her phone. Then she bolted upright. She read the texts from Rami inviting her to meet for a drink. How had she missed these?

Thom shifted in bed beside her.

That was how.

She checked the time. If Rami had gone to the bar, he wouldn't have been waiting long. She shot him a quick *OMW* and gingerly pushed back the covers and got out of bed. As silently as possible, she opened her closet and rummaged for something to wear. There, still on a hanger from the day she'd brought it home, was the *Team Nat* shirt she'd been supposed to give to Sara. Dread sank into her chest. What were the odds that her long-time bestie would wear it now? Or even show up to the event?

Nat shimmied out of her pajamas and into a simple black shirt dress. Still, if Sara did decide to show, and saw that she hadn't been given a shirt, that would definitely make it harder to heal their rift. Nat tiptoed back to the closet. She tucked a pair of knee boots under her arm to put on in the hallway, and carefully slipped Sara's shirt off the hanger. If Nat knew one thing about her best friend, it was that she absolutely loved a theme. She tossed the shirt over her shoulder. Maybe, if Nat was lucky, she still loved her, too.

She gave a quick look at Thom's sleeping form and crept out of her room . . .

Then crept back in. She grabbed a tube of bright lipstick off her dresser and tiptoed out into the dark apartment.

Sara's moving boxes had turned the space into a maze, and it took a minor feat of gymnastics for her not to stub a toe or bump an elbow as she inched toward the kitchen. She folded the shirt and placed it on the counter. Then she took one of the unpacked mugs, dropped in a bag of Sara's favorite tea and two spoonfuls of coconut sugar, and set it next to the shirt. She filled the tea kettle with water and plugged it in, so all Sara would have to do in the morning was push a button. It was the best Nat could do for a peace offering at the moment. She glanced at the frosty blue glow of the microwave clock and winced, hoping Rami was in a patient mood for what would seemingly be the first time in his life.

* * *

Nat pushed through the swinging pleather doors of the cocktail bar. She scanned the red-lit interior. Rami sat at the bar, sipping a bourbon. She smoothed her hair and walked over. The stool next to him was covered with his jacket.

"Saving this for someone?" she said.

Rami pulled off the jacket. "She has arrived."

She sat down, warmed by his now-familiar smell of beach water and spices.

"Thanks for meeting me," he said, sliding a fresh martini in front of her.

"Thanks for this." She took a cool, bracing sip.

"It's my pleasure."

Nat snapped her eyes to him. She wasn't used to such a soft tone of voice coming from her rival, or the way his melting brown eyes seemed to linger on her. "Yeah . . . me too," she confessed. "I guess I should be thinking about how to destroy you tomorrow, but . . ." She watched him flutter his long lashes and tighten his square jaw. "Honestly, it's just nice to see you."

"Really? I mean, I feel the same." His face was unguarded, and she could feel his happiness at seeing her. "That's why I wanted to talk tonight."

Relief, nerves, and excitement poured out of Nat in a rush of words. "Totally! No one can understand what I'm feeling right now except you, because we're the only two people stupid enough to get roped into this."

Rami put down his glass, softly cleared his throat, and leaned toward her. "Well, we make a good team . . ."

Nat nodded into her martini. "I mean, my new boyfriend just took me out to this amazing dinner, like the nicest food I've had in maybe my entire life, and I was basically a cold zombie to him all night."

Rami jolted. "Boyfriend?"

Nat winced at the word coming from his mouth in spite of herself. "He's literally perfect for me. I put in enough search filters to give SETI a run for their money, and my algorithm served him up to me on a silver platter." She gave him an "oops" shrug and held out a picture of Thom on her phone. "And he's also the hottest guy in the world, look."

232

"Thom?" Rami's face darkened.

Nat leaned in. "You know him?"

"Unfortunately, I do." Rami pulled the phone from her hand and squinted at the picture up close. His face darkened at some hidden memory. "He dated my sister for a year before he cheated on her with, like, a dozen other women, and basically treated her heart like his own personal gym rag."

Nat laughed as panic flared in her chest. She grabbed her phone back. "No, you must have the wrong person."

"You wish!" Rami hit her with a cruel smile and raised his glass in a salute. "Also, he used BeTwo to cheat, so hey, congrats and thanks for that."

"Again, *wrong* person. Thom told me that he'd just moved here and that he'd never used my app before then."

Rami pursed his lips in mock thought. "Well, he definitely has used your app in San Francisco, because that's how he got caught cheating on Sana. Her friend found his profile and sent her a screen grab." He smirked and shrugged. "Busted!"

Nat hunched over her cocktail. A thousand rationalizations flew into her mind like startled birds. Maybe Thom just wanted to impress her so badly that he was waiting to tell her the full truth. He said he already knew about the BuzzFill contest, so maybe he just wanted her to focus on winning before they had any complicated discussions, which was considerate, one could argue! But even her desperate mind couldn't quite swallow these excuses whole. Something jagged and dark still sank in her chest, especially since she was still sitting next to Rami. She recalled the awkward way Thom had asked if Rami would be at the interview — the interview that was the very next day.

"Speechless?" Rami swirled his glass with his long fingers. "Look, I'm sorry to tell you like this." He shifted with an awkward little *hmmph* and put a hand on Nat's shoulder. "I really can't believe I am cleaning up that asshole's mess a second time."

The warmth of Rami's hand only made Nat's heart ache harder. Now he felt sorry for her. Her feelings for him might be tangled up in chaos, but the one thing she knew that she didn't want from Rami was pity, especially not for her love life. She stiffened under his hand and cast him a hard look. "So that's what I am now? Thom's mess?"

Rami drew back like she was a hot stove. "Are you serious? No." He ran his hand over his face, and Nat could see the tiredness around his eyes. "I swear to God, I always say the wrong thing around you. Or maybe you just make me realize that I say the wrong thing around everyone."

Nat managed a bitter laugh. "I know the feeling." She bit her lip to quell the tears pooling in her eyes. She could still feel Thom's naked body on her skin. But how much of him was actually still hidden from her? She could imagine how stupid she would look to Rami if she told him that Thom was in her bed at that very moment. Even if Rami was telling the truth, what could she do about it now? And did it change anything? She still had to take someone to the interview tomorrow. She couldn't do better than Thom — for the contest, and maybe in real life, too. She took a heavy swallow of her martini and shrugged. "Well, whatever is in Thom's past is the past."

Rami laughed, then he scoffed, then she watched a shield form over his eyes like ice. "So, let me get this straight. You're OK being involved with a guy who I have personally witnessed treating women like shit, multiple times, and who has clearly also lied to you?"

"He's my ninety-nine percent match," Nat insisted. "There's no way he was that high of a match with your sister."

"That is dark as fuck." Rami's thick brows furrowed, and he shook his head. "Seriously, that is some chilling sci-fi shit that you just said."

"Why? Because I trust my own data?"

"Because you can't just admit it. Your algorithm can't capture the fact that he's a dirtbag! Because no algorithm can! Dirtbags just tell the algorithm what it wants to hear, and also what you want to hear too, apparently."

"You don't know what you're talking about." Nat scowled into his face. By this point, she'd argued with Rami many times, but this time felt different, and it wasn't because they were arguing about Thom. This time, his witty comebacks and uncanny ability to find the holes in her thinking didn't light a fire inside her that made her want to scream and order another round. This time it just made her want to cry.

But Rami continued. "And yet instead of owning up to this patently obvious fact, you'd rather ignore me and wait until some dickhead guy treats you just as poorly as he treated my sister." Rami rolled his eyes as another point occurred to him. "And yes, I know how hot Thom's accent is, OK?"

Nat scoffed. "You don't get it. People lie all the time!" Hurt panged in her heart as she spoke. "It'll turn out that they never really liked you, no matter how many times they said that they did. Or, best case scenario, they'll just change the way they feel about you on a whim! Poof!"

Rami's shoulders dropped, and his full lips twitched with sadness. He fixed her with a serious look.

Nat continued. "You can never trust that anyone really truly likes you, ever — never ever ever — no matter what they say or do."

Rami's coffee-colored eyes softened ever so slightly. He drew a long breath. "Do you really think that?"

Nat raised her palms at the obvious affirmative answer to that question. "I *know* that! I've lived that! Over and over again," she cried. "That's why my algorithm matters. It's compatibility data. *Data.* It's the closest thing I have to a guarantee that someone isn't going to just up and leave me!"

"Anyone would be an idiot to leave you, Nat." Rami shook his head and ran a hand through his curls, unwilling or unable to look at her. "But I'm saying that Thom *will* leave you." He sat up straighter, and then his eyes flashed into hers. "Or rather, that you should leave *him*, because you deserve better."

His words made the breath leave her body. Those last few syllables were like magic melting into her wounds despite the anger and adrenaline still coursing through her. She closed her eyes and drew in a shaky sigh. She wanted to take his hand and tell him that she was utterly exhausted, that she was glad he told her about Thom, that all of the pressure from the contest was making her act crazy to everyone in her life . . .

But Rami kept talking. "And the world deserves better than some shitty algorithm that treats us all like commercial products. But what do I know? Maybe you just enjoy dating your number one customer."

Nat's mouth fell open in shock. She hated Rami. His sparkly eyes, his shiny hair, and his pouty lips — she wanted to crush them all. "Got it. My app is trash; that's the point you've been making this whole competition — except no one seems to think that but you."

Rami nodded sadly. "Yeah, I know."

Nat put on her best mean girl voice, powered by the pain throbbing in her chest like an engine. "See, the thing is, we live in the twenty-first century so maybe you can just get over yourself and deal with it?"

"Can you?"

She rolled her eyes. "Good talk. I have a man waiting for me at home. Why'd you text me, Rami?"

He looked closely at his cocktail.

She watched his face for any sign of movement, but he was stoic. Thick brows knitted in thought, Roman nose pointed to his hands, long lashes down, and his espresso eyes closed to her. "Hello? You wanted to meet—"

"No," he interrupted, "I'm glad you've got someone for tomorrow." He sat up straight and fixed her with a flat glare. He brushed the hair off his forehead and jutted his chin. "I just wanted to give you the heads-up that I'm bringing someone, too. Her name is Allison." He paused. "She's great."

Something heavy dropped into Nat's stomach. She wished it were anger, but it very much wasn't. All she wanted was to go home, but even that was ruined — half-emptied into Sara's moving boxes and with Thom's checkered past waiting for her in bed. Heat stung in her eyes, so she narrowed them at Rami. "Awesome. We both won."

He grimaced with the last swig of his bourbon. "Looks like it."

"What a moment of optimism for the world."

"You're welcome, humanity."

Nat downed the rest of her drink with trembling hands. "See you and Amanda tomorrow, then."

Rami scoffed. "Allison. And don't worry, I won't introduce her to Thom."

Nat gaped at him. "Asshole," she said, turned on her heel, and left.

Rami slumped over his glass. "Yeah," he muttered. "I know."

CHAPTER 18

The day of the BuzzFill BuzzCheck Exclusive, Nat went to work, as usual. After the blow-up with Rami, she had crept back into bed with Thom and cried silently into her pillow before finally succumbing to exhaustion sometime around four in the morning. When he had woken her up with coffee and a kiss on the cheek, she hadn't been able to muster the energy to do anything but nod her thanks from bed and confirm their plans to meet up later. He also just looked damn good turning over his shoulder to wink at her as he pulled on his dress shirt — a force too powerful for anything like better judgment. Whatever train this was, and wherever it was going, it had left the station. All Nat could do was go along for the ride, or more likely, the trainwreck.

The interview was scheduled for early evening as part of the opening events for the BuzzForce Expo. So, she had eight long hours to try to stay calm. She did some rote running of numbers and smashing of bugs in the code, but her mind was all over the place. She mainly clicked around the internet, hoping to distract herself with clickbait articles about everything from the twenty-five things cat owners should never do, to elaborate casserole prep videos that she would never, ever, in a million years, be making. Still, she printed the recipes and put them in her purse.

It seemed to be the same for the twins, who were unusually fidgety but still kept to themselves all morning. Every now and then, Nat would look up to see them whispering to each other in a concerned, mirrored huddle. But whenever they met her gaze, they would smile brightly, wave, and scatter.

Nat slumped in her chair and thumbed open her phone to Sara's social media pages. It was pathetic to try and glean whether or not her supposed best friend was planning on showing up to the interview by stalking her posts — pathetic and a long shot in terms of getting any useful information — but Nat couldn't resist. Her feeds were the usual mix of sunsets, selfies, and salon memes. Nothing new, nothing that announced different plans for that evening, or that she was in the market for a new, non-shitty friend. Timidly, Nat scrolled down the grid to make sure Sara hadn't deleted any of the pics of them together. She hadn't. Nat sighed with relief and a flood of dopamine. Maybe there was still hope.

Before she'd left for work, she'd seen that at some point Sara had indeed taken the *Team Nat* shirt and the tea, but there had been no communication about any of it. Maybe she would show up wearing it. Or maybe she was just using it to wrap up some glassware in one of her moving boxes. Nat swiped away from Sara's page and let herself doomscroll her brain into numbness.

After lunch, a lush bouquet of flowers arrived from Thom with a note about how happy he was to be a part of this success with her. Nat stuck the note to the center of the office fridge with a magnet.

Only seven more hours to go.

* * *

Rami tossed in his bed. How dare Nat rob him of the simple, human pleasure of napping? On top of everything else! He checked the time again. It was barely past noon.

It wasn't like he wasn't tired. He'd hardly slept after getting home from the bar. Somehow, the heady mix of nagging guilt over Allison and crushing regret over not just missing, but completely shattering his window with Nat hadn't exactly lulled him into dreamland. He mentally waved goodbye to the version of his life where he was fresh-faced and perky for the interview. Nope, he'd be as worn out and stressed as ever.

He punched his pillow into a better shape and cracked his knuckle on the headboard. Perfect.

* * *

Nat's brain felt sticky and sore, like her mouth after she'd binged a whole bag of sour gummies, but this time she'd consumed hours of videos on the internet. Her ass actually hurt from sitting too long, which was truly a feat considering that she was a coder. She forced her stiff legs to stand and tried to stretch out the stabbing knots of pain behind her shoulder blades. Hadn't she just watched a demo about using, like, a sock, two straws, and a watermelon to fix back pain? She couldn't remember. Her mind was a blurry smear of sassy pets, miracle neck creams, banal observations that somehow felt profound, and enough conflicting information on healthy eating to keep her afraid of the grocery store for years to come. And yet she still had hours to kill before the interview.

She decided to stop avoiding her last resort and take a walk.

The rain had finally let up, and the San Francisco afternoon was crisp and gorgeous as Nat walked in the direction of the water-front baseball stadium. It was helpful and grounding to be near water, right? She was pretty sure that was something people said. A group of men in business casual polos and khakis approached her on the sidewalk. The one in navy blue with a salt-and-pepper beard shot her an approving look as she walked by. An ironic laugh rattled in her throat. Of course, now she was getting attention, after all those failed dates, and when she had Thom and was about to pronounce it to the whole world.

The idea still felt wobbly in her mind. She had Thom. She had a boyfriend. Her long, lonely dry spell was officially over, and quite possibly forever, since he met all her criteria to a tee. What more could she want, right? She'd listed out every possible thing.

A shadow darkened her thoughts as she walked another block. There was no way he really was the same guy who had cheated on Rami's sister, right? Nat had only shown him one picture in a dark bar, and Rami probably wanted to mess with her mind. If that was the same Thom — her Thom — it would mean he'd lied to her from day one, and why would he do that? Her mind flashed to how Eric had lied about his height on his profile and used much younger pictures of himself. Then there was her original profile, where she'd only put in whatever the data showed her was popular to make sure someone, anyone, would actually pick her. She jammed a crosswalk button and chewed her lip. What was the word Rami kept using to describe being on the apps?

Vulnerable.

It would have never occurred to her. She'd genuinely thought that fielding rejections through DMs and swipes would make it so that it didn't hurt. When she thought about how she'd been turned down by Jake back in London, Owen in the park, and a string of other guys throughout her life, what she couldn't forget were the looks on their faces as they'd let her know that they weren't interested. It was like looking into the cruelest mirror — seeing so clearly how very much someone didn't care about you, no matter how much you cared for them. She'd searched every cute guy's face since, always expecting to see that same dull sheen of dismissal. She'd never wanted to see that look on anyone's face ever again.

Nat reached the ballpark and cut around the back toward the seal statue. Seeing that stupid thing always cheered her up. So, she'd made BeTwo in the hopes that moving the romantic tri-al-and-error into pixels on tiny screens would prevent pain, and let her users protect themselves with matches based on data before making a personal investment and exposing their hearts. But the data was only as reliable as the users who entered it, and worse, there was no way to tell what was true until you met in person, anyway. So then what were all the hours spent on BeTwo even accomplishing?

She rubbed the giant baseball perched on the seal's nose and wished for good luck with the interview in a few hours. Now she knew from her own hours of swiping, and being unmatched and ghosted threads, and toe-curling awkward dates that those seemingly small digital actions *were* a type of personal investment — an investment of time. Instead of creating a shortcut around romantic vulnerability, she might have inadvertently made the path all the more twisted — literally and figuratively.

Despite the dimple of sunshine on the seal's cheery smile, or the way the waves in the bay glittered, her nerves crackled like static around her temples, and her heart felt like a lead cannonball lodged in her chest. She wanted to talk to Sara about it, but that was impossible. She wanted to talk to Jo, but she hadn't figured out a way to smooth things over, and asking if she thought their whole company was a mistake before their biggest-ever PR event probably wasn't the move. She could talk to Thom, but something inside her knew that he wouldn't get it. She could practically hear his lush rumble reassuring her that she was brilliant and her algorithm was incredible — which, for the first time ever, was not exactly what she wanted to hear.

The person whom she needed to talk to, of course, was Rami. But why would he help her? The fate of her whole career depended on proving him wrong. So, she would sit next to him and point to her handsome boyfriend and praise her dating app, and then the contest would be over, and she'd probably never see Rami again. If only that meant she would also stop thinking about the way his brooding eyes lit up when he made a good point, or how his dimples winked in his cheeks when he was really amused, or how safe she'd felt when he pulled her into his chest that night — all in those brief moments before she'd made him hate her again.

Nat leaned over the railing and let the salty sea breeze cool her face and lift the hair from her neck. She wasn't sure if she could get through the next few hours alone, even if she deserved to. She pulled out her phone and texted Sara.

> Nat: *I miss you so much it feels like my teeth are gonna fall out.*
>
> *I'm sorry I've been a terrible friend to you lately.*
>
> *Please let me make it up to you?*

She put her phone away and blinked back tears as a seagull screeched overhead. It was the best she could do, for now.

* * *

Rami steeled his nerves and waited for Allison to buzz him up to her apartment. The gleaming silver doors bleated their approval, and Rami pushed inside the slick apartment tower. It was so new, it still smelled like fresh paint inside. He'd watched this place being built, right over the footprint of, among other things, his childhood video store and a mom-and-pop taqueria that he used to love. Now it was a monolith of straight lines and shining glass in a city block full of derelict converted Victorians and the working families who clung to still being able to live in them. He pushed the elevator buttons and watched the doors glide silently shut. Getting himself worked up about gentrification was just a distraction, even he could see that. He needed to focus on his mission, no matter how unpleasant. He had come here to pick up Allison and escort her to the BuzzFill interview, yes, but he had also come here to break up with her. Hopefully, there was a way both things could somehow still happen, despite how impossible it was to imagine.

Allison answered the door in a frilly white dress that literally looked like an angel costume to Rami. He had to admit that the universe, or whatever, did have a good sense of humor sometimes.

"I'm not wearing this," she said in lieu of an actual greeting. "I'm just trying things on and this is what I was wearing when you got here, but don't worry." She gestured down her figure to what, in Rami's eyes, was a beautiful garment that complemented her curves and fair skin with an almost elfin perfection. "I know this looks awful."

"You look incredible, actually," he said as she spun away on a bare foot and disappeared into her bedroom. He slipped off his shoes and stepped inside. He had been to Allison's apartment only once before, and it had been late, and they had been drinking, and so he hadn't been in the state of mind to really take it in. To be fair, neither had she, and given her recent move, there hadn't been much to look at, anyway. But now more of her furniture had arrived, and Rami could examine the scrapes in the robin's egg blue paint of her small bookshelf, and the array of stone skulls that grinned between the spines of her books. They were mostly romance novels and a few of the usual novelty gift books about wet cats or rude birds that were the millennials' fruit cake. Nestled under a skull carved from rose quartz was a scribbled note. It read: *Abundance. I am the architect of my life!* He touched the edge with his finger and closed his eyes. "Polar bears," he whispered into the quiet. As if in response, loud rustling and a crash of hangers clattered from Allison's room. He had to save her from her wardrobe spiral, especially if she was about to stay home alone. "Can I help you?" he called into her room as he padded through the junior one-bedroom floor plan that he could only imagine cost most of her salary.

"Yeah, come look at this option!"

Rami took a deep inhale. Time to face the music. He leaned against the doorframe and immediately lost his calming breath. Allison twirled in a stunner of an emerald green dress. The neckline plumped up her soft breasts, the waist nipped in above her hips, and the skirt flared over her legs in a swooping hourglass. She was a vision. And he didn't feel anything close to what he should be feeling to see her.

"Good? Too much?" Her face was blotched and shiny with the effort of trying on several dozen looks, judging by the piles on her floor. Her jade green eyes blinked at him in full earnestness.

"Allison, you're stunning. Truly.".

Her pink lips perked up in a smile, and she smoothed her skirt a little. "Well good. And thanks."

Rami stretched his steps around the clothes on the floor to reach her and took her hand. "I can't believe you would go to all this trouble to pick something to wear just for me and this absurd interview."

"Of course!" She smiled at him, but her eyes wavered, ever so slightly, though they were standing close enough for Rami to notice. "It's important to you."

Rami squeezed her soft palm and guided her to sit on her bed with him. "It is important. That's why I have to tell you something." He took a deep breath and looked into her beautiful face. "You're a smart, funny, kind and cool person, and you are truly one of the most gorgeous women I've ever known, let alone been lucky enough to kiss."

Allison blushed with a small snort of breath. "OK, geez . . ."

"I, on the other hand, have acted like an absolutely selfish piece of trash toward you, and it has to stop." He watched her face go blank and then recoil, watched her eyes widen at him, and then narrow down to her hands.

"Yeah, that's true." Her voice was soft, and her chest heaved with fast breaths. "I know you're worried about this internet contest thing, but it's been feeling a little bit . . . wrong." She met his gaze with a more confident tone. "I mean, wrong between us."

He rushed to agree. "You're totally right and I'm so, so sorry. I should've never put you through this and we can just call it all off. It's not your problem to solve."

Allison sighed and chewed her rosy lip. He had been expecting her to cry. It didn't look at all like she was about to cry. In fact, her face looked brighter. "So, you'll show up to this thing with Nat all alone?"

The full weight of that reality swirled around him with a wave of dizziness. He shrugged it off. "Yes. I tried and I failed, fair and square." Freed from its facade of being Allison's happy boyfriend, his brain hit him with a new revelation. "This whole thing has been about me railing against how the apps make us treat each other as products, like dolls just to fill a need . . . and it really seems like that is how I have been treating you."

She gave a rueful laugh and looked at him. "You don't even really like me, do you?"

"I do! Allison, I do!" He knew this was only half of the truth. "But also . . . maybe not in the way that I thought."

She nodded. "I know. We don't have anything in common, really, and you talk about your work all the time and sometimes I can barely stay awake." She rolled her eyes in disgust. "And I said I wanted to hear about *Stargate* because I thought it was about astrology, and it was *not*."

Rami laughed in spite of himself. "A fatal mistake."

"In that moment? I kinda wanted it to be!"

Rami let the quiet settle around them. He couldn't dare bring up the contest. How could he ask anything more of her?

Allison cleared her throat with a pointed *ahem*. "You need someone more like Nat, don't you think?"

Her words hit Rami like bitter medicine. "Is it that obvious?"

She rolled her eyes with a nod. "I mean, I tried to ignore it but I saw the way you looked at each other in the check-in interview. And she really likes to talk about tech stuff." She wrinkled her freckled nose. "Like, even as much as you."

"That she does." Rami sighed. "She also found an actual boyfriend during this whole ridiculous charade, and I'm pretty sure that I'm never going to see her again after today."

"Well, that's too bad."

They sat side-by-side in silence for a beat. Allison took a deep breath and rolled her shoulders back with a sigh. "I just moved here, you know? I don't know anyone else, really."

"Did I take advantage of that?"

She shrugged. "Probably? But so did I." She twisted a strand of her red curls. "You seem like a nice guy, but also I think I just wanted some attention."

Rami nodded with a *hmm*. On principle, he refused to be triggered by being called a "nice guy," but he also knew that Allison meant it sincerely. "So, maybe we both kinda used each other a little bit."

"I think we did, yeah." She punched him lightly on the thigh. "It was still fun, though."

"It was, Allison. I'm glad I met you."

"Yeah, me too." She held out her palm. "Friends?"

He shook her hand. "Friends." He was about to ask her to celebrate their new understanding over a nice, spicy curry — *a joke* — when his eyes caught the time on his watch and broke the moment. Specifically, he broke a sweat. He raised his wrist to his face in the vain hope that he was simply misreading it. They were scheduled to be downtown in twenty minutes.

Allison grabbed his wrist. "Oh geez! We're gonna be late!" She bounded up and rushed to her dresser, grabbing makeup products like a mad scientist.

"We?" he echoed. "You're still coming?"

Allison scurried into the bathroom with fistfuls of colorful plastic tubes. "Yeah, I've always wanted to go viral again!"

Too many questions jockeyed for the front of his mind, but as always, sheer morbid curiosity won out. "*Again?*"

"You really didn't even google me, huh? That's so weird." She popped her face out of the doorway, newly glamorous in black lashes and red lips. "I posted this video of me tasting a pickletini at the sorority house one night and it got picked up by all the morning shows. I got sent so much free stuff, it was bonkers."

Rami's head swiveled as she breezed past him in a cloud of sweet floral perfume. He heard her gathering her keys and slipping into heels by the front door.

"I came *so close* to getting an SUV from a local dealership, but maybe this time I can get one of those cute little Vespa things!" she called. "Come on! We're gonna be late!"

Rami's brain blinked back online, and he knew that against all odds, he was being given a gift. Even if he didn't deserve it, he would be a fool not to just go with it and pay back his great karmic debt later. He hurried toward her. "So, you'll still pretend to be my girlfriend? On the internet?"

She winked a matcha-colored eye. "Just for tonight."

Rami's hands clutched at his chest, as if he were wearing a waistcoat and she'd just agreed to attend his ball. "You're an amazing woman. Let's get you a scooter."

CHAPTER 19

Jo met Nat at the door when she walked back into the office, already wearing her *Team Nat* shirt. Excitement buzzed off of her petite frame in a way that Nat could feel in the air. "Hey, how are you feeling? Do you want to practice what you're gonna say, or do some affirmation exercises, or do you just want some quiet time to get in the zone?"

Nat peered around the office. "Is Justin here?"

"No, he headed to the expo center to make sure the stage set-up was going all right." Jo's eyes frowned a little through her peppy smile. "Anything I can help you with?"

Nat nodded, searching for what to say. She had Jo to herself, and she knew that any more time spent doomscrolling might just liquify her brain for good. It was time to face what had happened between them. "Listen, can we talk?" she asked, gesturing to their ancient IKEA sofa.

Jo perched on the edge and searched her with nervous eyes. "Everything good?"

"Yes . . . actually, no." Nat twisted her hands in her lap as she sat next to Jo. In all the years that she had dealt with bullies and rejections and friends that turned their backs on her, she had never once talked to any of them about it. Why would she? So, she could hear exactly what was wrong with her? But as she searched Jo's patient but nervous expression, she realized that maybe that was actually the precise information that she needed. After all, how could she improve if she didn't know what to fix? Once again, it all came down to data. And data was something that she could handle. Nat took a deep breath. "You pocket dialed me one night, and I heard you telling someone that you really don't like me."

Jo's face went slack, and her eyes gaped before she buried her head in her hands. "Oh my God," she said. "When? What did I say? I'm so sorry! I was probably just venting about something and—"

Nat touched a hand to Jo's shoulder to stop her. "It's OK, you don't have to like me," she said. "We spend a lot of time together, and you probably know me about as well as anyone these days, so I guess I just want to know why, or like, why not?"

"But I do like you!" Jo looked at her with panic swimming in her eyes. "Also, I really like this job!"

"You don't ever need to worry about your job," said Nat, suddenly feeling like a monster. "I know it was unfair of me to ask you that, but I just . . ." She bit the inside of her lip. She felt like she'd waded out neck-deep into swampy water, but now the only way out was to keep going. "I don't have a lot of friends, OK? In my experience, people tend to keep me at arm's length, especially once they get to know me, and that's really the whole reason I started BeTwo — so people would know what they were getting beforehand and then maybe they wouldn't be disappointed and bail."

Jo narrowed her eyes as a realization hit her, and her face relaxed. "I see," she said. She took a few breaths, and Nat could practically see the thoughts turning in her head. "So, if that's why you started the app, why didn't you ever make a profile and use it?" Jo waved a hand toward the *Team Nat* shirt layered over her button-down. "I mean, before all this contest stuff."

Nat shrugged. "Well, I did use it to look for people," she said, starting on her standard line of defense. But the words felt hollow as soon as she heard them echo in the empty office. The loopy *Team Nat* cursive on Jo's shirt wove into her thoughts like a ribbon — if she couldn't be honest with someone wearing her name on their chest, when could she be? "I guess I didn't think anyone would really be interested in me." She gave Jo a sad smile. As incredibly difficult as it had been to say, once the words were out of her mouth, they sounded so small and childish, even if they were deeply true.

Jo nodded. "Yeah, I get that." She ran her eyes over Nat with a cautious expression and smoothed her sleek ponytail. "I don't know what you heard me say, but that's probably what I was talking about. It's gotten really depressing to come to work day after day and promote an app that's all about love and hope and connection, but yet the creator is so . . ." She trailed off.

Nat jumped in to try and help her out. "Annoying? Demanding? A totally selfish bitch?"

"No, it's like you were just *shut off*." Jo sighed and shook her head. "I get focusing on your career, but I never understood why you would make a dating app if you weren't going to date at all, and if you didn't even believe in having love in your life. Obviously, the algorithm is genius and all, but it started to just feel, I don't know, kinda bad vibes."

Nat closed her eyes and let Jo's words sink in, heavy even in their Gen Z patois. She was right, of course. Nat's confidence in her algorithm had never wavered, but she'd never managed to extend that confidence to her actual self. Instead, she'd hidden behind her work for validation because it was, objectively, really damn good, but also because she was afraid that her personality couldn't live up to anywhere close to that standard. It was one thing to make a "genius algorithm," and it was another to then get rejected by it. But those mistakes were all behind her now, right? Even though the contest with Rami had forced her hand, she had used BeTwo in earnest, and she had found a partner who wanted to be with her. So, what did Jo have to say about all of that? "Well, I have Thom now," she ventured. "I mean, you're right, about everything, but the situation has changed . . . hasn't it?"

Jo fixed her with a bright smile. "Thom! Yes, totally." She nodded and tucked a strand of hair behind her ear.

"Jo, please," Nat said. "Please just be honest with me." She felt the plea throb behind her eyes like a headache. "As a friend?"

A warm smile crept into Jo's heart-shaped face as she repeated Nat's words. "As a friend . . . OK." She scanned the ceiling and twisted her hands in thought. "I can totally see the Thom thing for you," she said.

"But?"

"But . . . I don't think you have to settle so soon."

Nat sat up straighter. "He's my ninety-nine percent match. Not exactly settling."

Jo smiled and nodded again. "Yes! That match is bananas high." Their eyes met with a laugh at the reference.

"But?"

"But . . . do you look at him the way you look at Rami?" Jo shrugged as a flush lit her cheeks. "I know, he's your competition, but once I saw you two together, I can't un-see it — in a good way. Justin and I have been talking about it non-stop since we watched you two at the rooftop interview. It was like, fireworks, explosions, you wanna kill each other but also rip each other's clothes off! It was way too cute." She giggled and then grew serious. "Sorry if that was overstepping."

Nat felt the truth of Jo's giddy admission swirl in her vision like stars. Rami. Of course, Nat knew just how deeply he had become lodged in her heart, but the fact that it was so obvious as to be a topic of conversation between the twins? That was a new data point — one that she didn't quite know what to do with yet, especially since she was hours away from publicly declaring her victory over him and his crusade against her app.

At least she had done something about the situation with Jo. She crossed her hands over her heart and gave Jo a warm look. "Thank you," she said. "And I'm sorry that I put you in this position. I'm gonna work on my personal friendships outside of work, I promise."

"We can be friends! I *want* to be friends!" said Jo. "You know, work friends, and you're still also my boss, so . . ." She gave a nervous laugh and trailed off.

Nat clapped her hands and stood. "As your boss, I officially demand that we get back to work." She glanced at the clock. "Which, today, means that I have to go report on my dating life on a livestream in front of a room full of strangers, just so I can keep this company from crashing to the ground."

Jo brushed some non-existent dirt off her shoulders. "No big deal, just another day."

"Right? Good thing my love life isn't confusing at all!" Nat gathered her things.

"I know! So grateful for that," chimed Jo, pulling on her coat and heaving a bag full of *Team Nat* shirts and swag.

Nat held open the door for Jo as they left. "And super good that the internet is full of generous, mentally stable people who won't rush to judgment." She turned off the office lights and locked the door. "Never been happier."

* * *

Nat and Jo approached the expo. It was in the same building as Tech-Talk had been, back when the whole, ridiculous bet started. There was, again, a line of people snaking around the entire block to get in. Neon pink and navy BuzzFill BuzzForce flags and banners flashed in the strong wind.

No turning back now.

Jo shouldered open the glass doors and jerked her chin toward Nat. "You coming?"

Nat shook her head. "You go ahead. Thom wants to meet out here so we can walk in together."

Jo smiled through a flicker of concern. "OK, well good luck out there," she chirped, stepping into the swirling crowd of people inside the expo. "See you on the other side!"

* * *

Nat and Thom settled into their director's chairs on the stage as producers scurried around them. Nat eyed the two empty chairs for Rami and Allison.

Thom squeezed her hand and surveyed the rows and rows of empty audience seats with gleaming eyes. "Not a bad way to spend an evening, right?" he said.

He had arrived at their designated spot right on time, and in a perfectly tailored dove gray wool suit. He wore a navy-and-pink paisley pocket square and navy socks with bright pink geometric accents under his toffee brown brogues. Of course, he had matched his accessories to the BuzzFill branding. It also explained why he had urged her to wear the navy-and-pink striped sweater she was currently sporting. She squirmed in it, wishing he'd just said it was to coordinate with his look, which was coordinated to the event. Instead, he'd given her a line about how the colors brought out her beautiful complexion, and now she wondered if that were even true.

"Exciting." Nat nodded and pulled on her denim jacket.

Rami approached the stage in a brisk walk-run. A curvy, red-headed woman wearing an emerald dress and a determined expression followed behind him. This, Nat guessed, was Allison. Even out of breath from clearly having rushed here, she was still prettier than Nat had hoped. Much, much prettier.

They took their seats next to her and Thom.

Nat felt Thom stiffen beside her at Rami's entrance. She put her hand on his leg to calm whatever storm was brewing. "Hey, lovebirds!" she sang to Rami, waving.

"Cool it," warned Rami.

"What? I can't be happy for the couple about to try and destroy me?"

Rami turned to Allison, whose curls seemed to naturally settle into perfect formation as soon as she sat down. "Just ignore her."

Thom leaned in and extended his hand to Allison. "Hello, lovely to meet you." He flashed a brilliant grin. "Don't worry, these interviews never last long and viral content has a mercifully short shelf life."

"Oh, I know," Allison answered, giving him a perky handshake.

Rami shot Thom a murderous look. "Isn't it lovely to see me, Thom?"

Thom chuckled. "Let's just keep it civil, mate."

"Hey, Nat." Allison gave a dismissive wave and tugged at her dress as she squinted into the beauty lights. "Is it supposed to be this hot up here?"

"Yep," V answered with unusual simplicity as they fastened lapel mics onto everyone in the group. "It's basically the surface of the sun, literally and metaphorically."

Nat shot Rami a cautious look while Tracy breezed in, flanked by assistants. He glared at Thom, his whole face puckered in an oversized frown like he'd eaten a lemon and then dedicated his life to scorching all citrus fruits from the earth.

Tracy perched on the stool and crossed her long, brown legs and smoothed her already liquid-glass-shiny hair. "Great, we're all here and looking cute?" She gave them an approving glance, letting her eyes linger a beat on Thom. "Outstanding. So, we're live in two minutes." She ran her tongue over her printer-paper-white teeth and smiled. "Dates, just keep it natural. Keep it fun!"

Allison nodded as if she'd received CPR instructions. "And those are all the cameras, right?"

Thom hit Tracy with his own dazzling smile and crossed his legs.

Tracy arched a laminated eyebrow and appraised him for a beat before she pointed a finger at Nat and Rami. "And you two? Remember, discontent makes good content."

Thom gave an approving laugh and elbowed Nat. "Oh, she's good," he whispered in a low rumble.

"Heh, yeah." Nat fidgeted with her jacket buttons as crew members wheeled in more cameras and speakers and tested audio-visual connections. Nat scanned the auditorium. She watched as Jo and Justin tapped away on their phones in the front row, wearing their matching *Team Nat* T-shirts. There was an empty seat next to them that they could have only been saving for Sara. Nat felt her heart clench. There were only a few minutes until it started. It looked like Sara had opted not to be on her team after all.

Then, seemingly all at once, V was shooing everyone out of the way, and attendees were streaming into their seats, and the lights were dimming, and the little green lights on the cameras were blinking.

They were live.

"Good evening, Buzzers!" Tracy cried, standing in front of the audience with her arms held aloft. Applause, or a stampede of elephants, filled Nat's ears. The stage lights glared in her eyes as Tracy gestured toward the four of them.

"Well, here's what you all have been waiting for — the big moment of truth in the #BeTwoChallenge." She began a slow walk in front of her guests. "Which kind of dating is better?" She stopped in front of Rami and Allison. "The old-fashioned way without apps to introduce us?"

Rami nodded with furrowed brows. Allison giggled and shrugged.

Tracy continued. "Or the modern way, with all of its swiping and sexting?" She gestured to Nat and Thom.

Nat gave a small wave as Thom seemed to give a kind of seated bow.

Tracy took her seat and turned to Nat. "Let's start with the side for technology. Here we have Nat Lane, creator of the app we all use, BeTwo, and the boyfriend she found through said app, Thom."

The crowd responded with polite applause. Thom sat up even straighter, raised an eyebrow, and adjusted his open shirt collar to show more of his skin.

"Nat, you obviously succeeded in finding a partner through your app, but how was the experience for you?"

"Amazing," Nat said without hesitation. "You know, Thom and I actually scored at a ninety-nine percent match, which is the highest possible percentage ever generated on the app."

She felt Rami cringe as Tracy nodded and fired her next question.

"Cute. So did you find that your algorithm was accurate with your other matches?"

Rami leaned in and gave Nat a pointed look.

Thom butted in. "Oh, now, let's not talk about the other matches while I'm right here, shall we? I might get jealous."

Tracy and the audience murmured with soft laughs as Rami rolled his eyes. "Wouldn't want that," he hissed under his breath.

Nat wanted to swat his attitude away like a fly. Instead, she gazed at Thom with adoring eyes and patted his thigh.

Thom took her hand and turned his charm on full blast into the cameras. "The point is, Nat's algorithm was so accurate, it matched me with another career-minded go-getter." He arched an eyebrow and brought a hand to his chin, the model of casually deep thought. "As the lead of an award-winning interior architecture studio, I don't have time to go on frivolous dates when I could be perfecting my new designs for dining chairs, chaises longues, and more, launching soon under the prestigious Design For All brand."

Rami caught Nat's eye again. He slow-blinked his round eyes as his face lengthened in mock disbelief.

Nat knew exactly what he meant. *This guy? Really?* But she just kept smiling. She noticed a very tall man in a silk shirt emblazoned with a snarling dragon sneak into the auditorium. She squinted. He held up a hand-scrawled *I Am Here for Rami* sign. She heard Rami laugh and point this out to Allison, who squeaked and wiggled a few fingers in greeting.

"All right," said Tracy. "Now, Rami and Allison, how did Cupid match you two IRL?"

Rami sprang into action. "You've heard of meet-cute? Try meat-cute! M-E-A-T!" He paused for laughter, but there was only a beat of silent confusion. "Because we met at a brunch!" he added, his pitch rising. "It was her birthday!"

"Oh, so you met at her birthday party?" asked Tracy.

"Well, no," said Rami. "We were both dining alone."

Allison squirmed. "I just moved here . . ." she added in a meek voice.

"That's right!" Rami raised a finger in the air. "I was the first person she met in San Francisco! Talk about fate."

Tracy zeroed in on Allison. "So, tell us, what drew you to Rami? You're a beautiful woman — you must have guys approach you all the time." She tented her fingers under her chin. "What made him stand out to you?"

"Well . . ." Allison twisted a strand of her curls with her index finger. "Like I said, I just moved here and I didn't know anyone else."

Nat scoffed. "That tracks," she muttered.

"And he's just so nice!" Allison gave the cameras a pageant smile. "And he wanted to show me all these cool places and, I don't know, I could only watch baking shows on my sofa for so long."

Nat let herself look Allison up and down, her eyes lingering for a moment on the spot where Rami's leg was pressed against her. She dropped Thom's hand and leaned in. "So, he was literally just better than being alone?" She gave the audience a stage-y smirk. "Have you tried my app?"

Allison's face dropped. "Sorry, that's not what I meant—"

"Oh, right, the magic algorithm that you trust more than the fact that I know your date is a liar." Rami glared at Nat and put a hand on Allison's shoulder.

"Wait." Tracy held up her hand. "Rami, are you saying Thom misrepresented himself on BeTwo?"

Nat balked. Tracy had jumped to that conclusion very quickly, even for a top journalist. She started to respond, but Rami cut her off.

He gave a loud and genuine laugh. "No, Tracy, that's the thing. He represented himself with perfect accuracy! BeTwo just doesn't have the *data* on whether someone cheats on their partner and treats women like trash."

A gasp went up from the crowd. Thom bristled beside Nat. "Now, wait a minute—"

But Tracy held up her hand to silence him. In her eyes, Nat caught a loaded, knowing glint of recognition. "I think I'm going to let Nat respond to that one, Thom."

Nat looked out into the crowd. Sara's empty seat stared up at her like a wine stain on a white dress. Maybe that part of her life was ruined, but there were Justin and Jo in their *Team Nat* shirts, counting on her to keep them employed. And an audience full of people staring at her. And an entire world that would be watching whatever she said next in perpetuity on the internet. Then there were the two men sitting next to her and her wildly different feelings for both of them. She wished she could start all over. She wished she believed more in what she knew that she had to say, but she said it anyway. "BeTwo said Thom is my perfect match, and I trust my algorithm completely."

Tracy shot her a pinched smile. "All right."

Rami crossed his arms. "So? Come on, who wins?"

Tracy scanned them for a beat with sharp eyes.

Rami gestured to himself. "Is it the couple who met by following the rules, fair and square?" He waved a hand to Thom. "Or the guy who cheated and got a second chance?"

The crowd gasped.

Thom turned to Nat with a clenched jaw. "Can you please control him?" he muttered in her ear with the tone of a threat.

Nat kept her eyes on Rami and leaned forward. "No, really, who wins?" She pointed to herself. "The couple who was united by a strategically perfect matching algorithm?" She waved a hand to Allison. "Or the guy who's clearly just using someone when she's lonely?"

The crowd gasped again, with a few boos this time.

Allison had gone pale and was looking at her hands.

Nat held Rami's furious stare.

Tracy cleared her throat. "Well, first I think our audience might have some questions about how closely either of you followed the rules . . ."

Now, Nat and Rami turned to Tracy together.

"What do you mean?" asked Nat. "We just met up for drinks a couple times!

"Yeah, and the kissing was a one-time thing!" said Rami.

Allison jumped in her seat. "You kissed?"

Nat scoffed. "It was a little more than that."

Thom huffed like he'd been punched and shifted in his chair.

"OK, fine, we kind of almost had sex, but we both agreed that it didn't mean anything, Tracy!" Rami was starting to gleam with sweat as his voice grew louder and more high-pitched. "Tracy, it was basically just a kiss!"

Tracy blinked, her face frozen in a stony expression.

Nat realized this must be what it looks like when someone with extensive media training cracks. She could guess that because she, for comparison, felt like waves of lava were radiating through her body as rainforests of sweat formed in her armpits. Nat wanted her old life back, and she would do it all differently this time. But since that was impossible, she just desperately wanted off this stage. "Just tell us who won!" she snarled.

Tracy grinned back into her professional self. "It looks like you both did. Now let's take a quick break!" She stood and drew the cameras away from Nat and Rami. "How about we throw to our live coverage of the BuzzFill Cuteness Overload Petting Zoo tent where I'm told there are baby sloths?" She clasped her hands in front of her chest. "Let's all look at some baby sloths for a bit."

The lights dimmed as V scurried forward to confer with Tracy.

Allison stood and pointed a finger at Rami's face. "This changes everything." She pulled off her mic and stormed off the stage.

"Bye," said Nat.

Rami jumped up and whirled to Nat. "Now I understand why you made such a heartless app."

He ran after Allison.

Nat turned to Tracy, who was pulling off her mic.

"So, that's it?"

Tracy gave her side-eye. "They literally left. And do you really want that trainwreck to continue?" She waved her glowing phone toward Nat. "Looks like the online mob is saying that you won, so just ride the trending topic for the next twenty-four hours and enjoy our open bar."

Thom stood up and smoothed his suit. "A stiff drink is definitely in order," he said coldly, but he turned and held out his hand to Nat.

Nat hesitated, but all she could seem to feel was the glare of the lights and the adrenaline crashing through her chest. She took his hand and followed him offstage.

CHAPTER 20

Nat leaned against a wall at the edges of the BuzzFill BuzzForce opening party. Thom swept toward her through the thick crowd with two glasses of champagne. She took one, staring into the bubbles, as he took a long, satisfied sip.

"So, you're not mad that I kissed Rami?" she said, wishing she had about three more glasses of champagne on hand.

"Not at all. People can be rather uptight and possessive in relationships, if you ask me." Thom shook his head and then patted his hair back into place. "I don't begrudge anyone a little fun." He winked at her. "Besides, the best man won."

Nat managed a weak laugh as Thom wrapped an arm around her. Given his history with Rami's sister, his words weren't exactly a comfort.

"Besides, controversy is the currency of the internet," he said. "You were like one of those catty housewives or something, and drama means followers for both of us. I can't wait to see what Lauren in social media has to say to me tomorrow," he said, surveying the party.

"So, you think I was mean?" Nat implored.

"Oh, my dear, vicious! You humiliated that poor girl." He planted a kiss on the top of her head.

Nat's stomach twisted. "Why did I do that?"

"That guy was going after your baby. You went all Mama Bear and it was fucking sexy." Thom roared very loudly. A few heads turned.

Nat's stomach lurched again. "But seriously," she said, still searching for an answer. "I don't even know her, and I'm not a mean girl . . . right?"

Thom shrugged and turned back to eyeing the crowd, as the twins maneuvered closer through the throngs of Buzzers. Their *Team Nat* shirts had been abandoned. They both looked like deflated balloons.

"Well, that's over with," said Justin, giving her a half-hearted fist bump.

Jo managed a tight nod. "Our high numbers are holding and people love you on socials . . ."

Justin rolled his eyes. "They kinda love Thom more though. #HotThom is a thing."

Thom frowned, as if in thought, but Nat could see his eyes light up.

Jo gave a forced grin. "So, hooray! Success!" She waved her fists in a tiny cheer.

Justin cleared his throat. "So, uh, did you see where Rami went off to, or have you talked to him, or anything?"

Even though she felt like she was standing in the middle of a dumpster fire, Nat had to smile at Justin's attempt to be nonchalant now that she knew the twins had been rooting for Rami all along. She wished Thom wasn't there so she could tell them that she needed to find him. Instead, she just shook her head and said, "Nope."

Thom grinned and raised his glass. "To the woman of the hour!"

Justin and Jo gave thin smiles and raised their glasses.

Nat pulled out her phone. "One second . . ." she muttered. "I need to check something."

As Thom clinked glasses with the twins, Nat wedged the champagne glass against her body and opened BeTwo — not the commercial version, but the one with developer settings that she could still poke around in. She had just consciously wished that Thom, her ninety-nine percent match, wasn't around so she could go chase down a different guy — the guy she really wanted.

She had to run those numbers.

She did a quick search of the cached user data. And in a few seconds, there it was — Rami's old profile. Her chest twinged as the words, *My heart is a little tender* jumped out at her. She switched to God mode, clicked a few dev toggles, and ran a match between his profile and her profile.

The number flashed on her screen.

Thirteen percent.

Nat closed her eyes and smiled. They would have never been matched by her algorithm, not in a million swipes. And that was everything she needed to know.

"I've gotta go do something . . ." she said, slipping her glass of champagne into Thom's hand. She shot Jo a reassuring glance and hurried off into the depths of the party.

* * *

Rami scanned the party crowd for Allison. She'd run out of the auditorium and onto the expo floor, and now she could be anywhere among the branded tees and stuffed backpacks of the opening party revelers.

He spotted her downing a cocktail at the bar.

He rushed over. "I'm so, so sorry. I should've told you about the kiss — kissing thing with Nat."

Allison turned to him, and his heart sank to see that this time tears were indeed pooling in her eyes. "But you didn't! You lied to me, even more than I already knew about."

He noticed several crumpled up, tear-stained napkins in front of her. His doing. "Yes, I did."

"It was really cruel of you to drag me through all of this when you liked Nat so much," she said, her green eyes flashing. "Yes, I suspected it, but you seemed so clueless and you kept insisting that you hated her. And then you kissed her! While you started something with me."

"I know," Rami mumbled.

"Why did you do that?"

Rami ran a hand through his sweaty hair. "I don't know. I can't stop thinking about her but she's also the embodiment of pretty much everything I hate, and you were, like, sweetness in human form."

Allison scoffed. "First of all, I'm not that sweet, and neither are you, Rami."

He winced. Had he really thought that simply getting a good person to date him would make him a good person? And still only ended up acting like a total shit, instead? Seemed like it.

"And as for Nat, you very obviously don't hate her, Rami. The opposite of love isn't hate — it's indifference, and a whole drama on the internet is not what that looks like." Allison stood up straighter and squared her shoulders. "I don't know what you were trying to prove with this competition, but if it was that you're a better person because you don't lie on the apps . . ." Her voice wavered a bit, and Rami braced himself for impact. "You kinda just ended up lying to my face instead."

Rami's stomach dropped with the truth of her statement. He felt like the biggest fraud in San Francisco, which was a high bar, especially at a tech conference. He forced himself to meet her blazing eyes. "You're right," he said. "I'm sorry, Allison. You didn't deserve that."

Allison sighed and tossed her copper hair. "No, I sure didn't." She knocked back the rest of her drink. "Can I say one more thing?"

"Honestly, the fact that you're talking to me at all instead of slapping me across the face is an unbelievable kindness." Rami leaned next to her. "Please, say anything you want."

"I don't want to be friends now, Rami."

"I know." He gathered up her damp tissues. "Wait here. Let me call you a car, OK?"

"Thanks. I really just want to go home." She wiped some mascara from under her eyes, put on a brave, tired smile, and sighed. "So, get me the heck out of here so I can never see you again, please."

Rami smiled back at her candor and ordered her a car — the premium ride, obviously. "Done."

Allison sighed and turned away from him, surveying the people milling around the party. "I guess this will be a good story to tell my grandkids one day," she mused into the air. She then simply walked away into the crowd. And in that moment, Rami was deeply grateful for her indifference.

* * *

Nat wedged her way through the boozed-up Buzzers looking for Rami. Several people greeted her with shouts and high-fives. She waved them away, even earning one muttered, "Bitch" as she pushed past a fan.

Finally, she spotted him leaving the bar.

"Rami! Rami wait!" She ran up to him.

For some reason, he seemed happy to see her. He took her hands and his face softened, but he said, "Listen, I have to tell you something but I also really have to get out of this awful party—"

"Wait, I need to tell you something too and you can't leave until I do."

His face wrinkled with confusion, but he nodded at her to go on. "You first, then."

She took a deep breath. "I was wrong, OK? My whole algorithm is wrong because, surprise, I don't want to be with Thom."

He nodded again. It was infuriating, and she loved it.

"I don't want to be with anyone else either. I want to be with you."

Rami's dark eyes widened. "You do?"

She showed him their thirteen percent match on her phone. "The data is very compelling."

Relief spread into his face. She saw the tension in his shoulders drop, and he gave her hands a gentle squeeze.

She stepped closer to him.

"I want to be with you, too," he said. "I can't stop thinking about you and our—"

Nat kissed him to finish the sentence. He wrapped his arms around her and kissed her back.

A camera flash went off.

She looked up from Rami's face to see Thom holding out his phone and smirking.

"Gotcha," he said.

Nat dropped Rami's hands and spun toward Thom. "What are you doing?"

Thom looked up from tapping on his phone with a casual glance. "Oh, just tweeting some viral content."

"Thom, I'm sorry." She summoned her most sympathetic tone. "But please don't post that pic."

"It's done," he said, slipping his phone back into his suit jacket. "And so are we." He smoothed his blond waves and lifted his chin, his gaze grazing the top of her head.

An audible wave of shock and amusement rippled through the crowd in "oooh's" and laughter at what, Nat could only assume, was Thom's post of her kiss with Rami. Several of the people around them whirled to look at the trio and immediately raised their phones, camera lenses out.

Rami covered his face with his hands and moaned in genuine frustration. "No, please, I can't be viral content anymore—"

Thom held up an index finger and cut him off. "Rami, don't. I've heard enough of your miserable whining for three lifetimes."

Rami's jaw clenched and his entire face hardened into an eerie stillness. His eyes welled with tears and fixed on the ground. "I can't do this."

Thom flashed a wolfish grin at the camera phones. "Are you crying, mate?"

Rami shook his head as he raised his gaze to Nat. His eyes were swimming with sorrow and panic as he took a step back. "I'm sorry. This is too much."

Nat reached for him. "Wait!"

Rami flinched and took another step into the crowd. He raised his hands in surrender and mouthed, "I'm sorry," before he turned and walked away.

Thom gave a slow clap as the circle of spectators tightened around them.

Nat swallowed back the panic flooding into her chest. The party lights glared off the ring of raised phones around her and Thom. She could imagine how unhinged she would look in all the videos, and how gleefully people would tear her apart in their hot takes. The truth was that she was doomed in the eyes of the internet, no matter what she was going to say next, so she figured that it might as well be sincere. "Thom, I didn't mean to hurt you."

"Hurt me?" Thom recoiled with a bitter laugh. He hugged her close but whispered like a snake in her ear. "Darling, we both got exactly what we wanted. You needed a date to win your little bet, and I got free placement on the homepage of *BuzzFill* plus a scandal where I look like the poor, mistreated victim." He released her with a performative frown, but she could see that his sapphire eyes were hard. "I just hope that love will manage to find me, too."

He gave her a quick two-finger salute, then stepped away into the crowd. Several women in tight dresses watched him walk by and began to trail him.

"Ugh," Nat muttered to herself as she elbowed away from the camera phones. "Ninety-nine percent my ass."

Microphone feedback squawked into her ears as Tracy took the party stage.

"*BuzzFill* Nation, are we ready to party?"

An exuberant roar sounded all around her as Nat zeroed in on her next move. She started toward the stage. "Yes, it's me, yay, BeTwo," she muttered as she squished through the crowd. She could sense yet more camera flashes and lenses held aloft in her periphery all pointed at her. "I did it, you're welcome, yay."

Finally, she reached the stage and clambered up. A few whoops went up as she hoisted her ass over the ledge like a gangly squirrel.

"Um . . . Nat?" Tracy's cat-lined eyes were murderous as Nat reached for the mic. "This is not a good look—"

Nat snatched the mic away and faced the crowd. "Hey, Buzz-people, whatever, internet. Guess what?" She heard the click of Tracy's heels running offstage. "My app, BeTwo, is a steaming pile of dog shit. Yep! Wanna know why? It's not because of my algorithm!"

The crowd hushed. She continued.

"You see, my algorithm truly does process bananas-high amounts of criteria to generate matches based on even the most minute factors. Chocolate or vanilla? Morning person or night owl? It can handle every single data point you throw at it! But you know what?"

She pointed to her chest, then wagged her finger in the air.

"Your heart doesn't care if someone likes the same bands as you, or is within your height range, or has a job we've categorically aligned with yours. That's not what we should be searching for. That's not what matters!"

She made eye contact with a few people in the front of the crowd. They weren't ignoring her or laughing or cringing. Yes, a few of them were obviously filming her. But a lot of the people she could see were simply listening.

"It's not a numbers game! Fuck the numbers! Maybe I match with someone ninety-nine percent, but maybe it's because of stuff I don't even care about or maybe it's stuff that I don't really even like about myself. Like, why *don't* I ever go hiking? Wouldn't it be great to find someone to introduce me to something new?"

A few people nodded.

"And maybe I match with someone just thirteen percent, but it's on all the things that actually make up who I am. Like someone who knows when I really need a laugh. Or will call me out on my bullshit because they're taking a totally different path . . . but we're heading in the same direction . . . And I really want to keep heading that way." She took a breath. "One hundred percent."

She held up her phone. The dev mode BeTwo app glowed into the crowd.

"So, I'm deleting my profile." She shook her head. "No, I'm deleting the whole app. As someone once said to me, dating isn't shopping. It's messy and surprising and unpredictable and it sure as shit needs to stay that way."

She tapped a few controls. Then it was done. BeTwo blinked offline for every last user. "I really should have made that harder to do," she muttered.

The crowd watched her in an eerie silence.

"OK, I'm done." Her heart raced. She was sweating hot and cold over every inch of her body, and she felt like she might never breathe normally again. "Speeches are hard, man," she said, starting to slink off stage.

A few slow, tentative claps began from the back corners of the room. Then there was a loud, familiar *whoop!*

Nat squinted into the stage lights. A bright pink blur was plowing toward her through the crowd.

"That's my girl!" It was Sara. Sara in her *Team Nat* T-shirt. Sara was pumping her fists and strutting through the crowd like a showy wrestler. "Give it up for Nat Lane!" she yelled and started clapping.

Tears flooded Nat's eyes as the crowd joined in with steady, if somewhat confused-seeming, claps and cheers. She met Sara's eyes and felt a laugh break out of her. What was her life gonna be now? But what did it matter now that she had her Team? Nat pointed at Sara, then she held the mic straight out in front of her, and dropped it.

CHAPTER 21

The next morning, Nat was curled up on the sofa in what she had officially dubbed her pink sweater of sadness. She imagined that she would be wearing it often now. Pixel purred on her chest. She'd barely slept all night between the many long and terrifying legal calls with her lawyers, her financiers, her landlords, and all of the other numerous people who made it clear that they thought she was out of her mind and wanted their money.

She wasn't thrilled with how things had turned out, but she stood by her decision. She was stepping down from BeTwo. The only question was what she would do next.

Sara entered holding the coffee pot. "Warm up?"

Nat held out her mug. "Good Lord, yes."

Sara maneuvered around the stacks of boxes to pour Nat a cup and take a seat next to her.

"You're my hero." Nat sighed as she took a hot sip. "And I'm the terrible friend who can't even help you move because I blew up my life last night."

Sara snorted in approval. "You sure did. I was worried when I knew I was going to miss the interview, but I think I saw the main event." She stretched her feet out on a moving box and rubbed Nat's shoulder. "And I'm sure you don't want a bunch of movers in your space today. This timing is truly the worst."

"Really, it's fine." Nat waved her concern away. "Nowhere to go but up."

"Well, you know that I'm still coming over all the time, right?"

"You better." Nat gave her a sly glance. "Just don't try and move back in because your room is now my office for my as-yet-undetermined new job."

Sara grinned. "You're welcome for leaving you all my good juju." She shifted to face Nat and rubbed Pixel's back. "So, you promise that you're OK?"

"Everything I said about the app was true." Nat scratched Pixel's tiny chin. "Besides, the board has to buy me out so I'll be OK for a while."

Sara nodded and decided to broach the more sensitive subject. "Any word from Rami?"

"Nope." Nat's face dropped. "Wouldn't have been the full BeTwo experience if I didn't get ghosted, right?"

Sara set down her mug and wrapped her friend in a huge, crushing hug. Pixel dove for his life and scampered away.

Nat giggled, squirming. "I still need to breathe!"

"No breathe. Only happy." Sara squeezed tighter.

Nat laughed and wriggled free. "I just need to say again that I'm sorry."

Sara waved her hand in front of her face in dismissal. "Dude, I get it. You were just trying to protect yourself."

"Yes, and also I was clinging to you and then punishing you for having your own life, and it wasn't fair."

"Well, that's accurate."

Nat felt a smile curl into her lips. "It is. And I don't know what I did to deserve the kind of friend who would stick with me, anyway, but I'm damn glad you're in my life."

Sara's normally cool eyes misted over. "Same. And I'm not going anywhere." She gestured to the towering boxes around them. "I mean, not literally, but you get it."

"OK, OK! Get out of here!" Nat laughed. "I've got to go clean out the office and tell the twins they're about to get fat raises from their new bosses as part of my exit package."

* * *

Nat unlocked the doors to the BeTwo office for the last time. The twins were on their way over from Oakland. That meant she had at least an hour to soak it all up before this place was closed to her forever. It still didn't seem like enough time to say goodbye.

She flipped on the lights and pulled a chair up to the bright blue sky in the window. Maybe she could still come by to toss some bread to the seagulls from the rooftops sometimes.

She heard the door open behind her. It seemed like the twins had gotten there sooner than she expected. She turned around.

Rami stood in the sunlight.

"Your roommate said you'd be here." A shy smile crept onto his face.

Nat sprang up from the chair and rushed to him.

He took her hands.

"You first," she said.

"No, you."

"One sentence at a time?"

"In alphabetical order." His eyes sparkled with the witty mischief she'd first swooned over, way back on that ugly couch. "Go."

Her voice came out soft but strong. "I was so convinced that I'd be rejected that I didn't let anyone see me."

Rami nodded. His face was open and fixed on Nat. "I figured that if I just dated women who seemed perfect on paper, nothing could go wrong."

"But you saw me, even my bad parts, and you liked me in spite of them."

A knowing smile curled into his face. "And you showed me how unsatisfying the so-called perfect match can be."

Nat narrowed her eyes with a memory. "I fought harder for the data inside my app than I did for the people who use it." The ghosts of her online dates flickered in her mind. "Using my app was pretty awful, actually."

Rami's dark brows angled with a thoughtful frown. "But people don't need technology to make them act like jerks. I proved that we can still do that the old-fashioned way."

She squeezed his hand. "So, I don't want to be scared of being seen anymore."

He squeezed back. "Because being scared is kind of supposed to be part of it."

"Yeah." She watched his full lips move with his breath. "That's how you know it matters."

He leaned closer to her with a dreamy expression. "That's how you know it's worth fighting for."

Nat hooked her arms around his shoulders. "Was that a good speech?" she whispered.

"I have some notes, but . . ." He wrapped a hand behind her head and kissed her.

When they came up for air a few moments later, Rami leaned back with an urgent look. "Wait, you're not losing this sweet office, are you?"

Nat cringed. "I have definitely left BeTwo."

"No!"

"It's fine, really." She smoothed one of his curls. "I still own my algorithm." She shrugged inside his arms. "And I have other ideas. Probably."

"But I really do have some notes," he said. "On the app! On how to make it better," he hedged. "Or, I mean, less bad."

"Yeah, I have some ideas, too." She nudged him with her elbow. "Because some of your thoughts weren't half-bad."

"I can surprise myself sometimes." He sighed. "I just thought we could version something with broader efficacy if we combined our approaches."

The deeply nerdy way he'd phrased that pinged in Nat's heart. "Well, then I guess this is a very inappropriate way of announcing that you're hired." She ran a hand over his chest. "For whatever we make next," she whispered, locking back onto his lips.

A few moments later, Rami came up for air again. "Wait." He searched her shining eyes and elfin smirk. "We're not making a dating app though, right?"

"Oh, hell no."

Then they smiled at each other and kissed again, and for a long, long time.

ONE YEAR LATER

Nat and Rami searched for their booth on the floor of the Tech-Talk Expo. They were in the airplane hangar-sized General Exposition Hall, stuffed with other people debuting their new app or database or cloud service or what-have-you across hundreds and hundreds of small tables.

"I think it's back there," said Nat, pointing to a dark corner by some restrooms.

Rami consulted their map. "Yep, section Triple-Z. That's us."

They hauled their boxes over to their designated rickety folding table.

"Is there a section Quadruple-Z?" Nat asked as she laid out their brochures and promotional enamel pins.

"I think that would technically be the toilets," said Rami, booting up their demo machines.

Nat laughed and reached for another box to set up.

For a while, they worked in silence, handing each other binders and locating dongles and unfurling their banner in orchestral precision.

"Should we go say hi to Tracy?" asked Rami. "She's probably around here somewhere, right?"

"Are you kidding? She's an influencer now. She's probably sky-diving with hedgehogs or something as we speak." Nat adjusted their QR code placard.

"Oh, yeah! I just saw her TikTok recipe for vegetable soup." He nodded and set out the final stack of brochures. "Looked pretty tasty, honestly. We should try it."

"Sounds good."

They stood back and admired their booth. In big blue letters, their banner read: *Perfect Catch: A Weather and Fishing Optimization App.*

She tucked her hand into his back pocket. "I love it," she said.

He wrapped his arm around her shoulders. "I still think *Data Streams* was a better name."

Nat heard a familiar voice calling through the maze of booths. "Nat? Are you . . . anywhere?"

"Oh no, I think Sara is lost." She stood up on a chair and waved her friend over. "Follow my voice!"

Sara appeared from behind a life-size cut-out of a cartoon gopher riding a cloud in the iconic pose from *Dr. Strangelove*. "I feel like I'm in a humans-versus-aliens movie right now, and I'm rooting for the aliens," she said, giving Nat a hug.

"Hello, hello!" said Ian, stepping up behind her.

Rami sputtered. "Wait. Did you two arrive together?" He staggered back like he had just made an exciting discovery in the chemistry lab. "Like, *together*-together?"

Sara scoffed through a creeping blush. "No! We just both exited the labyrinth at the same time."

"Good morning, Sara," said Ian, with a cordial bow.

"Yeah, hi, anyway, you guys. You're at Tech-Talk!" Sara raised her eyebrows and wiggled her fingers. "Where it all began just one year ago . . ."

Happiness swirled inside Nat as Rami winked at her. "Yeah, we know."

Sara elbowed Rami. "Wanna go make some outrageous bets on a livestream, for old times' sake?"

Rami raised his hands. "Well, a romantic might say I won that bet, so . . . maybe."

Sara tilted her head. "Yeah, not sure there were any winners in that epic crash-and-burn." She wrapped an arm around Nat's shoulder. "The memes are still pretty popular, you know."

"Yes, I know." Nat sighed. "My mom keeps sending them to me because she doesn't understand that they're making fun of me."

Ian cleared his throat. "Well, anytime love prevails is a 'W' in my book," he intoned.

Nat frowned at Sara. "Where's Jax?"

"They swore they could get bagels and still come find us in this mess." She shrugged and checked her phone.

Ian cleared his throat and made a show of inspecting the booth. "I happened to run into Sara, and was it Jax you said? I ran into them on the way in, and so they will be bringing me a bagel, as well." He put his hands behind his back and rocked on his heels. "Coincidence. That's why."

Rami squinted at him. "You're being weird. Weirder."

Ian shrugged and scooped up a handful of their free buttons.

Sara rushed to fill the silence. "I don't see what the big deal was about the app, anyway. Meet how you meet. Date how you date, right?"

Ian nodded as he fastened an enamel catfish to his lapel. "Of course. Different approaches are all just part of life's rich pageant . . . the spice of it, etcetera."

Sara picked up a brochure and tapped it against Ian's shoulder. "Totally. Keep it safe and people-focused, but then, yeah, let's have some fun."

Ian and Sara smiled at each other through the hum of the expo center.

"OK," said Rami, squinting at them. "Is there . . . ? Never mind."

Nat sighed and checked the time. "We only have fifteen minutes before Jo's talk about her start-up consultancy and I promised her I'd be in the front row." She held out a demo phone. "Do you guys wanna see what lures to use, to catch the most fish, given the most likely weather at your precise location, indexed against historical fish migration patterns — or what?"

"Hell yeah, we do!" said Sara.

"Don't keep us in suspense!" said Ian.

"Well, you might be the only people in the world who care about this besides my mom's fishing group . . ." said Nat, loading the demo.

"The Bass Betties are my girls," said Rami.

"But here we go!" Nat turned the screen to her friends. "I think it just might be my favorite thing that I've ever made." She winked at Rami. "For now."

THE END

ACKNOWLEDGMENTS

Publishing a novel has been a lifelong dream of mine, and like all wonderful things, it only happened because of the many wonderful people who gave me their time, knowledge, support, and love along the way.

I've had some form of this story in the works for almost a decade, and have been working toward publishing a book for even longer, so my list of people to whom I owe my thanks is long, and I can't possibly do the journey to get here full justice. But I will try!

Thank you to the brilliant and caring writer and teacher Janis Cooke Newman — you taught me how to unlock all of the half-formed story ideas swimming around in my brain and spin them into a coherent narrative. My time soaking up your wisdom and forming friendships in writing groups and at the incredible Lit Camp retreat truly changed my life, and gave me the tools for a career in fiction and teaching. Your ability to see the missing pieces in a scene or an entire narrative arc is unmatched, and this book would not exist without your crucial insights.

Thank you to my dear friend, Sarah Youree. You listened to many of my teary real-life stories that inspired Nat and Rami's bad dates. You believed in my first steps into the romcom genre, and read and edited them in comic form. Having your eyes on this manuscript gave me the courage to believe in it. Your counsel, love, honesty, and intelligence never cease to inspire me and fill my heart. I am so damn grateful to have you in my corner and in my life.

Thank you to my dear friend, Vincent Perea. Your support and advice, kindness and humor, and truly over-the-top talent and brilliance have been a constant beacon and joy in my life. Our friendship means the world to me, and your creativity has been inspiring me for 20+ years and counting — a true privilege.

Thank you to my sweet family. Dad, you encouraged me to keep going when I was in the thick of rejections. As I said to you then, everything that I love about myself is something I get from you, and I am so grateful that I got to be your daughter. Mom, you've never stopped believing in me — from encouraging my creativity as a child, to soothing my heartbreaks, to supporting me through a long and circuitous path to get here, and always making sure that I believed in myself. I could never have done this without you. Kent, my loving, supportive, and protective big brother — thank you for being my friend and always looking out for me. Vanessa, my brilliant and caring sister-in-law, and one of my very first readers — I knew that if you liked the book, it couldn't be that bad! Elliot, my kind and cool nephew — thank you for being my buddy and always making me smile!

Thank you to Holly Faulks, my dynamic agent. I am so fortunate to have you on my side. Thank you for believing in Nat and in my take on this genre and this modern way of love.

Thank you to my wonderful editor, Becky Slorach, and the entire team at Choc Lit. You all saw the heart in Nat and Rami from the start, and your love for these characters has made me so grateful to call Choc Lit my publishing home.

Thank you to Stuart Kelban, Cindy McCreery, Richard Lewis, and Beau Thorne in the MFA screenwriting program at UT

Austin, for seeing a first version of this story and helping to get it, and my narrative thinking, into shape.

And thank you to: Galadrielle Allman, Sarah Bardeen, DB Finnegan, Noah Sanders, and Kurt Wallace Martin — the best writing group I've ever been a part of. Andrew McClain — an early reader, writer of my favorite joke in the whole novel, and an outstanding DM. Andy Lane — my intrepid guide to the shadow realm. Deepthi Welaratna, my dear friend and creative co-conspirator — I'm so lucky you were by my side for my real-life San Francisco time. Morgan O'Brien — it'd be hard to write a love story if I didn't believe in love; here's to our next chapter. Lou Lou, Bertie, and Tina — my constant companions.

THE CHOC LIT STORY

Established in 2009, Choc Lit is an independent, award-winning publisher dedicated to creating a delicious selection of quality women's fiction.

We have won 18 awards, including Publisher of the Year and the Romantic Novel of the Year, and have been shortlisted for countless others. In 2023, we were shortlisted for Publisher of the Year by the Romantic Novelists' Association.

All our novels are selected by genuine readers. We are proud to publish talented first-time authors, as well as established writers whose books we love introducing to a new generation of readers.

In 2023, we became a Joffe Books company. Best known for publishing a wide range of commercial fiction, Joffe Books has its roots in women's fiction. Today it is one of the largest independent publishers in the UK.

We love to hear from you, so please email us about absolutely anything bookish at choc-lit@joffebooks.com.

If you want to receive free books every Friday and hear about all our new releases, join our mailing list here: www.joffebooks.com/freebooks.